*Clint swallowed. H...
killing him.*

He was enjoying spending time with Alison and her little girl. Enjoying the three of them, together. It wasn't very exciting, but it was very nice.

A man could get used to this.

The unbidden thought surprised Clint. Unnerved him.

God help them all, but he was falling for Alison O'Hara, and little Hannah, too.

And admitting it scared him to death.

This fatherless little family deserved a better man than he. Lots better.

Yet, for some crazy reason, they seemed to want him....

Dear Reader,

As the beautiful fall foliage, sweet apple cider and crisp air beckon you outside, Silhouette Special Edition ushers you back *inside* to savor six exciting, brand-new romances!

Watch for *Bachelor's Baby Promise* by Barbara McMahon—October's tender THAT'S MY BABY! title—which features a tall, dark and handsome bachelor who takes on fatherhood—and the woman of his dreams! And romance unfolds in *Marrying a Delacourt* as bestselling author Sherryl Woods delivers another exciting installment in her wildly popular AND BABY MAKES THREE: THE DELACOURTS OF TEXAS miniseries. Sparks fly when a charming rogue claims the wrong bride in *Millionaire Takes a Bride* by Pamela Toth, the first book in HERE COME THE BRIDES—a captivating new trilogy about beautiful triplet sisters by three of your favorite authors. Look for the second installment next month!

One tiny baby draws two former lovers back together again in *A Bundle of Miracles* by Amy Frazier, who pays tribute to National Breast Cancer Awareness Month with this heartwrenching novel. Fierce passion flares in *Hidden in a Heartbeat* by Patricia McLinn, the third book in her A PLACE CALLED HOME miniseries. And not to be missed, talented new author Ann Roth unravels a soul-searching tale about a struggling single mom and a brooding stranger in *Stranger in a Small Town*.

I hope you enjoy all of our books this month as Special Edition continues to celebrate Silhouette's 20ᵗʰ anniversary!

All the best,

Karen Taylor Richman
Senior Editor

Please address questions and book requests to:
Silhouette Reader Service
U.S.: 3010 Walden Ave., P.O. Box 1325, Buffalo, NY 14269
Canadian: P.O. Box 609, Fort Erie, Ont. L2A 5X3

ANN ROTH
STRANGER IN A SMALL TOWN

SPECIAL EDITION®

Published by Silhouette Books
America's Publisher of Contemporary Romance

To Kim Bergstrom—
Thanks for pushing me so hard.

To Brian, Rachel, Stephanie, Kathryn, Mom and Dad,
for always believing in me

 SILHOUETTE BOOKS

ISBN 0-373-24356-1

STRANGER IN A SMALL TOWN

Copyright © 2000 by Ann Schussler

Visit Silhouette at www.eHarlequin.com

Printed in U.S.A.

ANN ROTH

has always been a voracious reader, reading everything from classics to mysteries to romance. Of all the books she's read, love stories have affected her the most and stayed with her the longest. "Is there anything more powerful and moving than a love that triumphs over seemingly insurmountable odds and ends in happily ever after?"

While in college Ann was lucky enough to meet and marry her own real-life hero. Today they live in the Seattle area with a finicky cat who rules the house. They have three wonderful college-age daughters.

It had long been Ann's dream to pen emotional love stories. In 1999, she won the Romance Writers of America Golden Heart Award for Best Long Contemporary with *Stranger in a Small Town*. Winning the prestigious award pushed her toward her goal: publication. "Yes, dreams can come true!" she says.

Ann would love to hear from readers. You can write her c/o Box 25003, Seattle, WA 98125-1903.

IT'S OUR 20th ANNIVERSARY!
We'll be celebrating all year,
Continuing with these fabulous titles,
On sale in October 2000.

Desire

 #1321 The Dakota Man
Joan Hohl

 #1322 Rancher's Proposition
Anne Marie Winston

#1323 First Comes Love
Elizabeth Bevarly

 #1324 Fortune's Secret Child
Shawna Delacorte

#1325 Marooned With a Marine
Maureen Child

#1326 Baby: MacAllister-Made
Joan Elliott Pickart

Special Edition

#1351 Bachelor's Baby Promise
Barbara McMahon

 #1352 Marrying a Delacourt
Sherryl Woods

#1353 Millionaire Takes a Bride
Pamela Toth

#1354 A Bundle of Miracles
Amy Frazier

#1355 Hidden in a Heartbeat
Patricia McLinn

#1356 Stranger in a Small Town
Ann Roth

Romance

 #1474 The Acquired Bride
Teresa Southwick

 #1475 Jessie's Expecting
Kasey Michaels

 #1476 Snowbound Sweetheart
Judy Christenberry

 #1477 The Nanny Proposal
Donna Clayton

 #1478 Raising Baby Jane
Lilian Darcy

#1479 One Fiancée To Go, Please
Jackie Braun

Intimate Moments

#1033 Who Do You Love?
Maggie Shayne/
Marilyn Pappano

#1034 Her Secret Weapon
Beverly Barton

#1035 A Thanksgiving to Remember
Margaret Watson

#1036 The Return of Luke McGuire
Justine Davis

#1037 The Lawman Meets His Bride
Meagan McKinney

#1038 The Virgin Beauty
Claire King

Chapter One

Heaven above, it was hot. Alison O'Hara wiped the sweat from her brow with her arm and surveyed the hand-lettered Room for Rent sign she'd just hammered into the draught-hard ground. Aside from a few dirt smudges, it looked good. And from its place near the road, it was visible to passing cars.

Now, if she could just find a boarder…. Crossing her fingers, she sent a silent plea heavenward. The sign had to work better than the newspaper ad, which had run for the past six weeks and hadn't elicited a single phone call.

Shading her eyes from the harsh July sun, she glanced up the two-lane highway, then down. Heat danced in waves over the pavement, but that was it; there wasn't a single car in sight. But just beyond a clump of dusty poplars, a man trudged slowly toward her. He was big and dark, and he wore faded jeans, a black tank top and a grim expression. At his side loped a ragged, panting dog.

Alison frowned. She lived several miles from town, and the few strangers who passed by did so on wheels, not on foot.

Both his stony look and his pace lightened as he caught sight of her and hurried forward. Her heart pounding, she snatched up the rock she'd used to pound in the sign. Thank goodness Hannah had gone swimming with Jimmy Burton and his parents. She made sure the man saw the rock. "Stop right there."

"Easy, ma'am, I mean no harm." Hands up in a gesture meant to calm, he hesitated at the edge of her pebbled driveway. Sweat glistened on his forehead and dampened his shirt. "My name's Clint Strong, and my truck broke down a few miles up the road. I'd like to use your phone."

Clutching the rock, she quickly assessed him. He was tall and muscled and could tackle her in a heartbeat. But he appeared too hot and tired to bother. And his poor dog looked even worse, scrawny and filthy and weary.

They both looked like strays, and, wise or not, her heart went out to them. In the same situation, she would expect kindness from strangers, and she saw no reason to deny this man the use of her phone. A few years back she might even have invited him in. But now she was older and smarter. And there was Hannah to think of.

"Come on, then." She gestured toward the house. The stranger fell into step beside her. Neither spoke, and only the crunch of their shoes on the pebbles broke the silence. Near the old wood front steps, she stopped. "Wait here. I'll bring it out."

"And a phone book, too, please."

She returned a few minutes later with lemonade, the phone book and the phone, its beige cord stretched as far as it would go. Clint had moved to the foot of the steps, where he stood stiffly and waited. The dog lay sprawled under a dusty elm tree, panting in the heat.

"Here." She set the phone and phone book down and handed Clint the ice-cold drink. "I thought you'd be thirsty."

"Thanks. You thought right." His appreciative smile erased years from his face and melted any doubts about her safety.

This man wasn't here to steal or hurt. She couldn't help smiling back.

His eyes were as dark and warm as midnight in August. "Uh, I didn't catch your name."

Underneath that sweat and grime, he was darned good-looking. Her stomach fluttered. "Alison O'Hara."

"Good to meet you, Alison." He sat down on the bottom step. The moment he did, the dog jumped up and, wagging his tail, sniffed the glass. Alison laughed. "You can have a drink, too, fella."

From the spigot on the side of the house, she filled an old plastic bowl. Then she sat down beside Clint, careful not to sit too close.

The house faced west, and the afternoon sun beat down mercilessly. Sweat trickled down her neck. "Your truck picked a bad day to break down." She lifted her heavy ponytail off her nape. "It sure is hot."

"Sure is." Clint's eyes strayed to her breasts, then to her lips, then to his glass. Tipping it in a salute, he drained it, his Adam's apple bobbing. With a satisfied sigh, he wiped his mouth with his hand. "That's the best lemonade I've ever tasted."

"I made it myself, from fresh-squeezed lemons." Alison couldn't help staring at the ugly red scars that crisscrossed his fingers and the back of his hand. A person's fingers were so sensitive, and his had been badly hurt. The pain must have been unbearable. She winced.

Beside her, Clint stiffened and set the glass between his feet. "Not a pretty sight, is it?"

"What?" A guilty flush prickling her cheeks, she quickly raised her gaze.

His expression shuttered, he spread his fingers and stared down at them. "My hand."

Alison bit her lip. "It looks like it hurts."

"Not anymore." His mouth compressed into a thin line, as if he were still in pain. Stripped of warmth, he looked remote and hard.

Seeking to bring back his smile, she scooped up the empty glass and forced a cheery note to her voice. "Would you like a refill?"

"No, thanks."

He reached for the phone book, brushing her arm in the process. It was an accidental touch, brief and casual, but it set her nerves humming. Interest flared in his eyes before he bent his head toward the directory.

"I need a mechanic for my truck." His voice was gruff. "Any suggestions?"

"There's only one garage in town. Chuck's."

She watched Clint thumb through the pages until he located the number and dialed it. A crease formed between his dark eyebrows as he listened. A moment later he hung up. "He's out fishing, closed until Tuesday. Just my luck," he muttered, turning to Alison. "There must be someone else."

"Not that I know of."

He plowed a hand through his hair. "Well, hell, if they just close up like that, what do people around here do when their cars break down?"

Alison knew only too well the answer to that question. Her station wagon stopped running at least once every other month. She shrugged. "Walk...or get a ride from someone."

Clint rolled his eyes. "I can't walk all the way to Tallahassee. I need that truck."

"Well then, you'll have to wait until Chuck gets back."

He groaned. "But it's only Friday. That's four days from now."

He'll need a place to stay. Alison's mind spun with the thought as she bent to rebuckle her sandal. Was this divine providence or what? Out of the corner of her eye, she studied Clint. Despite the scowl that came and went, he seemed decent enough. His dog, though thin and dirty, certainly showed no fear of him. He wasn't the nice, elderly lady she'd envisioned for a housemate, but Flatville, Indiana, population 4,753, wasn't exactly a haven of renters.

Besides, she was in no position to pass up this opportunity, not with Millie remodeling the restaurant and Alison's waitress position on hold. Jobs in the small farming community were hard to come by, and she hadn't been able to find other work. Even after selling some of her antique furniture, she'd been forced to withdraw money from an already meager savings account. Now it was almost empty.

She needed rental income for food and necessities, and the man sitting beside her was her best bet. Her only bet. Straightening, she offered her best smile. "While you're waiting for Chuck, you'll want a place to stay. I have a room to rent. You may have seen the sign by the road." The furrow between Clint's eyebrows deepened, so she quickly added, "Your dog's welcome, too, at no extra charge."

"He's not my dog, he just followed me here." Clint shifted restlessly. "Look, I can't leave my truck sitting on the highway all weekend. Is there a tow truck in Flatville or have they gone fishing, too?"

Alison ignored his sarcastic tone. No sense upsetting him further. She smiled politely. "You're in luck. My friend Millie owns the only tow service in town, and she doesn't fish. She'll haul your truck over to Chuck's." She gave him the number.

A moment later he'd arranged for Millie to pick him up. He handed Alison the phone book. "At least that's taken care of. I'd better call Tallahassee. They're expecting me Monday morning." Angling his hip off the step, he slid a wallet from his back pocket. "I don't carry credit cards, but I'll give you cash."

His wallet looked about as thin as the dog. Alison's hopes for making money faded. She accepted two dollars from him, tucking the bills into her pocket. "You're not from Florida. You don't have a Southern accent."

He studied a scrap of paper extracted from his wallet. "No, but there's a construction job waiting for me, if I make it in time."

She didn't want to appear rude and listen in on his conversation, so she went inside to give him privacy.

But his voice was loud, and she couldn't help over-hearing as he swore. He didn't seem to have much patience.

She waited until he hung up, then stepped through the screen door. "What happened?"

"It's after five in Florida. Nobody answered."

The heavy rumble of Millie's truck sounded in the distance. Clint stood and started toward the road. He hadn't said whether he was staying. Alison hurried down the steps. Thin wallet or not, he was better than nothing. "If you're going to stay here, you may as well leave your dog with me."

He frowned. "Looks like I don't have much choice."

Relief flooded her. She bit back a shout of glee. She had a boarder.

But what'll I do when he leaves?

And what about the rest of her money troubles? The bank note was due in four weeks, and rent from *ten* boarders couldn't pay that.

Alison pushed away her worries and focused on the positive. For the next few days she had a guest to see to. Things were definitely looking up.

They had to be.

"Chuck's Auto Shop is just a few miles down the road," Millie Allen said as the huge tow truck lum-bered toward downtown Flatville through the slanting afternoon sunlight. With Clint's help, the fiftyish woman had anchored his half-ton Ford securely to the back.

"That's good," Clint replied. The woman talked a blue streak. Though he hadn't asked, she'd volunteered a wealth of information about herself and the town.

Childless and widowed young, she'd somehow managed to run the towing business her husband had started, as well the area's main restaurant. He'd learned that most of the town's inhabitants farmed or ran local businesses and that Flatville was suffering its worst drought in a decade. Things he didn't care about, but he listened anyway. Trapped in the truck, he had no choice.

"Crime is almost nonexistent here," she told him. "The streets are safe and folks trust each other. This is a wonderful place to live. But some of our kids go off to college and never come back. It's a crying shame, because Flatville's a great place to raise a family." She eyed him hopefully. "With the population slipping, we sure could use a newcomer or two."

He pretended not to notice. He stayed away from small towns. They were all alike, full of nosy people who made it a point to know everyone else's business.

"Enough about me and Flatville." She braked as a cow and her calf ambled across the road. "What about you, Clint? What line of work are you in?"

For all she'd told him, he figured he owed her an answer. He skipped over his past white-collar job as an insurance fraud investigator and cut to the present. "Construction."

"Construction?" she repeated, widening her eyes in surprise.

She probably wondered how he managed with his hand. Glancing at it, he shrugged. "It's not as bad as it looks." He flexed his fingers to demonstrate. "I'm great with a saw and hammer."

The answer seemed to satisfy her. She nodded once. "I know something about that. I'm remodeling my restaurant. It'll be open again by the middle of August. It's going to be a honey of a place, the nicest Flatville has ever seen." She glanced at him. "It's a shame you won't be around to try my fried chicken with creamed gravy and homemade biscuits."

Clint tried to look like he was sorry. "I'll be long gone by then."

"So where are you from?"

"No one place. I travel the country, wherever work takes me."

"You like all that moving around?"

As long as it kept the demons at bay. Clint shrugged. "There's a big job in Tallahassee. That's where I'm headed. They're expecting me to report for work Monday."

Millie frowned. "You won't make it in that truck of yours. Look, there's a bus station halfway between here and Indianapolis. If you need a lift there—"

Clint shook his head. "I won't leave the truck."

Besides his tools, it was the only thing of value he owned, paid for with money earned from back-breaking, honest labor.

Her brow lifted. "It must mean a lot to you."

"You might say that." He could have bought a brand-new, state-of-the-art truck with some of the insurance proceeds. He shuddered at the thought. *Death money.* After nearly four years, the pain was still too close to the surface. He pushed it away.

He would never touch that money. Never.

He stared out the window. "Is there anybody besides Chuck who could take a look at the engine?"

Millie chewed her lip and considered the question.

"Not that I've heard of, and believe me I'd know. You'll just have to do like the rest of us. Sit back and wait. At Alison O'Hara's, you've got a fine place to do both." A smile lit the tow truck driver's creased face. "She's a darling girl and a great cook."

"Is she?" Clint thought about the woman who'd brought him fresh-squeezed lemonade and loaned him her phone. She was a little slip of a thing, nice enough, but too thin for his tastes. Except for her hair. Wild, thick, copper-gold in color, even in a ponytail, it cascaded halfway down her back. The sun glinting off it was the prettiest thing he'd ever seen. He remembered the way her breasts had raised as she'd lifted the heavy locks off her neck.

She might be small, but she was all woman.

He shifted in his seat. Sex hadn't interested him for years, since the fire. His body had picked a hell of a time to wake up.

"How old are you, son?" Millie glanced at him, then signaled and pulled into the turn lane.

"Thirty-three."

"Alison's twenty-seven," she replied, as if he'd asked.

She turned onto Flatville's main road. Tired-looking trees and weather-beaten shops lined the street. Though it wasn't yet dusk, lights winked on as they drove slowly past. "There's my place over there." She pointed to a gutted one-story building.

Clint leaned forward to see it. "It looks like a good location."

"It is." Millie beamed. "We're the only upscale restaurant in town. Add to that terrific food and friendly service, and you know why business has always been great. I know Alison will be glad to get back to work.''

"She works for you?'' Clint rested his arm on the back of the seat. "What does she do, cook?''

"Goodness, no.'' Millie laughed. "She's a waitress, one of my best. With the tips, there's good money to be made.'' Glancing at Clint, she lowered her voice. "I shouldn't tell you this, but my temporary closing has really hit her hard. I know she's struggling, even though she'd never admit it. She's even sold off some of the beautiful antique furniture her aunt left her.'' Millie's forehead wrinkled as she paused and rubbed her chin. "She'd be mortified if she knew I'd told you. So let's make this our little secret.''

"Okay,'' Clint promised, wishing Millie had kept quiet. The last thing he needed was someone else's problems weighing him down.

"It's a godsend you're staying at her place,'' Millie continued. "And I'm sure you'll enjoy yourself.'' A cryptic smile hovered on her mouth. "While you're here, you may as well look around. This is a great town.''

A moment later she slowed to let a sleek, black Mercedes pass. The expensive vehicle looked out of place amid the modest cars and pickups parked along the street.

"Who owns that?'' Clint asked, curious despite himself.

"Vincent Cahill.'' She spat out the name. "He runs the bank.''

Until now, everything she'd said about the people in Flatville had been positive. Clint lifted an eyebrow. "You don't like him much.''

"There's not much to like." She pursed her lips. "His father, Morton, may he rest in peace, was a banker with a heart. I think Vincent has greed instead of blood in his veins."

She signaled, and they pulled into the parking lot under Chuck's red-and-white revolving sign. Other than a few old cars, the lot was empty. A chain-link fence and a few lights were the only security offered.

Clint didn't like the setup. Over the years he'd learned to distrust people. Hands on his hips, he turned to Millie. "You sure it's safe to leave the truck here?"

"Safe as can be. I'd stake my reputation on that. Like I said, we don't have much crime here. Now come on, let's unload. Then we'll pick up my car and I'll drop you back at Alison's."

Warning bells sounded in Clint's head. Leaving the truck, sleeping under the attractive Alison's roof— neither felt like wise decisions. But at the moment they were the only choices he had. With a terse nod he helped Millie unhook the truck.

Chapter Two

Catching the plump feather pillow under her chin, Alison deftly slipped on a fresh white pillow case. Any minute Millie would bring *him* back. Clint Strong, the man who'd rented a room. With his dark, somber eyes and sober expression, he seemed to carry the weight of the world on his shoulders.

And what broad shoulders they were. Sun-browned and muscled. *Sexy.* With a sigh, she clasped the pillow close. Then she caught a glimpse of herself in the beveled oval mirror across the room. Wiping the dreamy look off her face, she quickly settled the pillow beside its mate.

What in the world was she thinking? A good-looking man passing through town on his way to someplace else was trouble. Hannah's father had proved that. Alison smoothed the hand-quilted spread over the double bed, then backed away from it.

She turned up the fan. Even though a big elm
shaded this side of the house, up here it was hot and
stuffy. She pulled open the blue eyelet curtains and
raised the window higher. Out front, the dog barked
as tires crunched over the gravel drive.

He's here. Alison's stomach jumped. She watched
him emerge from Millie's silver convertible sports
coupe.

He was a big man, so big it was a wonder he'd
managed to fit in the small car. His dark hair was
windblown and wild. He stretched, then combed his
fingers through it, exposing a broad, tanned forehead.
High cheekbones and a strong, straight nose gave him
a noble air, like an Indian chief.

Alison sucked in a breath. Heaven above, he was
handsome.

The dog licked Clint's hand and wagged his tail
joyfully. Clint's mouth quirked into an almost smile,
and he rubbed between the animal's ears. Satisfied,
the dog trotted to the plate of food Alison had set out,
sniffed it and finished his dinner.

Clint hoisted a small, battered suitcase and a duffel
bag from the trunk. His muscles rippled beneath his
tank top. Setting the bags down, he walked to the
driver's side. Alison couldn't help noticing the way
his snug, faded jeans accented narrow hips and long
legs. Resting an arm on the car, he said something to
Millie, then straightened and waved as she drove off.

Suddenly he looked up, straight at Alison. His eyes
widened, then lit with awareness, and she knew he'd
caught her staring. A smile tugged his mouth. Her
pulse skyrocketed.

It had been years since she'd reacted so viscerally
to a man. She didn't like the feeling. Physical attrac-

tion only got a woman into trouble. Jerking her gaze away, she turned from the window and headed for the stairs.

If only Hannah were here. Surely her daughter's lighthearted laughter would ease this strange tension in Alison's stomach. But the little girl was still off swimming with Jimmy Burton and his parents. She wouldn't be home for another hour.

Soft doorbell chimes summoned Alison to the door. She wet her suddenly dry lips. She was silly to feel like this, shy and nervous. For heaven's sake, the man was a boarder, nothing more. Pulling in a calming breath, she pasted a smile on her face and swung open the screen door. It squeaked loudly. "Hello, Mr. Strong."

"Clint," he corrected.

The eyes that met hers were whisky-brown and flecked with gold. Why had she thought them dark?

"Clint," she repeated, tasting the name aloud for the first time.

His expression softened and warmed, as if he liked the way she said his name. The pleasure that gave her made no sense. Was she so hungry for a man's attention? Flustered, she beckoned him inside. "How long are you planning to stay?"

The sober expression returned. "Through Tuesday morning, until the truck is fixed. How much do I owe you?" Alison told him and he dug into his pocket. "I'd like to pay up front. This is for me and the dog, for four nights."

"Thank you." Alison accepted his payment, stuffing the bills into the pocket of her Bermuda shorts. "If the repairs take more time, you're welcome to extend that." She tried a smile but, nervous as she was, failed.

The grim set of his mouth didn't help matters. "Let's hope not."

Alison pressed her lips together. Plainly, the man was not happy to be here. But he was her first boarder, and she was determined to make his stay here as enjoyable as possible. Using her best friendly waitress manner, she looked up at him. "You probably want to unpack and clean up before dinner. Come on—" she gestured toward the narrow stairway "—I'll show you your room."

He followed behind her, his footsteps heavy on the old wood stairs. As usual, the step halfway up groaned. Though he didn't speak, she felt his eyes on her. Heaven only knew what he was thinking. Probably wishing he were someplace else.

She would change his mind, work hard to make him like it here, to make him feel comfortable. That way, if Chuck needed a few extra days to work on the truck, Clint would stay here and not in the Flatville Motel on the other side of town.

He had to. She needed the money too much to fail.

Half an hour later Clint rolled up the cuffs of his wrinkled but clean chambray shirt. After a shower and shave, he felt refreshed. A full night's sleep would be even better, and tonight he was tired enough to sleep like a dead man. Too tired for bad dreams.

He headed down the hall, toward the stairs. Clattering pots and pans mingled with the mouthwatering aroma of fresh-baked strawberry pie. Clint licked his lips. From the smells, he guessed Alison was as good a cook as Millie said.

What else was Alison good at? He started down the steps. Was there a man in her life? Not that he cared. He just wondered.

He remembered following her upstairs earlier. Her softly rounded hips and cute little behind had tempted him mercilessly. And those legs... He shook his head. He'd gone way too long without sex. She was too thin, not even his type. He liked his women with plenty of curves. Yet, there was something about her....

"Oh, I'm setting the table, setting the table," a cheery voice sang out, interrupting his thoughts.

A young child's voice.

Stunned, he stopped at the bottom step and gaped unseen at the little girl in the dining room. Where had she come from?

She was freckle-faced, with drooping pigtails the same coppery color as Alison's hair. He didn't have much experience with kids, but he guessed she was about four. The age Erin would be.

But Erin was dead.

Pain hit him like a hard punch to the stomach. Gripping the wooden banister, he fought the urge to turn around, grab his bags and run.

Suddenly the child spotted him. Her brow furrowed a moment, then smoothed as she smiled—a wide grin that exposed a dimple in her cheek. "You're the boarder man. I'm Hannah. I'm almost five years old, and I'm setting the table for you, me and Mama." Puffed up with importance, she carefully laid a fork beside a neatly folded linen napkin, then tilted her head at him expectantly. "Didn't I do a good job?"

Alison hadn't mentioned a child. If she had, he sure

as hell wouldn't be here. He cleared his throat and backed up a step. "Uh, yeah."

Hannah's smile faded. "What's the matter, mistah?"

Luckily, Alison chose that moment to push through the door, saving him from having to reply. Balancing a bowl of coleslaw in one hand and a steaming platter of corn on the cob in the other, she smiled. "I didn't realize you'd come downstairs, Clint." Her gaze traveled from him to Hannah. "I see you two have met."

"We sure have." Under different circumstances, the warmth lighting Alison's face would have stirred him. Now it only added to his agony. He lifted the platter from her arms and set it on the table.

Hannah stuck out her lower lip. "He doesn't like me, Mama."

"What?" Alison's eyes widened and the smile vanished. "I'm sure you're wrong, sweetie," she said brightly. "Everyone likes you, including Mr. Strong. You must have misunderstood." The warning look she leveled at Clint sent a clear message. *Be nice to my daughter.*

He knew his reaction was irrational. Hannah couldn't help it if she dredged up painful thoughts of Erin. Slowly he turned to the girl. "I like you fine, Hannah."

Arms stiff at her sides, the little girl chewed her bottom lip, staring at him with big eyes. At least the crease between Alison's eyebrows had eased.

"Sorry I was gruff." Guilt spurred him to stick out his hand. "Okay?"

"'Kay," Hannah replied after a brief hesitation, and allowed him to clasp her small hand in his.

Frowning, she stared at his fingers. "You gots scars and so do I. Wanna see?"

She let go of his hand to pull up her T-shirt. A long, vertical scar ran from midchest to just above her navel. His heart gave a painful tug. Poor kid must have had surgery. "What happened to you?"

"My heart used to have a hole in it, but now it's fixed." She glanced at Alison. "Right, Mama?"

Alison nodded, her face a mix of emotions. "Right, sweetie. Thanks to a great surgical team, you're good as new."

"Uh-huh." Hannah nodded, then eyed Clint soberly. "Did you have an operation, too?"

"No." He stretched out his fingers and stared at them, the scars an ugly reminder of the past. "I burned my hand."

He felt Alison staring at him, the same way she had earlier this afternoon. Tensing, he waited for her questions. Luckily, none came. He liked it that she didn't pry.

Hannah, however, was entirely different. "How did you do that?" she asked.

"In a fire." He clamped his lips shut.

"Fire is hot. You're not supposed to touch it or you'll get burned," she said, sounding like an adult.

Truer words had never been spoken. Clint nodded gravely.

"Can we eat now, Mama? I'm starved. I set the table just like you taught me. We had plastic spoons and forks at our picnic today," she informed Clint. "I saw a fish jump up, right in the middle of the lake. He maked a big splash." She wrinkled her nose and giggled. "Isn't that funny?"

She didn't seem to expect a reply, so Clint listened

politely as she jumped from one subject to the next. Alison rewarded him with an approving smile.

"Come on, sweetie, you can help me with the pork chops." Placing her hands on the little girl's shoulders, she guided her daughter forward. "We'll be right back, Clint. Please sit down."

They disappeared into the kitchen, leaving him alone with his thoughts. Hannah had stirred up memories better left buried, and God, he hurt. His hands clenched into fists as he fought back the pain. More than anything, he wanted to go upstairs, pack and leave. Now.

He glanced at the linen tablecloth, the fresh flowers in the crystal vase at the center of the table. Obviously, Alison had done this for him. And she'd cooked a meal that smelled too good to pass up. Despite his pain, he was hungry. Ravenous. He'd leave after dinner.

But Alison needed his money. And with a child to care for, he'd feel like a jerk if he asked for a refund. Hell, she could keep the money. He had a couple hundred dollars stashed in his duffel for emergencies. He'd find another place to sleep. He'd even bunk in a field if he had to, mosquito bites and sweltering nights be damned.

Because now he couldn't stay.

Not with that little girl around, torturing him with reminders of what could have been. Bad enough he couldn't sleep at night. He didn't need the constant reminder in the daylight hours, too. Watching her small, animated face, listening to that innocent prattle, hit too damn deep.

His fingernails bit into his palms. If only he could go back and change that terrible night four years ago.... But that was impossible, and there wasn't a damn thing he could do about it now except try to survive each day.

Sometimes even that was hard. He sighed wearily, unfisted his hands, and with sheer will forced his thoughts to the upcoming meal.

Alison glanced at Hannah's empty plate. Her daughter had eaten a huge meal tonight, and that pleased her. "More dessert, sweetie?" she asked, pointing the strawberry-coated spatula at the remains of the pie.

Hannah patted her rounded stomach. "No, Mama, I'm full to the tops of my eyebrows."

"Clint? Seconds on pie or coffee?"

"No, thanks." He laid his napkin on the table. "That was delicious."

Alison dipped her head. "Thank you."

The compliment would have pleased her if his voice wasn't so gruff. He'd been stiff and aloof throughout the meal, eating as though he'd rather be someplace else. If it hadn't been for Hannah's excited chatter, the meal would have been uncomfortably silent.

"Will you play with me, Clint?" Hannah's small face tilted hopefully toward him.

"Can't." Abruptly he stood. "I've got things to do."

"I can help you." Hannah stood, too. "And then we'll play. Guess what, I turn five on August third. That's in twelve days, right, Mama? We're having a party here with cake and ice cream and balloons and everything. I hope I get another Pretty Pony, so my pink one doesn't get lonesome. Her name is Princess, and she likes to play. Wanna take turns brushing her?''

"Uh," Clint jammed his hands into the front pockets of his jeans, "I don't think so."

His stricken expression told Alison exactly what he thought of that idea. She understood that children made some adults uncomfortable, but he seemed more than ill at ease. He flat-out disliked Hannah. Alison balled her napkin in her fist. An innocent child! Somehow her daughter had offended him. Surely he realized she meant no harm. Though, by the stony frown on his face, that didn't appear to be the case.

Since Clint's rent entitled him to sit-down meals shared with both Alison and Hannah, they'd best straighten out the matter right away. Alison intended to do that, but not in front of her daughter.

She touched her child's sun-bronzed arm. "Mr. Strong wants to be alone right now, sweetie. Why don't you help me in the kitchen? You can fill the sink." Over Hannah's head, she sent Clint a look that she hoped conveyed her need to speak with him before he disappeared upstairs.

"Can I put in the soap, too, and make bubbles?" Hannah hopped enthusiastically from foot to foot.

Alison nodded. "I'll even let you wash the silverware. Why don't you get an apron from the bottom kitchen drawer."

"Oh, goodie!" The little girl skipped off.

In the silence left in her wake, Clint crossed his arms. His face was dark and shuttered. "Why didn't you tell me you had a daughter?"

"I didn't realize it mattered."

Pain flashed in his eyes. "Well, it does."

Stung, Alison moved quickly around the table,

snatching up silverware. "Is it Hannah, or do you dislike children in general?"

"It's not your daughter," he stated quietly. "It's me."

The ache in his voice stilled her. Gripping a handful of knives and forks, she turned to him.

He rubbed a hand over his face. "Maybe I should—"

A clamor outside stemmed whatever he'd been about to say. The dog barked excitedly, and a beat later the doorbell rang.

"Who can that be?" Alison frowned and set down the silverware. She didn't get much company at night and wasn't expecting anyone.

"Somebody's come to see us." Wearing an adult-size apron that hung to her ankles, Hannah darted from the kitchen. The hem tangled with her sandals and tripped her. She landed hard on her stomach. Her eyes widened, then she screwed up her face and began to cry.

The color drained from Clint's face. He looked as if he wanted to go to her. Instead, he gripped the back of a chair. "Is she all right?"

He looked scared to death.

"I'm sure she'll be fine," Alison soothed, both for her child and her boarder. She knelt down and pulled Hannah close. "Where does it hurt, baby?"

"My knee. Oweee." Hannah dragged the word out in a long wail.

Alison examined the knee. "You've scraped it, but it's not even bleeding. See? I'll kiss it and make it better."

"'Kay." Hannah sniffled.

Clint released a breath. "Thank God."

For the brief instant his unguarded gaze hooked with Alison's, she saw relief and, behind that, pain. Something inside him was hurting. An irrational urge filled her to reach out and comfort him as she had Hannah.

The doorbell rang again, twice in rapid succession. Clint jerked his attention toward the sound. "Why don't I get that for you," he offered, and looking relieved, strode rapidly from the room.

Alison urged her daughter to her feet, then quickly tucked up the apron so the little girl wouldn't trip again. "Wait here, Hannah."

She reached the door as Clint swung it open. Jenny Ross, the antique dealer who'd sold some of Alison's furniture, stood on the top step, inside the glow of the porch light. Though she and Alison were friends, usually Jenny called before dropping by. And she never visited outside regular business hours.

So why was she here now? Had she finally found a buyer for the matching wing chairs? Alison hoped so, because she really needed the money. But Jenny looked too serious for that.

Oh dear, did the woman who'd purchased the claw-foot sofa want to return it and get her money back? Alison's stomach twisted at the thought. She firmly pushed away the depressing notion. Those kinds of things didn't happen.

Did they?

Please let this be good news. It had to be, she figured, because her luck had taken a decidedly positive turn. Didn't Clint's arrival prove that? He was handsome and a paying boarder, to boot.

Alison's thoughts quickly turned to his less-than-warm treatment of Hannah and she frowned. Make that a twist in her luck. Perhaps Jenny was here to twist it again in a more positive direction. Ever hopeful, Alison swallowed, mentally crossed her fingers and prepared to greet her guest.

Chapter Three

"Jenny." Surprise flickered across Alison's face, and something else Clint couldn't read. "What a surprise," she said through the screen door. After a slight hesitation, she opened the door, wincing at its loud squeak, and beckoned her visitor inside. "Please, come in."

Clint studied the tall blonde, who looked to be in her mid-thirties, nearly a decade older than Alison. Unlike Alison, this woman sported a sleek, movie-star hairdo and a fancy white suit that clung to her trim body. She reeked of sophistication and success.

In the darkness outside, the mutt barked. Pausing in the threshold, Jenny glanced over her shoulder. "That's some watchdog. When did you get him?"

"He's not mine, he belongs to my boarder." Alison glanced at Clint. "Clint Strong, meet Jenny Ross."

"A boarder, eh?" Disapproval flashed across Jenny's face as she and Clint shook hands.

Clint wondered why. Maybe she was one of those rigid, moral types who didn't like the idea of a man sleeping under Alison's roof. Well, she could rest easy, because he was leaving tonight. And this was his cue to head upstairs and pack. But he stayed put.

"I'm in the antique business." Jenny handed Clint a business card.

Clint remembered what Millie had said earlier, about Alison selling some of her antiques because she needed money. This must be the woman she'd hired.

"Who is it, Mama?" Hannah called from the dining room.

"Jenny Ross, sweetie."

"Oh. Hi, Jenny," Hannah sang.

"Hi, sugar," the blonde replied.

The child showed no further interest in greeting her mother's visitor. "Can I fill the sink and wash the dishes now?"

"*May* I fill the sink," Alison corrected without taking her eyes from her guest. "Go ahead. I'll be there soon." A pucker creased Alison's forehead as she tucked a wayward strand of hair behind her ear. "What brings you out here on a Friday night, Jenny?"

"Something that couldn't wait. I'd like to talk to you."

"Oh?" Hope flickered across Alison's face, then, as she glanced at Jenny's subdued expression, worry. "What is it?"

"Mama, I need help turning on the water," Hannah called out.

"Guess I'd better get Hannah started." Alison offered an apologetic smile. "Would you like coffee? There's half a pot left from dinner. Or, I could make fresh."

Jenny shook her head. "Don't trouble yourself. I'll drink what's already made."

"How about you, Clint?" Alison asked.

"No, thanks." He had enough trouble sleeping at night without adding more caffeine. Besides, he had no interest in hanging around, listening to what was none of his concern. He'd go upstairs and pack. And when Jenny left, he'd talk to Alison, tell her he couldn't stay.

"I'll be right back." Alison gestured toward the living room. "Make yourselves comfortable." Pivoting, she hurried toward the kitchen.

"Nice meeting you. Good night." Clint nodded formally at Alison's guest.

To his surprise the antique dealer leaned forward and lowered her voice. "Would you mind sticking around? I may need your help."

"What for?"

"Convincing Alison to sell the rest of that living room set." Jenny glanced toward the big chairs and the small couch between them. "She already sold the big divan, and now she wants to sell the chairs. But I doubt she'll part with that love seat."

The antique in question didn't look like much to Clint, just a faded flowered sofa, too small to get comfortable on. "What she decides is none of my business," he said brusquely. "You're the salesperson, you convince her."

"Convince me of what?" Alison reappeared, carrying a wicker tray.

Caught, Jenny looked sheepish. "I thought I'd tell

Clint about Rose Murphy," she said, deftly skirting Alison's question. "She was Alison's great-great-grandmother. She and her husband, Michael, built this house almost a hundred years ago. Of course, it's been modernized, but it's one of Flatville's oldest standing structures. There's a portrait of Grandma Rose in the living room. Come on, I'll show you."

Clint didn't want to see it. He didn't want to do anything but leave. But then Alison glanced at him, her expression a mix of fierce pride and vulnerability. For some reason she wanted him to see the painting of her ancestor. What the hell. He followed them into the living room.

Jenny sat demurely on one of the big wing chairs, waiting until Alison passed out the coffee before continuing the story. With a shake of his head, Clint declined a cup and remained standing.

Alison set the tray on a marble-top table that looked old but solid. She sat down across from the other woman, sinking into the sagging cushions on a brightly flowered sofa that seemed out of place with the rest of the furniture.

"There she is, Rose Murphy, circa nineteen hundred." With her cup Jenny indicated the portrait over the fireplace. "Wasn't she a beauty?"

Without moving from his place near the wall, Clint studied the painting, drawn to the young woman looking out from it. It was easy to see the family resemblance. Her eyes were the same green as Alison's, and the women shared the same brilliant copper-colored hair. "She was pretty, yes."

His gaze dropped to the pale-blue dress that covered Rose Murphy from neck to ankle and then to the heavy gold chain around her neck. A glittering pendant hung from it, a large, oval diamond, circled with emeralds that rivaled her eyes. Intrigued despite himself, he whistled. "That's some necklace."

"Isn't it?" Jenny nodded. "It would be worth a small country today. Unfortunately no one knows what happened to it. But that's Alison's story. She should tell you."

"I don't think Clint wants to hear it." Alison lifted a skeptical eyebrow at him.

He didn't, but hell, he was stuck here, so why not? He shrugged.

"All right." She set down her coffee and leaned forward, her eyes on the portrait. "When Rose and Michael emigrated here from Ireland, they brought two items with them. This love seat—" she indicated the small couch next to Jenny "—and the necklace you see in the painting." Alison's expression softened, as if the tale touched her deeply. "No one knows where the necklace came from, but it had been in the family for generations. The story goes that Rose planned to pass it to her oldest daughter in her will, as her mother had passed it to her. If that had happened and the tradition had continued, today the necklace would be mine."

She shook her head. "But it didn't. A few years after that portrait was finished, Michael Murphy died. Sometime after his death, the necklace disappeared."

"What happened to it?" Clint asked.

Alison met his gaze. "No one knows. Some say it was lost."

"And some say she sold it to save the land and house," Jenny said, fixing Alison with a meaningful look Clint couldn't ignore.

Moneywise, Alison was hurting. A shame, but not his problem.

"Anyway, that's the story."

Jenny and Alison looked at Clint as if they expected him to comment. "Interesting," he replied.

"It would be more interesting if she had the necklace." Jenny turned to Alison. "Now...I've got a business proposition for you."

Whatever it was, Clint wanted no part of it. He glanced past the dining room, toward the stairs. "Uh, why don't I leave you two alone."

Alison nodded, then focused on Jenny. "Go ahead."

Before Clint was through the room, the antique dealer began to speak. "Finally, after six long months, I've found a buyer for your chairs. He wants them right away, and he'll pay top dollar. Cash."

"Yes!" Alison laughed. "That *is* good news."

Her obvious relief shouldn't have mattered to Clint. It didn't, he told himself. She needed the money. Anybody would be happy for her.

"But there's a catch," Jenny said.

Without thinking, Clint stopped in the archway and turned around, waiting to hear it.

"What is it?" Alison asked in a sober voice.

"He won't take them without the love seat."

She groaned. "Come on, Jen, you know I don't want to sell that piece."

"Yeah, yeah, sentimental value and all that. Will you tell her?"

The blonde rolled her eyes at Clint, but he didn't respond. Crossing his arms, he leaned against the wall.

Jenny turned her attention back to Alison. "Look,

hon, antique buyers haven't exactly flocked to your door. This is a great opportunity for you, one that may not come your way again. What do you say?''

Alison bit her lip, apparently torn. Finally she let out a sigh and lifted her chin. "Can I think about it?''

"Sure, but don't wait too long." Jenny stood up. "I'll put the buyer off for a few days."

"Thanks." Standing, too, Alison glanced at Clint, her thoughts plainly visible. She seemed embarrassed that he'd heard about her troubles, but also full of confusion over what to do.

"Take care," Jenny said at the door. She and Alison embraced. "Call me when you make up your mind."

The screen door squeaked and banged shut. In the darkness the mutt yipped excitedly as Jenny walked to her van and drove off.

Releasing a breath, Alison sagged against the heavy oak door. She looked uncertain and weary. She looked as if she could use another hug.

For some reason Clint wanted to do just that, to take her in his arms and hold her. But that would only lead to trouble. Stifling that urge, he hung his thumbs from his belt loops and walked toward her. "That's some pushy saleswoman."

"She comes across that way, but actually I consider her a friend. She's only trying to help." Alison said nothing further, but the pucker of worry reappeared between her eyebrows.

Her problems were none of Clint's affair, and he didn't pry into other people's affairs. Still, he had to know. "Are you going to be okay?"

"Hey, it's only furniture." She offered a tired smile. "I'll be fine."

She didn't look fine. Exhaustion clouded her eyes and echoed in her slumped shoulders. Forgetting his decision not to touch her, he cupped those slender shoulders and steered her back toward the living room. The bones beneath her warm flesh felt fine and delicate, too delicate for the fatigue weighing them down. "Why don't you sit on the couch and relax. I don't mind doing the dishes," he offered before he had time to think.

Alison jerked. "Oh, my gosh, Hannah! Excuse me." Ducking from his grasp, she dashed from the room.

Clint followed her, stopping in the kitchen doorway. The little girl stood on a chair in front of the sink, her hair, apron and clothes soaking wet. Soapy water had sloshed onto the tile counter and the faded linoleum floor. Looking pleased with herself, Hannah gestured toward the sink brimming with bubbles. "Look, Mama, I filled it all by myself, and I only got a teensy bit wet."

"A teensy bit? Hannah Rose O'Hara, you look like a drowned rabbit." Alison's mouth twitched, then she burst out laughing.

After a startled moment Hannah giggled. Their mirth tickled Clint. He couldn't stifle his grin.

The cuckoo clock chimed ten. Too late to leave tonight. Tomorrow he'd look for another place to stay.

He thought about the love seat. Would Alison sell it? Even though it was none of his business and he didn't care, he was curious. Hell, with his truck broken down and the mechanic off fishing, what else was there to occupy his time?

* * *

Clint knew he was dreaming.

He stood in his front yard and looked up at the bedroom window. He could see Lynn through the glass, cradling their newborn daughter. Love and tenderness filled him.

"Erin misses her daddy. Come upstairs," Lynn called out, smiling.

His heart full, he grinned back and turned the knob. The door was locked. Suddenly smoke blurred his vision.

"Help us!" Lynn cried, panic lacing her voice.

"Where are you? I can't see," he shouted. Gripped with fear, he pounded against the windows until his hands ached, but they remained shut.

"Please hurry." The edge in Lynn's voice tore through him.

"Hang on, I'll save you." Terrified, he kicked the door down. Groping his way forward, he ran up a stairway filled with smoke and flames. He couldn't get to the top. Angry and frustrated, he lengthened his stride and took the stairs two at a time, but the faster he moved, the farther away his wife and daughter seemed. Lynn's screams echoed helplessly in his ears, then slowly faded and died.

"No!" Clint bolted upright.

Oh God, oh God. His heart pounding, he switched on the lamp. The sudden light hurt his eyes, and he blinked. It took him a moment to remember where he was. This wasn't Seattle. There was no thick smoke, no burning flames here, only freshly painted, pale-yellow walls and framed prints of peaceful country scenes.

This was his room at Alison's house. He glanced

around, at the colorful, braided rug that lay over a worn but gleaming hardwood floor and the fragrant flowers in the antique pitcher on the bedside table. Her warmth and cheeriness were everywhere, taunting him with memories he didn't want to recall.

Rubbing a hand over his face, he swung his legs over the bed. Four years ago he'd lived in a place like this, *home,* with a wife and a brand-new daughter. They'd been happy there, a family.

Until the fire. He'd been out, buying disposable diapers, when an arsonist he'd sent to jail for insurance fraud years earlier took his revenge and torched the house, intending Clint as the target. Instead, his wife and baby had died.

Agony shot through him, the pain as familiar as his shallow breaths. If only he'd remembered to buy the diapers during lunch, he could have stopped the fire or at least been there to save his family.

It should have been him who died. Why couldn't it have been him?

Move. He had to move or his thoughts would drive him mad. Blindly he reached for his jeans and tugged them on. Bare-chested and barefoot, he stumbled down the dark stairs. Somehow he ended up in the kitchen.

Through the open window above the sink, he heard the frogs croaking. Heart pounding, he braced his hands on the counter and stared out into the night. Moonlight wreathed the backyard in silver and shadow. His life was like that, more shadow than light.

"What are you doing down here?" Alison padded softly toward him.

He spun around. "Did I wake you?"

"No." She switched on the light over the sink.

Like him she was barefoot. A shapeless pink robe hung to just above her knees, and what looked like the hem of a white T-shirt peeked from under it. Her brow creased. "Is there something wrong with your room?"

"Everything's fine." He shoved his hands into his pockets. He didn't feel like talking, but he *was* in her kitchen in the middle of the night. He owed her an explanation. "Sometimes I can't sleep." He turned to leave.

"I don't usually have that problem." Her soft voice stopped him. She swept her hair over her shoulder. "I guess I'm wound up tonight, stressing over that love seat. I was going to make myself a cup of hot milk. I'll make enough for both of us."

He didn't want the milk or her company. But he wasn't ready to go back to his room. Grudgingly he shrugged. "Why not?" Crossing his arms, he leaned his hip against the counter. "When I was a kid, my mother sometimes fixed warm milk for me before bed."

Surprised, he clamped his mouth shut. He didn't talk about his family. Why now?

"You're lucky." Alison pulled a carton of milk from the refrigerator. "Mine was too busy trying to make ends meet to have time for that." She emptied the milk into a saucepan and turned on the burner. "You'll find the place mats in the top drawer."

Clint located them and laid them on the round oak table. "Anything else?"

"The mugs are in the cabinet to your left."

He set the mugs on the mats. Then he shoved his hands back in his pockets and leaned against the kitchen counter. Alison stirred the milk with a long wooden spoon, her movements slow and easy. For some reason, watching her soothed his nerves. But the dream hovered at the edge of his mind, threatening to pull him back into hell. Clint swallowed. If he got her talking, maybe it would fade faster.

"Have you always lived in this house?" he asked.

"No." She shook her head, the motion causing gentle ripples in her unbound hair. "My mother and I lived in Indianapolis until I was twelve. It's a big city, much different from Flatville. I never even knew we had family here. Or anywhere, for that matter."

Clint barely listened to the words. He'd been right, the sound of her voice helped edge out the darkness.

"That winter, my mother died in a car accident." Alison's spoon scraped rhythmically across the bottom of the pan. "Since we moved often, we didn't have many friends there. It was a bad time for me. I was really scared, and so alone."

Clint nodded, but didn't speak. He understood loneliness. And pain. He spent his days running from it. But some nights it caught up with him while he slept. Stifling a shudder, he gripped the counter behind him and forced his attention on Alison's voice.

"...and then I found out about Aunt Phoebe," she was saying. "She was my only living relative, and she lived right here in this house. I moved in with her."

She paused and looked at him, one eyebrow raised slightly, as if she expected him to reply. "Sorry about your mother," he said, his voice gruff.

"Thank you. That was a long time ago and I've put it behind me. Now that I'm older, I know that coming here to live with Aunt Phoebe was the best thing that ever happened to me." A soft smile lit Alison's face. "She'd never married, and I'm sure taking me in was a big adjustment for a fifty-year-old woman. But she never acted like it. From the funeral on, she opened her arms and treated me like a daughter. I learned about my ancestors and my roots from her. We had ten wonderful years together." A wistful look on her face, Alison stared into space at something only she could see. "I sure do miss her." She sighed.

To Clint's dismay, tears filled her eyes. If she cried, he didn't know what he would do. He'd best keep her talking. "Uh, what happened to her?" he asked.

"Unfortunately she died of cancer, just before Hannah was born." Thankfully, Alison swiped her eyes and resumed stirring the milk. "Battling the disease took all her savings, everything but this." Her gesture swept the room. "When she died, she left me the house and the adjoining twenty acres and all her possessions. I love this old place," she said, and adjusted the heat. "There was no mortgage then. But when Hannah needed surgery, I borrowed against the property to pay for the operation."

The worried frown on her face bothered him. "The operation was a success, right?"

"Oh, yes. She's perfect now. The only aftereffect is that scar you saw…and a big old mortgage."

A heavy sigh escaped her lips. So it was debt that clouded her face. Curious despite himself, Clint eyed her. "Where was Hannah's father during all this?"

Alison's eyes blazed. "I don't know and I don't care." Pressing her lips together, she tapped the spoon against the metal rim of the pot. "The day he found out I was pregnant, he wrote me a goodbye note and left town. Nobody's heard from him since.''

What kind of man walked out on a woman pregnant with his baby? Clint frowned. ''He sounds like a first-class jerk to me.''

''Oh, he is. But I'm glad he came along.'' Alison turned off the burner. ''Because without him, I wouldn't have Hannah.''

She poured the steaming milk into the mugs, then sat down. Clint didn't want to sit at the table, didn't want her to look at him. She might see something in his eyes and realize the kind of man he was. A man no better than Hannah's father, a man who had let down his family when they needed him most. But Alison gave him a gentle smile and beckoned him to the table with the warm expression in her big, pretty eyes, and he couldn't resist. Scowling, he sat down across from her and cupped his mug.

''I've talked your head off tonight.'' She puckered her mouth and blew on her milk, then tasted it, licking her lips with enjoyment. Even though he was an emotional wreck, his body stirred. Damn, she was sexy.

''Now it's your turn,'' she said in that soft, soothing voice. ''Where are you from, Clint?''

''Seattle. I used to own a place up there.'' Pain clutched him. Why had he mentioned the house? He gulped the hot milk, not caring that it seared his throat.

''Used to?'' Alison prodded.

Sexy as hell, but nosy. He didn't need or want her inquiries. ''What is this, twenty questions?''

He saw by the expression on her face that his rudeness shocked her. Maybe she'd get the message and stop digging in places she had no right to go. His chair scraped across the linoleum as he scooted back and abruptly stood. ''I'm turning in now. Thanks for the milk.''

Setting his mug in the sink, he left her sitting at the table alone.

Mourning doves cooed to each other outside the window when Alison awoke. Through a crack in the curtains she saw the pale light of dawn.

The moment she opened her eyes, she thought about Clint Strong. She hadn't expected to see him in the kitchen last night. Wearing only a pair of snug-fitting jeans, he'd looked dark and lean and sexy. And she'd looked like a frump in her old pink robe.

Not that it mattered.

Solemn and grim-faced, he'd seemed lost in a world of pain he didn't want to share. Though she barely knew him, her heart ached for him. She shouldn't have tried to draw him out. But he'd listened to her as if he were genuinely interested, as if what she said was more important than his own problems. It was a lovely feeling, one she'd never experienced. She'd wanted to return the kindness.

Instead her questions had driven him away. He'd practically sprinted out of the kitchen. That was the last thing she wanted. What if he decided to leave now and stay at the motel across town? She wanted him to feel welcome, to stay here.

Lord, Alison, don't be a fool. Clint was the last thing she needed in her life. Like Hannah's father, he was a drifter, here only until his truck was fixed. If she were smart, she would remember that he was a boarder, a means to an end. She wouldn't pry again.

Besides, she had troubles of her own to occupy her

mind, money troubles that Clint's rent couldn't solve. There was the bank note to pay, due in exactly four weeks. The only way to pay it was to get a loan. Without a job, that was impossible.

Alison released a weighty sigh. If only Vincent Cahill hadn't turned her down when she'd asked for an extension. But he had. If Millie's restaurant reopened in time and Alison proved she was working there again, she could get that loan. If not, if she didn't come up with the money in time, she could lose the house and land that had belonged to her family for generations.

Foreclosure. The ugly word raised goose bumps on her arms, despite the warm summer morning. Alison hugged her cotton blanket close.

That was not an option, not with a daughter to raise. The property was Hannah's birthright.

Too well Alison remembered her mother's continual moves from apartment to apartment, and the uprooted, flighty feeling that came with it. Hannah needed security and stability, a home she could count on. *This* home.

Alison hoped and prayed that Millie's restaurant reopened in time. For now, that was all she could do. That and selling the love seat along with the wing chairs. Tossing back the covers, she rose.

Early this morning, she'd come to a decision. The money from the sale would replenish her savings. It wasn't enough to pay off the note, but it would help cover emergencies. Sorrow filled her. She hated to sell part of her heritage.

She rooted through the dresser until she found the shorts and matching T-shirt she wanted. The pale-aqua color set off her hair. Not that she wanted to catch Clint's eye. She just felt like looking nice, after looking so dowdy last night. She tossed on her robe, then tiptoed toward the bathroom, stopping to peek into Hannah's room. The little girl was curled in a ball, still asleep. Farther down, Clint's door was closed, indicating that he, too, slept.

Good. There was time to start a hearty breakfast, the kind that set a friendly, welcoming tone. Alison showered quickly, dressed and pulled her hair into a ponytail, just in time to hear the heavy front door open and the screen door's loud squeak. The dog woofed twice, then was silent. Clint must be up.

Slipping into a pair of sandals, she hurried downstairs. She heard the deep rumble of his voice through the screen door before she saw him. "Good boy."

Dark and unshaven, in jeans and a black T-shirt and no shoes, he was hunkered down beside the supine dog, rubbing his furry stomach. The animal wriggled in ecstasy.

"Think you're something, don't you?" His tone was gruff, but his mouth quirked.

Not quite a smile, but close.

Even though Clint couldn't see Alison, she smiled back. Her spirits lifted. The day had started better than she'd hoped.

"Good morning," she said, and moved through the squeaking door and down the steps. At this hour the air was damp and warm, but not yet unbearable.

"Back at you."

The haunted look of last night was gone. His eyes traveled slowly over her. The interest in them made her feel attractive and glad that she wore her best shorts. Cheeks heating, she slid her foot through the dew-laden grass. "You're up early. I thought you'd sleep late."

"I had to call Tallahassee to check on that job. Being it's Saturday, the office is closed. My bad luck." He shrugged. "I'll try again first thing Monday." He eyed her. "That's why I'm up. What about you?"

"I like to get up before Hannah. It's my thinking time, my time to get things done. I decided to sell the love seat."

The sober expression returned. "Are you sure you want to do that?"

"I don't have much choice."

He nodded, gave the dog a final pat and stood. "I'm sure your grandma Rose would approve."

The words were exactly what she needed to hear. She smiled sadly. "I hope you're right. I'm going to ask Jenny to pick it up this afternoon."

The dog scrambled up. Wagging his tail hopefully, he approached Alison and shoved his head into her hands, nudging away the heavy feeling in her chest. Laughing, she scratched between his ears. "What's up, dog?"

She glanced at Clint in time to see his intent expression.

"What?"

"I like the way you laugh." Frowning as if he disliked paying her the compliment, he cocked a hip against the step railing and crossed his arms.

Still, the unexpected words pleased Alison. "Thank you."

Clint held her gaze. An awkward beat of silence played between them. Luckily, the dog yipped.

"Shh," Alison warned the animal. "You'll wake Hannah."

"I think he's hungry."

"I'm just about to make breakfast. I'll fix him a plate of eggs. How do you like your coffee?"

"Black, and strong enough to cut with a fork. Need help?"

"No. Sit down and relax."

Fifteen minutes later, when she brought out a plate for the dog and a mug for Clint, he was sitting on the bottom step.

"Thanks." He took it from her and sipped with relish. Then he pointed it toward the screen door. "Those hinges are almost rusted through. That's why they squeak. After breakfast, I'll head into town, pick up my toolbox from the truck and get you some new hinges."

His offer surprised and pleased her, but she couldn't accept his help. He was a boarder, not a handyman. She shook her head. "You're a guest, Clint. You're not supposed to fix things around here."

"Hell, I can't sit around and do nothing." He shrugged. "You're lucky the door hasn't fallen off and hit Hannah. Let me take care of it."

"When you put it that way...all right. How much do you charge?"

"Nothing. I don't want your money."

Things were tight, but she wouldn't take charity. "I can afford it."

He shook his head. "Forget it."

Hands on her hips, she frowned. "Well, what *do* you want?"

His gaze dropped to her mouth. "I—"

The squeaky door cut off whatever he'd been about

to say. "Mama, why are you and Clint arguing?" Rosy with sleep, clutching the tattered blanket that had been with her since infancy, Hannah padded down the steps.

"Good morning, sweetie. We're not arguing."

"Uh-huh. Clint doesn't want your money. Why don't you, Clint? I gots twelve dollars in my Dalmatian bank. Mama says if I save it, someday I can go to college." She sat down beside Clint and looked at the dog, still bent over his breakfast. "Why doesn't your dog got a name?"

"He's a mutt, a stray," Clint said. "He doesn't belong to anyone."

The corners of Hannah's mouth turned down. "But everyone belongs to someone."

Clint winced as if she'd slapped him. "Not everyone, Hannah. Sometimes it's better to be alone."

Wide-eyed, the child stared up at him. "Are you alone, Clint?"

He glanced at Alison, then studied his mug. "You're a lot like your mother. You ask too many questions."

Oblivious, Hannah plunged ahead. "You wouldn't be lonesome if you had a doggie. Why don't you want him, Clint?"

Shadows darkened his face. "It wouldn't be fair to him."

"Well, he needs a name. Can I give him one?"

"If you do that, you'll have to keep him." He lifted his eyes to Alison. "Better ask your mama."

As if the dog understood, he left his meal and trotted over to Hannah. Cocking his head, he wagged his tail and did his best to look cute. Beaming, Hannah patted his head. "Look, Mama, he likes me. Can I keep him, please, please, oh, pretty please?"

Hannah rounded her eyes in that adorable way Alison couldn't resist. She looked at the dog. He needed a flea bath, shots and heaven knew what else. Vet and dog food bills mounted in her head. But Clint didn't want him, and she couldn't very well turn the poor animal loose again. She let out a sigh. "I suppose so."

"Yippee!" Hannah clapped her hands. The dog woofed once and licked her face. Giggling, she hugged him. "I gots a name for him. Barker, 'cause he likes to bark."

"It suits him," Alison said. "Let's go in now. Breakfast is ready."

"Come on, Clint." Hannah slipped her hand inside his. He stiffened and looked as if he wanted to bolt.

Alison led them up the steps and opened the door. It was obvious now that Clint didn't dislike Hannah. But she did make him uncomfortable. He almost seemed *afraid* of her. Why?

Alison wished she knew. Maybe he simply needed time to get used to Hannah. Or perhaps there was some other, deeper reason for his skittish behavior. She could waste ages wondering. It was best to focus on the positive. Clint was here and he'd paid her. For now, that was enough. It had to be.

Chapter Four

Clint felt lucky as he deposited two door hinges and his other purchases on Flatville Lumber and Hardware's cluttered counter. When he'd come into the store an hour earlier, half a dozen shoppers were waiting to pay for their purchases. Now, he was the only one.

"You're new around here." The round-faced, balding man who peered up at him through gold-rimmed bifocals looked like he belonged in a Norman Rockwell painting. For that matter so did the store itself, with its shelves crammed with locks and nails, tiles and flooring, fixtures and paint, and every building gadget a man could want. "My guess is you're planning to fix a door."

"That's right," Clint said. Alison had finally agreed to let him repair the front door, but only if she paid for the materials. And she'd insisted he borrow her car until his truck was fixed. Anxious to get away from her and Hannah, he'd agreed, driving into town right after breakfast. The old station wagon had rattled and groaned as if it was on its last legs, worse than his truck.

She needed a new car, and that wasn't all she needed. Clint thought about the worn places in the runner on the stairs, the freshly painted but warped cabinet in the bathroom that didn't quite close, the faded linoleum in the kitchen. Evidently, she'd been hurting for money for a long time. Because she needed the rent, he'd decided to stay at her place. It was only for three more nights. If he kept to himself, he could handle it.

He slid his wallet from his back pocket. "How much do I owe you?"

"Wait a minute, son, till I place you." The clerk slowly rubbed his chin. "I heard tell Arliss Maxwell's college boyfriend is down here visiting, but you're a might old for college." Rocking back on his heels, he looked Clint over from head to toe. Suddenly he snapped his fingers. "I know, you're that fella rentin' a room from Alison O'Hara. Clint Strong, right?"

Like all small towns, news traveled fast. Clint nodded. "That's me."

Reaching across the counter, the clerk shook his hand. "Tom Farley, at your service. Find everything you need?"

"And then some." Clint gestured toward the dazzling array of supplies and tools. He couldn't have chosen a better place to pass the morning. "You've got a great store here."

"Thanks." Tom beamed. "The wife and I built it from scratch, back in 1960." He leaned his elbows on the counter. "That Alison's one sweet gal, isn't she?"

Clint thought about how she'd looked this morning, wearing those shorts that showed off her legs. They were nice legs, long and slender. And that beautiful, wide mouth was made for kissing. She sure *looked* sweet. Not that he would ever find out. "Uh, yeah," he said, frowning. "How much did you say I owed you?"

"Haven't added it up yet." Curiosity lit Tom's eyes. "I saw her last week, when she bought wood and paint for that rental sign. Guess it worked, huh? She brought Hannah with her." He chuckled. "That child is cute as a golden retriever pup. Never had a daughter, and I don't have any granddaughters yet, but if I did, I'd want 'em just like Alison and Hannah."

Clint remembered how the little girl's small fingers felt cupped in his, how he'd wanted to push her away and hold on at the same time. His heart pulled painfully. He cleared his throat. "How much?"

"Well now, let's see," Tom said. "Which door is it that's giving them trouble?"

Was everyone in town so damned inquisitive? Clint stifled the urge to roll his eyes. "The screen door at the front of the house. The hinges are rusted through."

"You got the right tools for the job? 'Cause I can lend you some."

The offer surprised Clint. As a person who moved frequently and kept to himself, he was used to suspicion and mistrust, especially from a man who barely knew him. "I'm all set for tools, but I appreciate the offer."

Tom eyed the hinges. "You sure you want that brand? Let me tell you a thing or two about what our climate will do to that finish."

Clint gave up on getting out of there anytime soon. Hell, what was the hurry, anyway? He had the time, and he would rather spend it here than at Alison's. Decision made, he relaxed.

For the next half hour, between ringing up purchases, Tom traded information with him about the merits of various hardware and tool brands. When the store owner found out Clint's occupation, he asked Clint's opinion on treated versus untreated wood for a back porch. Clint gladly gave his view. This was the kind of conversation he enjoyed, focused on work instead of on him.

He ended up exchanging the hinges he'd selected for the ones Tom recommended. A few minutes later he paid and ambled toward the door. "Thanks, Tom."

The store owner nodded. "Don't be a stranger, now. Anything you need, just ask."

Clint left Flatville Lumber and Hardware with a sack of supplies, an earful of advice and what felt like the beginning of a friendship.

It was a funny feeling, a warm feeling. He shrugged it off. He didn't plan on sticking around, and he didn't want to make connections to Flatville or anyone in it. Not even Alison.

Especially not Alison.

Alison. When she'd handed him the car keys this morning, things between them were all business. But then she looked into his eyes and smiled. "I'll see you soon," she said in that soft voice, and he wanted to stay right there with her. Hell, he wanted more than that. He wanted to pull her into his arms and kiss her senseless.

He frowned. He had no business thinking about her that way, no business at all. The late-morning heat was already relentless. He kept to the shaded side of Main Street as he headed toward the car a few blocks away. A woman with a child and money problems meant nothing but trouble. He needed a woman out for a good time and nothing more. Which definitely put Alison off-limits.

With luck, his truck would be fixed by the first of the week. Then he'd leave. Meanwhile he would stop thinking about her and keep his distance.

He crossed into the next block, where the shell of Millie's restaurant stood. Right now it was only a roof and walls, with blue plastic taped across the window holes. It was Saturday and there were no workers around, but the front door gaped open.

Reluctant to hurry back to Alison's, Clint peered through it. The walls were roughed in, but that was the extent of the remodel. If Millie expected to open in a few weeks, hard work and long days lay ahead.

Suddenly Millie appeared through a doorway across the unfinished room. Worry wrinkled her brow, but when she spotted Clint, her forehead smoothed. "Why, hello there, Clint. What are you doing here?"

"I was just passing by on my way to the car." Acutely uncomfortable at being caught snooping, he shifted his purchases and turned to leave.

"Do you have time for a tour?"

He didn't care about the restaurant, but Millie looked so pleased to see him, so anxious to show him around, he couldn't turn her down. Besides, he had plenty of time. He stepped across the threshold and into the room. Hot air assaulted him. Without insulation the inside of the building was at least ten degrees hotter than outside. Sweat beaded his brow.

Millie fanned herself with her hand. "Land, it's hot. They're supposed to install the air conditioner right after the windows and insulation. Cool air will be piped through the ceiling, here and over there." She pointed at the rafters. "This is what it's going to look like when it's finished." Opening her enormous handbag, she pulled out a sheaf of folded papers.

Clint studied the drawings. Despite himself, he was impressed. He whistled. "Very nice. It's going to be huge."

"With the crowd I draw, I need a big place. Come on, I'll show you the rest of it." Bubbling with enthusiasm, she escorted him through the building, showing him the kitchen and pantry. They ended up back in the dining area. Millie gestured at the large space. "Imagine how it will look, packed with customers. Alison and the other servers will have plenty of work."

Clint imagined Alison waitressing here, earning wages and desperately needed tips. He wondered how Millie's contractor planned to finish by the middle of August. Hands low on his hips, he surveyed the area. "There's a lot left to do."

"I know." Millie frowned. "Rusty Jones and his men left work early yesterday. He promised to come in today to make it up, but it doesn't look as if he's going to show."

"It's none of my business, but do they know your time line?"

"Of course. Rusty's girlfriend, Stella, waitresses for me, so he knows. And the dates are in the contract." Millie glanced at Clint's face, then drew her eyebrows together. "You don't think they'll make it."

"That depends. How many on the crew?"

"The three men who work for Rusty and a few subcontractors."

Clint shook his head. "Unless they're prepared to work day and night, it'll be tough."

For a moment Millie stared at him. Then she pressed her lips together and shoved the drawings back in her purse. "That settles it. I'm going to find a phone and call Rusty right now." She marched outside.

Clint followed her. "Good luck, Millie. It'll be a nice place when it's finished."

"Thanks." She pulled the door shut. "It's a shame you won't be here to see it." She looked disappointed.

Clint didn't reply.

She shrugged. "Maybe someday. Jenny says Alison is selling that love seat this afternoon. It's nice that you'll be there to help them carry it down the front steps." Millie shook her head. "With all that family history tied up in it, selling it has got to be hard on Alison. I'm stopping by this afternoon to help her plan Hannah's birthday party and lend her moral support. See you then." With a wave she hurried off.

Clint didn't plan on seeing Millie or Alison or Jenny, other than to load the chairs and love seat into Jenny's van. He intended to fix the screen door and then make himself scarce. When he reached the car, he unlocked the door and opened it.

The interior felt like a sauna. Dripping sweat, he rolled down the windows. Alison was bound to be shook up when that furniture was gone. It was part of her history, her family, and meant a great deal to her. She'd said she would be fine, but he wasn't sure of that.

He shouldn't care, didn't care, he told himself as he pumped the gas pedal and waited for the motor to stop burping. Still, he'd better stay close but out of view. Alison might need a friend. She might need him.

What makes you think you could help anybody? a small voice in his head taunted. He turned up the radio and pulled into the street. Someone had to be there for her. Besides, there wasn't much else to do until his truck was fixed. It might as well be him.

The scent of cinnamon wafted through the living room as Alison set a plate of fresh-baked snickerdoodles on the coffee table beside the sweating pitcher of iced tea. Though the temperature outside was well over ninety, she'd baked several dozen cookies. Cooking and its wonderful, homey smells always lifted her spirits.

Now, with two floor fans and the big elm shading the front of the house, the room was comfortable enough. She and Millie could easily pass the afternoon in the living room to plan Hannah's birthday party.

Hands on her hips, Alison surveyed the space. This was the last time the living room would appear this way, and she wanted it to look perfect. Moving to the end table, she rearranged the flowers in one of the two antique, cut-glass vases she and Hannah had filled with wild black-eyed Susans, daisies and buttercups from the meadow behind the backyard.

She glanced at the secondhand couch that had replaced the lovely old sofa sold months earlier. In a few hours it would be the only furniture left in the room besides the tables, lamps and vases. And Rose's portrait.

Alison bit her lip. Thank goodness Jimmy Burton's mother had invited Hannah swimming again. Alison had readily accepted the invitation. It gave her time to plan her daughter's birthday party.

More important, she didn't want Hannah around when Jenny picked up the furniture. Alison didn't want her daughter to know how sad it made her. The little girl would only worry, and Alison knew firsthand how that felt. From the time she could talk, her mother had shared every one of her money woes with her.

Frowning, she brushed a thread from the new chintz slipcover she'd sewn to brighten up the used couch. Feelings of helplessness and bad dreams were not what her innocent child deserved. No, it was better that Hannah be away until after the furniture was gone and Alison had a chance to put on a happy face. She would downplay the whole thing, tell Hannah they'd buy new furniture someday. And when Hannah was old enough, Alison would try to explain why she'd sold off part of her daughter's heritage.

Forgive me, Rose. Alison glanced at the painting. Her great-great-grandmother seemed to look right at her. Alison swore she saw compassion in those green eyes. A feeling of peace settled over her, and she knew her ancestor understood.

Just as Clint had said she would. How had he known?

Suddenly Barker yipped, and tires crunched over

the gravel drive outside. Through the window Alison watched Millie's convertible screech to a stop in front of the house. The dog's ragged tail wagged as he trotted over to greet the visitor. She patted him briefly, then, looking preoccupied and worried, Millie hurried up the stairs.

Alison opened the screen door which, thanks to Clint, no longer squeaked. "Hello, Millie."

"I know I'm early, but oh, Alison, I'm so upset." The normally unflappable woman cast a distressed gaze at her. Her face was so red, she looked apoplectic.

Alarmed, Alison took the woman's arm and led her to a chair. "Sit down, Millie, and take a deep breath. I'll get you some iced tea."

"Thank you, dear." While Millie waited for Alison to pour her drink, she glanced around the room. "Your slipcover looks great, and so do the flowers." She accepted her glass, pressed it to her forehead and closed her eyes. "I was hoping to see Clint. Where is he?"

Alison hadn't seen him since he'd fixed her screen door right after lunch. He'd seemed withdrawn and uncomfortable, just as at dinner the night before, responding to Hannah's and her attempts at conversation with one-syllable replies. Not at all like at breakfast, when he'd seemed friendlier, more open. She sighed. She'd thought things were going to be easier between them, but she'd been wrong. "I don't know where he is," she replied.

"Right here." He'd slipped into the room so quietly Alison hadn't noticed. In jeans and a black T-shirt, with his arm angled against the doorjamb, he looked like a modern-day James Dean.

Her breath caught. His eyes sought hers, dark and hot. Awareness flooded her, and confusion. Every time she saw the man, his mood shifted. Her cheeks warm, she poured him a glass of iced tea and one for herself, then took the wing chair opposite her boss and friend. Clint remained standing.

For a split second Millie seemed to have forgotten her troubles. She eyed Alison, then Clint. A smile played briefly at her lips, but quickly faded. "I'm glad you're here," she said to him. "I was just about to tell Alison my troubles. Maybe you can help."

He shot a longing look at the front door, as if he wanted to walk back through it. Alison held her breath. Was he going to run away or stay and listen? To her relief he lifted an eyebrow and shrugged. "What's up?"

"I took your advice, Clint, and phoned Rusty this morning." Millie glanced at Alison. "Are you ready for this? Last night he walked out on Stella and moved in with Maris Watkins. She works at the Cut and Curl," Millie explained to Clint.

"What?" Shock rendered Alison speechless. She tried to picture the tall, skinny contractor romantically involved with the voluptuous hairdresser, and failed. "But Rusty and Stella were engaged. From what Stella said, they were planning a fall wedding."

"Not anymore." Ice cubes clinked as Millie swirled her drink and looked from Alison to Clint. "The rat didn't even break the news in person, just left a note propped on Stella's kitchen table. Of course she's devastated."

"I would think so. Poor woman." Alison understood too well how her friend must feel. The scenario—leaving a note on the table—bore an uncanny resemblance to what had happened with Hannah's father. Only he'd left town. "She probably needs a shoulder to cry on. I'll call her later. I'll bet eventually, when she has time to think, she'll realize she's better off without him."

"Well, I'm not." Millie wrung her hands. "Rusty won't be showing up at the restaurant today. He said he would because he's behind, but he must have changed his mind. His crew won't work without him. I just hope he'll put in a full day on Monday. Even though he signed a contract, he doesn't seem to care that I've got a deadline and he's so far behind."

Alison gripped her glass. It was bad enough, struggling to make ends meet while she waited for the restaurant to reopen. Now, instead of opening in the middle of August, it might be longer. Her stomach knotted. Without that job she couldn't get a loan to pay off the note in time.

She felt Clint's gaze on her and turned to see his eyes narrowed, as if he were trying to read her mind. Not wanting him to see her fears or upset Millie further, she lifted her chin. "Surely they can catch up."

"At the rate they're moving, I don't see how." Millie sank back against her chair.

Alison felt sick. She set down her glass with shaking hands, spilling tea on the coffee table. Clint handed her a napkin. His expression dark and unreadable, he watched her mop up the mess.

Millie sank back against her chair. "What do you suggest I do, Clint?"

His brow creased as he thought about that. Finally he shrugged. "Offer a bonus if they finish ahead of schedule," he suggested. "Deduct money from your bill if they don't meet deadline."

"Now, there's a smart idea," the older woman mused. "Is that doable this far into the project?"

"I don't see why not."

Deep in thought, Millie reached for a slice of lemon, dropped it into her tea and looked up at Clint. "You seem knowledgeable about this sort of thing. Could you write up something about a bonus or a penalty for me? I'll gladly pay you for your—"

"No." His mouth clamped shut.

Alison's jaw dropped open, and Millie jerked as if he'd slapped her. They both stared at him.

His expression grim, he glanced at Alison and then Millie, then cleared his throat. "I can't get involved. You know that. There's a job waiting for me in Florida."

"I understand." Millie looked as if she wanted to cry.

Clint shifted his weight and shoved his hands in his pockets. "Look, you're better off taking care of this yourself. In fact, you and your contractor should hash things out together. Give him another call and tell him you need to talk. Be firm and don't take any excuses."

"All right," the older woman replied, but she looked doubtful and no less ready to break down.

Small wonder. *Firm* was not a word usually associated with the softhearted Millie. Heaven only knew how her talk with Rusty would turn out.

Hopefully, well. If not…

Alison wanted to cry, but she managed to hide her distress. The restaurant had to open on time.

Otherwise how could she get a loan to save the house?

* * *

"You've got wonderful ideas, Millie." Alison offered her friend another cookie. Problems with her contractor had dampened the older woman's spirits, but not her appetite. Yet, in typical fashion, after a few moments of hand wringing, Millie had pushed her troubles aside and jumped into planning Hannah's fifth birthday with gusto. "Thanks to you, Hannah's going to love her party."

"I've enjoyed helping. That child is like a granddaughter to me." Millie glanced toward the near-empty cookie plate. "You haven't eaten a single snickerdoodle. You really ought to." Over her glasses she eyed Alison with affectionate concern. "You could stand to gain a few pounds. Besides, it'll make you feel better."

"I'm not hungry." Unlike her friend, Alison couldn't ignore her problems. The way her stomach was tied in knots, she couldn't eat a bite.

Millie looked sympathetic. "I wish I had better news about the restaurant." The worry she'd pushed aside now filled her face. "I really wanted to reopen on schedule."

"I know you did." Alison tried a reassuring smile and failed.

Suddenly her eyes filled. *Oh, no.* If she didn't get a moment alone, she was going to lose it in front of Millie. The woman was upset enough. Alison snatched up the empty plate from the coffee table. "Jenny will be here soon. She'll want cookies. Excuse me."

She felt Millie's eyes on her back as she headed toward the kitchen.

Unbidden, her thoughts turned to Clint. If only he were here. For some odd reason she felt better with him around. Certainly not because of his disposition. He'd been so abrupt when Millie had asked for his help. After that, he'd stayed around only long enough to find out when Jenny was coming so he could help carry the furniture to her van. Then he'd beat a hasty retreat.

Alison brushed a wayward lock of hair off her face. What a fool she was to wish him near! He couldn't wait to get away from her and Flatville. And he would, too, as soon as Chuck returned to town and fixed the truck.

The tears she could no longer hold in check gathered in her eyes. Blinking them back, she quickly filled the cookie plate. Her money worries had made her an emotional wreck. Her low spirits had nothing to do with Clint Strong. She barely knew the man. It was the news about the restaurant coupled with losing the rent money, she told herself, not the man, that made her feel so blue.

There would be another boarder, and Millie's restaurant would reopen.

But what if those things didn't happen in time?

"Think positive," she murmured. Shoving her negative thoughts aside, she lifted her chin and returned to the living room.

Jenny drove up a few moments later. As Alison beckoned her inside, the antique dealer's eyes filled with concern. "Are you all right?" she asked in a low voice.

"Millie's here, we'll talk later," Alison murmured. In a louder voice she said, "Clint offered to help move the furniture, but he's not here yet. We don't need him. We'll move it ourselves."

Jenny waved the suggestion aside. "Honey, never

turn down a man's offer of help. I've been working since dawn. I could use a rest."

"Then come and sit down," Millie called from the love seat. "Alison made snickerdoodles."

"That's an offer I can't refuse." Jenny sank onto the secondhand couch, selected a cookie and took a bite. "Mmm. As usual, this is to die for." She popped the rest of the treat into her mouth and chewed with relish. "You're a great cook, Alison. Someday, some lucky guy is going to snatch you up."

"Right." Alison snorted, but a pang of longing shot through her, so strong it hurt. What would it be like to have a man who adored you, a man you could trust with your heart? With her track record, she'd probably never find out.

"Like Clint Strong." Jenny sighed and glanced at Millie. "Is he a hunk, or what?"

Licking crumbs from her lips, Millie nodded. "He's attractive, all right."

"I've always liked the strong, silent type," Jenny said. "Too bad I've got a boyfriend in Indianapolis." She winked. "But Alison doesn't. Hmm."

"Get real." Alison brushed a crumb from the cushion. She could feel the eyes of both women on her. Caring for Clint could only lead to heartache. "Anyway, Clint's leaving soon, so what does it matter?"

Jenny shook her head. "Hey, it's only Saturday. Chuck's not due back until Tuesday, right? You've got time."

"For what?" Alison asked.

Jenny's eyes lit, and a smile bloomed on her face. "Why, to woo the man with your home cooking and charm."

Alison's face heated. "Very funny," she quipped,

but the idea appealed to her more than she cared to admit. "You know I'm not running that kind of place."

The antique dealer wiped her fingers on a napkin. "Well, I would if I were you."

Millie glanced at her watch. "Land, look at the time. I've got to scoot. See you both later."

Alison rose and held the door open for the older woman. "Take care, Millie. And don't worry, things will work out," she said, as much for herself as for her friend. "They always do."

When Millie's car headed down the driveway, Jenny frowned. "You don't look so good. You're not reneging on the furniture deal, are you?"

Alison shook her head. "I need the money."

"So, what's the matter?"

Alison didn't like the idea of sharing her problems, but she couldn't carry the burden alone any longer. She released a heavy sigh. "I've got a big problem, and I don't know what to do."

"I'm here for you." Jenny patted the cushion beside her. "Sit down and tell me all about it."

Clint tromped through the woods abutting Alison's yard. Afternoon sun dappled the ground between the trees, striking the ivy and wildflowers with splashes of brilliant light. Stopping between two huge oak trees, he inhaled deeply. The earthy smell, the quiet of the place might have soothed his mind if Millie's words weren't echoing in his head.

Why the hell had she asked him for help? He couldn't get involved.

In the distance he heard Barker's excited woof. The dog had sniffed out a rabbit and, with an enthusiastic yip, disappeared after it. Clint wished he could disappear as easily. For now he was stuck.

Birds chattered merrily around him, but he barely noticed. He remembered Alison's dismayed expression at the news about Rusty Jones. Her hands shook, and worry clouded her eyes when she understood she wouldn't be able to get back to work as quickly as she'd hoped.

With a mortgage to pay and a daughter to care for, she might be in trouble. *Was* in trouble, he amended. Financial trouble.

There must be a way to help her.

Clint swore and pushed through a tangle of vines beneath his feet. Her problems weren't his concern. He eyed the tall tree in his path. Unlike the others, this one had few leaves on its branches, and those were brown. It was obviously dead. His nerves taut, he snapped a barren branch from the tree. Oh, for a saw and an ax. Nothing cleared his mind or exhausted him enough to sleep at night like hard, physical labor.

He thought about going back to Alison's and finding the tools to start now, but the afternoon was slipping away. With that antique dealer arriving soon, he'd better get back to load up the chairs and love seat. He grimaced. The thought of Alison selling the furniture that meant so much to her worsened his bad mood.

Turning around, he headed back toward the house. He'd take care of that dead tree in the morning. There was nothing else to do, so why not?

In the distance he heard voices and the roar of Millie's sports coupe as she drove off. He left the woods and moved to the side of the house.

Except for Jenny's van parked out front and Alison's old Chevy in the weathered carport, the driveway was empty. No doubt, the women were waiting for him. Clint strode across the front yard. Through the living room window, he heard them.

He hadn't planned to listen, but their voices carried easily on the heavy afternoon air.

"I had no idea things were that bad," Jenny said in a tone exuding sympathy.

"Please don't tell anyone," Alison urged.

Clint heard the worry in her voice and crept closer.

"You know you can trust me," Jenny said. "Gosh, this must be hard for you. First the furniture and now the house. I hope you can hold on to it."

"Me, too," Alison murmured fervently.

Her desperation tore at Clint. He frowned. Alison's money troubles were worse than he'd thought. He wanted to see her face. He edged behind the bushes, where he could look in the window without being seen. Jenny and Alison sat beside each other on the old, sagging couch. Though Alison held her head high, her hands were locked so tightly in her lap her knuckles were white.

"Here's an idea." Jenny laid a hand on Alison's arm. "Keep the house but sell the land. You can use the money from the sale to pay off the mortgage."

"That's not an option, and you know it," Alison replied without hesitation. "The land and the house have been in the family for generations. They belong together. Someday they'll be Hannah's." She bit her lip. "But I *am* willing to sell the rest of the antiques, except for Rose's portrait. None of it means as much to me as holding on to our property."

Jenny nodded. "All right, I'll put out the word. The

dining room and bedroom sets should sell quickly. They'll bring in a pile of money.''

"That'll help, but it won't be enough." Alison glanced at the portrait above the fireplace. "Sometimes I wish I had Rose's necklace. If I did, I'd sell it. That would solve all my problems.''

"But you don't have it. That necklace is long gone.''

"I know." She released a weary sigh.

"Maybe I could lend you the money," Jenny offered. "How much do you need?''

"You're a true friend," Alison said.

Clint saw the tears glistening in Alison's eyes. His heart tugged painfully.

"But I could never borrow from you. Besides, you don't have forty thousand dollars.''

"Forty thousand?" Jenny gasped. "You're right, I don't.''

Clint frowned. How did Alison plan to get her hands on that kind of money?

As if she read his thoughts, she replied, "I talked to Vincent Cahill last week. If the restaurant opens on time and I can prove I'm working there again, he'll give me a loan. If not..." She shuddered, then squared her shoulders. "I've got one month to figure out what to do.''

Cahill. The name sounded vaguely familiar. Cliff searched his mind until he remembered. Ah, yes, the man who ran the bank. Millie had said he was cold and greedy.

"That's not much time." Jenny frowned. "I think you should ask Vincent for an extension.''

"I already did, and he turned me down. But I suppose I could try again. I'm sure he's heard what happened with Rusty Jones and that Millie's restaurant is behind schedule. Maybe you're right.'' Hope filled Alison's voice. "He might understand and give me more time.''

Clint didn't share her optimism, not after what Millie had said. Dammit, Alison needed the restaurant to open on time. That or a pile of cash from somewhere. But who besides a bank had that kind of money?

Out of the blue the answer came. *He* did, sitting in a savings account up in Seattle. Insurance proceeds. From the fire, from the loss of his home, his wife and his child.

Death money.

Clint winced as the familiar anguish lurched through him. He wouldn't touch that money. Ever. And he didn't want to think about it or the past, not now. With the strength that had come from years of practice, he pushed the memories and the accompanying pain from his mind.

Alison's troubles were none of his affair, and he refused to get involved. Period. But listening further couldn't hurt.

"It's worth a try,'' Jenny said.

Alison nodded. "I'll call the bank first thing Monday. And, hey, don't worry about me. I'll be okay.''

"Now you sound like the Alison I know and love.'' Jenny opened her arms and pulled Alison into a hug.

The gratitude on Alison's face touched Clint. After the fire he'd shunned the friends who'd offered him support, preferring to keep to himself. For the first time he wondered what he'd given up.

When Alison pulled away from her friend, she looked both grateful and relieved. "Thanks, Jenny. I feel better now that we talked. I'm glad I have you to confide in.''

''That's what friends are for.'' The blonde frowned and glanced at her wrist. ''I'd like to load up that furniture. I wonder where Clint is?''

Stifling an oath, he squeezed out of the bushes as quietly as he could and moved quickly toward the porch.

Chapter Five

At daybreak on Sunday, Clint gave up trying to sleep and headed outside. Alison came into the yard just as he located the saw and ax, hanging neatly on the wall in her carport.

Even in the first rays of dawn, her unbound hair shimmered over her shoulders and down her back like burnished copper. She wore flip-flops on her feet and that same shapeless pink robe. Hardly attractive, yet the way the fabric draped gently over the curve of her breasts and her rounded hips sparked his imagination.

"Good morning. Up early again, I see." She tossed her hair over her shoulder, the gesture reminding him of a young, carefree schoolgirl. But she was no kid, not with those womanly curves.

Neither was she carefree. Clint didn't like the worried frown that marred her face or the dark circles under her eyes, but he understood. She could very well lose her home unless she came up with big money, and fast.

But that was *her* problem. So why did he keep thinking about that insurance money idling in his savings account? Maybe...

Scowling, he dismissed the thought before it formed and grabbed the ax and saw. "There's a dead tree a few yards into the woods," he said in a gruff voice. "I thought I'd cut it down. It'll make great firewood next winter."

Slipping off the ax's leather guard, he tested the blade for sharpness. It wasn't razor sharp, but it would do. He slipped the guard back into place.

Alison was going to ask that banker, Vincent Cahill, for an extension, but Clint doubted that would work. She needed that waitressing job at Millie's. Damn Rusty Jones for screwing up. Damn Millie for asking Clint for help. And double damn his fool thoughts for straying into matters that were none of his business.

Frustration mixed with an anger he didn't understand shot through him, and he gripped the handle so hard that the old scars on his hand ached. *Easy, man.* With an effort, he forced himself to relax. He needed to get away from Alison. Now. He hefted the ax over his shoulder and grabbed the saw.

Tiny puckers appeared between her eyebrows. "Wait a minute, Clint."

He knew what she was going to say. "No need to pay me," he quickly replied. "Just drop me at Chuck's first thing Tuesday."

She looked surprised. "Well, all right. But what about breakfast? Aren't you hungry?"

"I already ate a bowl of cereal. Honey Flakes have always been a favorite of mine."

He realized he'd been waiting for the soft smile that suddenly lit her face. "That's Hannah's favorite, too, but there's too much sugar in it. I only allow her to eat it on special occasions. Please, let me make you a real breakfast."

The thought of sitting across the table from Alison, sipping coffee and talking, was all too tempting. And daunting. She didn't know he'd heard the conversation with Jenny. "No, thanks." He turned away from her. "I'd better get started now, before it gets too hot."

He beat a hasty retreat into the woods, where he felled the old maple, chopping it into fireplace-size logs and hauling it to Alison's depleted woodpile. To-morrow he'd be good and sore, but just as he'd hoped, the physical labor had wiped his troubles from his mind. For a while. As soon as the job was done and he'd finished carting the logs to the side of the house, his problems flooded back.

Not just his, but Alison's.

He frowned. Dammit, somehow he had to stop—

Hannah's squeal from the backyard, followed by a giggle, interrupted his thoughts. He winced. The darned kid was always laughing.

Alison called out, "Thank you for watering the garden, sweetie. Now let's finish filling the washtub for Barker's bath."

Despite his dark mood Clint's mouth quirked. At last the mutt was getting a much-needed bath.

A moment of silence followed, then a loud splash. Barker yipped, and Hannah shrieked gleefully. "Watch out, Mama!"

"Ooh, that water's ice-cold." Alison's laughter filled the air like a lilting wind chime. The pleasant sound was infectious. Clint grinned. It was impossible not to.

He shook his head. Despite her problems, she seemed determined to remain cheerful. How did she do that?

"Stand still, Barker. I've got him now," Alison said, a smile in her voice. "Okay, Hannah, I'm ready for that flea shampoo."

More silence. Then the little girl's voice rang out. "Oh, we're washing, washing, washing our doggie, goodbye all you fleas," she sang in her child's tuneless soprano.

Her sweetness touched a place deep inside Clint, a place long ago closed off. The fatherless little girl had survived heart surgery without losing her innocence. Would her mother's money troubles force her to grow up before her time?

Without thinking, he moved toward Alison and Hannah, stopping at the edge of the backyard. Wearing a faded yellow baseball cap that dripped water, Alison squatted over an old tub, scrubbing the reluctant dog with a brush. Hannah stood a few feet away, hands on her knees, watching intently. Like her mother she wore a baseball cap, but hers was adorned with prancing pink horses and turned backward. When Hannah saw Clint, she skipped toward him.

"You weren't at breakfast. I missed you, but Mama said you were cutting down a tree. Jimmy's daddy chopped a tree once. He said a bad word when a branch hit his toe. We're giving Barker a bath," she continued, jumping from topic to topic as she always did.

"So I noticed." Clint glanced at Alison. "How's it going?"

Alison wrinkled her nose. "Barker's not very happy, but at least he'll be clean."

A white T-shirt, wet from the squirming dog and almost transparent, clung to her. Underneath, Clint saw her thin lace bra, the kind that showed a woman's nipples. Alison's were pink, and beaded from the cold water.

Desire rolled over him like a bulldozer. His body responded like a randy teen's, and his jeans grew uncomfortably tight. *Damn.* Tearing his gaze away, he shifted and prayed she wouldn't notice. He cleared his throat. "You're all wet."

"I know." Alison laughed, but her smile quickly faded, as if she noted his hunger. The brush in her hand stilled. To Clint's surprise, her eyes darkened. He swore he saw mutual yearning there.

At that moment Barker scrambled from the tub. Water sloshed over the edge and onto Alison. "Hey!" She jumped back.

"Where are you going, Barker?" Hannah cried.

A few yards away, the dog shook himself off and pretended not to hear.

Clint shrugged. "I guess he's had enough."

"But he's not finished." Alison dropped the brush and jumped up. Water dripped from her drenched cutoffs and ran down her long, smooth legs. "That's flea shampoo. The directions said to rinse thoroughly. We'd better catch him, Hannah."

"Okay, Mama." The little girl hopped up and down with excitement and ran after her mother and the dripping dog. "Come on, Clint," Hannah called over her shoulder, "we need your help."

He hesitated. What did he care about the damn dog?

Then Alison laughed and glanced at him, her brow raised in question. He shrugged. Why not? He followed her and Hannah around the side of the house.

Between the mutt's excited yips and the kid's squeals, the place sounded like a madhouse. Swiveling his head, the soapy dog loped into the front yard. With three humans in close pursuit, one of them giggling, he quickly made a game of the chase, stopping close enough to encourage, but far enough away to prevent anyone from catching him.

Finally Clint figured out what to do. Glancing at Alison, he hunkered down, feigning nonchalance. She smiled and nodded her understanding.

He sure liked that smile. His mouth quirked into a semigrin.

"What are you doing?" Hannah asked.

"Tricking Barker," Alison explained, keeping her voice calm and easy. "Let's chase him toward Clint, and he'll grab hold of him. Ready?"

"Okay." The little girl eagerly complied. "Oh, Barker, here we come," she sang out and skipped toward the animal.

Alison and Hannah came at the dog from opposite sides. He whished past them and headed in Clint's direction. Lunging forward, Clint caught the animal around his middle. "Gotcha, mutt," he said, then toppled over backward.

The world blurred as Clint wrestled the dog. Cold water soaked through his T-shirt and jeans as the big animal lay prone on his chest. The smell of wet fur filled his nostrils. Finally the dog gave up. On his

back Clint stared at the dog's soulful brown eyes. A
moist black nose prodded his chin.

Hannah clapped her hands. "You got him, Clint."

"Or maybe he got me," he quipped.

Hannah giggled. Alison laughed. A strange, rusty
sound came from his lips, and he realized he was
chuckling with them. It had been a long time, and it
felt good.

"The poor fella looks so miserable," Alison said.
"Let's get this over with." She reached for the mutt.

"I'll carry him. You don't want him to escape
again." Holding tight to the wet, squirming canine,
Clint struggled to his feet.

Five minutes later the freshly rinsed dog shook
himself off and quickly trotted away. Alison gave
Clint a thumbs-up sign. "Mission accomplished. You
were great, Clint. We couldn't have done it without
you."

The pleasure he felt over the simple words surprised him. He hid his feelings under a shrug.

"Clint, you're filthy," Hannah said. Wet and
muddy, cap askew and hair falling down, the little
girl could have been describing herself. Hands on her
hips, she pressed her lips together in a gesture similar
to what Clint had seen Alison use. "You need a
bath."

Clint looked down at his drenched, mud-smeared
shirt and jeans. "I guess I do."

"We all do." Alison laughed and made a futile
attempt at brushing the dirt streaks from her legs.

"Sometimes Mama lets me get clean with the hose.
Want me to spray you?" Hannah gazed hopefully at
him.

He needed a long, cold shower, but not from the

little girl. "No, thanks. I thought I'd go into town. I'd better get cleaned up." At Alison's puzzled look, he added, "Your ax needs sharpening. The hardware store's got what I need to hone it."

"I'll pay for it," Alison began.

"No need to." Clint held up his hand. "It won't cost much. Besides, I'm the one who dulled it. I'll take care of it."

"Thank you." Her eyes were soft and warm. "You didn't get much of a breakfast. Have lunch with us before you go."

He'd had enough of her and her daughter for one day. He opened his mouth to decline. "All right," he said, surprising himself.

"Great." Her pleased smile dazzled him. She glanced at her daughter. "Why don't you fill the wading pool, Hannah? You can swim this afternoon."

"Goody!" The little girl skipped toward the hose.

When she was across the yard, Alison turned to him. "Thank you."

"For what?"

"Fixing the screen door. Cutting down that tree and sharpening the blade. Helping us with Barker." Standing on her toes, she leaned her palm against his chest and kissed his cheek.

He hadn't been touched in a long time. Through his wet shirt the pressure of her palm felt warm and sweet, her lips, soft and gentle. Fresh desire shot through him. "I had to fill the time *some* way," he said gruffly. "It was no big deal."

"Just the same, I appreciate what you've done for us." Her hand slid to his arm as her gaze sought and held his, the gentle pressure of her touch burning him.

"I'm very glad you're here, Clint Strong," she said in that soft, sweet voice.

Heat radiated from her body. Her scent, flowery and womanly, invaded him. Of their own accord, his hands cupped her shoulders. Awareness darkening her eyes, she leaned into him.

He knew he was in trouble, big trouble. Any minute now he was going to kiss her. *Let go of her…now,* the voice in his head warned. "Alison," he groaned, dropping his hands and backing away, "I've got to clean up."

He swore disappointment clouded the eyes searching his face. "Of course," she said.

Turning away, he strode toward the house.

Monday night, acting on automatic pilot, Alison wiped down the kitchen counter. She'd always considered herself upbeat, but now, after Millie's news about the delay in opening the restaurant and the fact that Clint would soon leave, she no longer felt optimistic. Instead she felt weary and listless, as if the weight of the world sat on her shoulders. Releasing a heavy sigh, she wrung out the dishcloth and hung it on the hook beneath the sink.

She'd managed to put on a cheerful face for Hannah, but now that her little ray of sunshine was asleep, with Barker at the foot of her bed, Alison could let down her guard. Despite her troubles she smiled. Hannah and the dog had formed a quick, deep bond.

She turned off the large overhead light and stood in the dark. What would happen to the animal if she lost the house?

"No," she muttered, and flipped on the small window light. Losing her home and land was not an option. Period. But how was she going to come up with forty thousand dollars?

Deep in thought, she headed for the back porch.

Outside, the crickets greeted her cheerfully. Lightning bugs flashed through the air, still warm and thick but cool enough to be comfortable. A waning half-moon lit the sky.

Alison barely noticed any of it. Hating the uncertainty clinging to her, she sank onto the top step. Her feelings reminded her of the bad times, when she and her mother had lived hand-to-mouth.

On top of that, Clint was leaving. Sadness filled her. Drawing up her knees, she wrapped her arms around her shins and stared into the darkness. He was a drifter. He'd never promised to stay. Yet, in just a few days she'd gotten used to him. Even his gruffness. She smiled. She knew now that his brusque manner concealed a heart of gold. Why else would he fix her door and take down a tree and not ask for payment?

She remembered the scratchy feel of his face against her lips yesterday, the solid chest she'd leaned into. Her heart thudded. She liked Clint Strong. Too much, considering he was about to walk out of her life.

So did Hannah. Her daughter had taken to Clint right away, soaking up his scant attention like a dry sponge.

Alison frowned. Never in her wildest imaginings had she suspected that Hannah needed a man in her life. She'd thought a mother's love would be enough for her child.

The screen door opened, then closed softly behind her. "Hey, there." Clint's footsteps echoed across the old wood as he crossed the porch and sat down beside her.

This morning he'd reached the foreman in Tallahassee, who'd agreed to hold his job two more days. He'd also contacted Chuck just after dinner tonight, and the auto mechanic had promised to look at the truck first thing tomorrow, then call and let him know how quickly it could be fixed. With all the good news, Clint seemed more relaxed. "It's a nice night. Look at all those stars."

Still hugging her shins, Alison stared up at the black, star-studded sky. "When I was little, I thought they were diamonds. I always believed that if I could just reach up and grab one, our worries would be over. Later, after I moved here, I thought Rose's necklace must be a star. If I could figure out which one it was, it would be mine." She laughed sadly. "What a naive fool I was."

She felt Clint's gaze on her. "Once upon a time, we were all innocent. Like Hannah. The poor kid thinks the world is a beautiful place." He snickered. "Someday she'll learn the truth."

He sounded so cynical. Alison gave him a sideways look. "Most of the time, it *is* beautiful, Clint, even if there are a few ugly patches."

"You've got that backward. We live in a pit full of pain and ugliness." His eyes glittered in the dim light. "If we find beauty now and then, it's just a fluke."

Heaviness filled Alison. What had happened to him, to make him look at things that way? She let go of her legs and straightened. "I'm sorry you feel that way."

"I'm surprised you don't." His face in shadow, he

shifted beside her. "Look at your own situation, Alison. You're so bowed down with money worries, you haven't cracked a smile since we washed the dog."

"Am I that easy to read?" Her self-conscious laugh started and ended abruptly.

"Let's just say you'd never last in a poker game."

"I see my problems as a hurdle, something to get past. They're not a permanent condition."

"No?"

He didn't ask her to explain, but she wanted to. "I may as well tell you. I have to pay off a note, secured by the house. That's all."

He lifted an eyebrow. "And this is a hurdle you can get past."

She shrugged. "Sure."

Though he didn't reply, his shadowed face and silence seemed to mock her.

"Okay, so I am a little worried. If I don't have the money in three and a half weeks, the bank will take the house from me. I need a loan, and the only way I can get it is to start working at Millie's again."

There, it was out. Ashamed, she hunched her shoulders and stared down at her sandals.

Clint touched her cheek, his hard, callused fingers somehow comforting. "Hey, you were laid off. That's nothing to be ashamed of," he said softly.

The eyes that met hers were dark and full of compassion. Alison sensed that he didn't usually let himself feel such things. That he did, for her, filled her heart. She tried to smile. "Well, it's certainly nothing to be proud of. I've made a real mess of things. I should have put more money aside."

"A woman raising a child on her own doesn't have much extra to save. You're too hard on yourself." He tucked a lock of hair behind her ear. "Like you said, this is a temporary situation. Things will work out."

She wanted so much to believe him. Grateful for his words, she leaned into his hand.

Suddenly Clint's eyes warmed, the way they had yesterday after she'd washed the dog. He glanced at her lips, and Alison knew: he wanted to kiss her. And she wanted him to, even if he was a drifter and about to leave. She caught her breath, waiting. As if he read her thoughts, he quickly dropped his hand and looked away.

A beat later he cleared his throat. "So, what are you going to do?"

"Pray that Rusty and his team work harder and faster and the restaurant opens on time. Meanwhile, I'm managing okay. I've sold off the living room furniture, and I've asked Jenny to sell more. And there's the money from renting the spare bedroom. You're my first boarder."

Clint's jaw tightened. "And now I'm leaving. I guess you'll have to figure out some other way to save your house." His tone was flat, his eyes focused on the dark shadows in the yard.

He didn't care after all. She must have misunderstood earlier. Stung, she lifted her chin. "It'll be easy to rent again. Who knows, maybe I'll move in with Hannah and rent out my bedroom also. With enough income I might be able to get a loan to pay off that note."

"What if you don't find a boarder?" Clint asked, still staring straight ahead.

The question scared her. She pressed her lips firmly together. "Then I'll find some other way. I won't lose my home. Someday it will be Hannah's."

He turned to her, his expression guarded. "It means a lot to you, holding on to this place for her."

"Everything," she replied softly. "When I was little, we were always moving. I didn't stay more than a few months anywhere until I moved to Flatville. I want Hannah to have roots here in this town, in this house that was built by her ancestors."

For a beat Clint was silent. Suddenly he cupped her shoulders. "Listen to me, Alison. I don't want anything holding me down ever again," he said fiercely, as if defending himself. "I move when I feel like it, go where I want to go." His gaze held her as firmly as his grip. "Is that clear?"

Alison swallowed. He couldn't wait to leave town, leave her. She'd known that, but still the words hurt. To her horror, tears filled her eyes. "Y-yes," she said, and pulled out of his grasp. "I have to go in now." Jumping to her feet, she spun away from him.

"Wait." Clint rose and grabbed her wrist, pivoting her around.

"Let go of me," she snapped, angry and upset, but something in his face, raw, unmasked agony, caught at her heart. "What is it?" she asked.

He shook his head. "I didn't mean to hurt you."

"I'm all right." Shoving her pain aside in her need to soothe him, she stroked his face.

Clint tensed and started to pull away. Suddenly he groaned. "To hell with it," he muttered, and closed his eyes. Turning his head into her palm, he touched his soft, warm lips to the sensitive underside of her wrist.

Her stomach fluttered. "Oh," she said, her voice breathy.

Slowly he worked his way up her arm, each kiss

longer and warmer than the one before. Heat flared and then shot through her, and with it, the sudden need to sit down before her legs gave out.

As if he knew, Clint pulled her close and held on tightly. "I've wanted to taste you since the first time I saw you. God help us both, I can't resist you any longer."

Lowering his head, he kissed her.

His lips were hot and insistent and wonderful. He tasted of after-dinner coffee, smelled of sunshine and man. Wanting, needing to get closer, Alison threaded her fingers through his thick, black hair and sank against him.

Clint groaned. He was fully aroused.

Tracing the seam of her lips with his tongue, he urged her mouth open. Alison welcomed him inside. He kissed her again and again, stroking his hands up and down her back, pressing her closer. Never had a man made her feel so alive. When at last he gripped her hips and lifted her, fitting the part of her that ached against his flagrant need, she moaned with pleasure. "Clint," she panted against his mouth, "Please—"

Suddenly still, he tore his lips from hers and set her back on her feet. Breathing hard, he released her. "Hell."

Dazed, she opened her eyes. "What?" She touched her lips, puffy from his kisses.

He stared at her mouth, and his eyes smoldered as if he wanted to kiss her again. Curling his hands into fists, he backed up a step and cleared his throat. "It's late. You should get some sleep, and I need to pack."

"Right." Her face heated.

Her blatant hunger had scared him. It scared *her*.

Lowering her head, she smoothed down her shorts. What in the world had come over her? Clint was a drifter. Caring for him would only break her heart. She'd learned that painful lesson with Hannah's father.

The sooner Clint left, the better. She looked up at him. "I'll drive you to Chuck's as soon as your truck is ready."

"Thanks." He turned to go.

Despite Alison's feelings, the brusquely uttered word seemed a harsh end to what had just happened between them. "Sweet dreams," she whispered to his back.

Clint made a strangled sound in his throat, then swung around to face her. "Not tonight," he said, his voice husky. His gaze raked over her, making her feel naked and thoroughly desired.

Alison's knees felt weak all over again. She grabbed for the railing, sinking against it, and watched him stride away.

Chapter Six

"Why are you leaving us, Clint?" Hannah asked. Strapped into her car seat, she sat directly behind the driver's seat.

Alison slowed to let a cat cross the road and glanced at Clint. Though her face was smooth, her eyes held the same question.

He swore silently. Those big, warm eyes were what had gotten him into trouble last night. His gaze lowered to her lips. Even turned down at the corners, her mouth was impossible to resist. It would be easy to wipe that frown from her face. He'd lean over, pull her close, and her soft lips would part, inviting him inside. Sweet, so sweet.

He thought about the way she fitted against him, warm and yielding, and the way she responded to his kisses. His blood heated.

If she knew what you were, she never would have kissed you.

Shifting, he stared out the window. Dusty green fields and drooping trees rolled by as Alison sped toward town.

Kissing her last night had been a mistake, a big mistake. Thank God, he would be out of here in a few hours. He'd never have to worry about going near her again.

"Why, Clint?" the little girl persisted.

Swiveling in his seat, he turned to her. "Chuck phoned a while ago," he said gruffly. "He says my truck's almost ready. I need to pick it up now because there's a job waiting for me in Florida, and I have to get there by tomorrow."

"Oh," Hannah replied solemnly. Instead of making up one of her usual songs, she shot out her lower lip and stared at him with round eyes. She didn't want him to go.

For some reason he was touched. He frowned. Kissing Alison, letting her kid get to him—he was losing his mind.

Suddenly the car seemed too small. He had to get away from them both. Downtown Flatville was a few miles down the road, but no matter. He'd walk. He pointed to a clump of trees. "Drop me off there."

Alison's brow furrowed. "But Chuck's shop is a long way from here."

"Save yourself the time and gas," Clint said.

"No." Her chin lifted stubbornly. "After all the nice things you've done for us, I *want* to take you all the way to Chuck's door."

Grudging admiration filled him. That willful streak would help her hold on to the thing she valued most—

her property. Hell, what did it matter if he stayed in the car? Another few minutes wouldn't kill him. Within a few days he'd be hard at work in Florida, and Alison, Hannah and Flatville would be no more than a distant memory. He shrugged. "Your choice."

With a satisfied nod, Alison rounded the corner. They finished the trip in silence. At last she pulled into the concrete lot of Chuck's Auto Shop. The double-wide garage doors were flung open, with the country music station turned up so loud the floor of the car vibrated. Inside the garage the hood to the truck was up. Oblivious to Clint's arrival, Chuck stood bent over it. A good sign.

Clint couldn't wait to get in there and check the progress. He hopped out of the car. "Thanks for the ride."

Alison followed him around to the trunk. She unlocked it and watched him retrieve his suit and duffel. Setting them down, he turned to her.

Despite the loud music, the silence between them was thick and uncomfortable. Clint kicked a rock and watched it skitter across pavement. Well, hell. Other than a few talks and some sizzling kisses, they hardly knew each other. So what was the big deal? "Good luck with that note," he finally said. "If I run into anyone looking for an antique dining room set, I'll send them your way."

She flashed him a brave, fleeting smile. "Don't worry, I'm resourceful. I'll figure out something."

"I'm sure you will." Clint frowned. He hoped to hell she didn't lose her home.

She searched his face. "If you ever pass through Flatville again, there's a place for you at our house."

"I'll remember that," he replied, knowing he'd never return.

"I guess this is goodbye, then." Reaching up, she touched his face. "I hope you find what you're looking for."

Her palm felt strangely soothing against his cheek. For a brief moment peace settled over him. Relishing the feeling, he closed his eyes.

Peace of mind, that was what he wanted.

"Clint?" Hannah called out over the radio.

Her voice jerked him out of his short reprieve. He'd never find peace. With his ugly past, he didn't deserve it. Backing away from Alison, he glanced at the car. "Yeah, Hannah?"

"Can I have a goodbye hug and a kiss?"

He started to shake his head, but her little face was puckered with worry. She was far too young to hold an expression like that. "Why not?" he said, and headed around the car.

She was reaching out her arms as he pulled open the door. They wrapped tightly around his neck. She smelled of cherry bubble bath and fresh air, all little girl and naiveté. Her rosy lips smacked sweetly against his cheek. For some reason his heart tugged.

Pulling back, he gently jerked a pigtail. "Goodbye, smart stuff. Be a good girl and listen to your mother, you hear?"

"Okay." She nodded obediently. "Clint?"

Now what? "Yes, Hannah?"

"You gots to kiss Mama goodbye, too."

The innocent request threw him. Kissing Alison was dangerous.

Pulse jumping, he studied Alison. Those pretty eyes were full of sadness and yearning as she lifted her face to him. Fool that he was, he wanted to hold her again. One final embrace and then he'd put her out of his thoughts permanently.

Leaning down, he kissed her. He meant it to be a brief, light kiss, a last goodbye. But she threw her arms around his waist and hugged him hard. Her soft body pressed against him from shoulder to thigh, quickly wiping his thoughts from his mind.

He felt good, being held, damned good. Wrapping his arms around her, he drank in her sweetness. For a moment he wanted to stay with her, sink to the ground and make them both forget their troubles.

But that wasn't right. He didn't want to stay, couldn't. And she deserved a better man than him. Steeling his will, he released her.

Her cheeks were flushed prettily, her eyes dark with desire. Breathless, she hugged her waist, as if she were holding on to the warmth they generated together. "Goodbye, Clint," she whispered, and headed for the car. At the door she paused and looked over her shoulder at him. "Take care of yourself."

"Back at you," he said.

Feeling strangely empty, he watched her drive away.

"You mean to tell me it's not fixed?" Clint roared four hours later.

He'd thought when Chuck phoned and told him to hurry over that it meant the truck was ready. No such luck. After a long, tedious morning, the mechanic had finally directed him to turn the ignition and press the gas pedal. The engine turned over and sputtered loudly, then died. Clint stuck his head out the window. "What's the matter?"

The mechanic lifted his head from under the hood and held up a palm. "Turn it off." Clint did and waited while Chuck tinkered with the motor. A moment later the man straightened, nodding. "Okay, try 'er again."

As soon as Clint turned the key, the engine coughed, making loud, unhealthy noises, but still refused to run. "Keep cranking," Chuck directed.

Clint frowned. Obviously, something had gone wrong. Sure enough, after a minute the engine backfired, and a nasty burned smell filled the air. With a feeling of doom in his belly, he turned off the ignition and exited the cab. "Why won't my truck run?"

The ruddy-faced man rubbed the back of his sunbaked neck. "Well now, that's a tough one. The timing chain keeps slipping. Beats me as to why." He pulled a package of gum from the bib of his overalls and offered Clint a stick. Clint shook his head, his small store of patience rapidly dwindling as the mechanic peeled off the paper and popped the gum into his mouth. For several seconds he chewed loudly. "Looks like I'll have to take her apart again and see if I can figure out why."

At Cliff's murderous expression he stopped chomping and held up his hands. "I won't charge you."

"That's not the point," Clint snapped. Chuck's lips tightened, and Clint realized his temper would only slow the man down. With an effort he softened his tone. "You've done that twice already, and it's not working. Is there something else you can try?"

Chuck pulled his ear and looked at the concrete floor while he chewed some more. He was slower to talk than molasses in winter. Clint waited. "I could put in a new timing chain if I had the part. But I don't. I'll have to special order it from Indianapolis.'' He rubbed his chin and studied the truck. ''She's an '85 Ford. I reckon they'll have the part.''

Great, just great. Clint rolled his eyes. ''How long will that take?''

''If we're lucky, tomorrow, but no longer than a couple of days. It's gonna cost more, too.'' He frowned. ''No sense gettin' mad, Clint. That won't help.''

Clint *was* mad, and frustrated. But Chuck was right. What good would hollering do? With an effort he again reined in his temper. ''You're right,'' he said through gritted teeth. ''The deal is, I'm supposed to be in Florida tomorrow morning, for a job. I was prepared to drive all night to get there.''

''Not in this truck, you ain't.''

Forgetting his resolve to stay calm, Clint swore. He was already two days late. There were other men, equally suited to the job, and the company wouldn't hold his place much longer. A sick feeling flooded him. His stash of money was dangerously low. He needed that job. He needed out of Flatville. ''Do you have a phone?''

''In the office.'' Chuck gestured toward the opposite end of the garage. ''Through that door. Come on, I'll show you.''

Five minutes later Clint hung up the telephone in despair. ''Well, I lost that job.'' He plowed his fingers through his hair. ''Now what am I supposed to do?''

''That's a real shame.'' Looking sympathetic, Chuck pulled his ear. ''If it's work you want, you can find it right here in Flatville. Everybody knows that Rusty Jones and his crew are way behind on Millie's restaurant. I'm sure they could use an extra hand. In fact, I know it. Tom over at the hardware store told me Rusty was in there yesterday, looking for help."

If Rusty wanted help, then Millie's no-nonsense talk with him must have paid off. Not that Clint cared. He glared at the mechanic. "Don't you understand? I don't want to stay here."

"You don't have to stay forever, just till your truck's fixed. And while you wait, you may as well help out Millie." Chuck shrugged. "Besides, living here ain't so bad. Folks are friendly, and the fishin's great." He grinned slyly. "And Alison's here."

It didn't surprise Clint that Chuck knew about Alison. Not in this town. "I realize that," he growled. "So what?"

"So, she's got a room to rent, and you need a place to stay. It's a great setup. You could work on Millie's restaurant and spend the rest of your time at Alison's."

Clint narrowed his eyes. "You've thought it all out, haven't you? What if I don't like those choices?"

"Well then, leave." Chuck shoved his hands in his overalls. "Ain't nobody stoppin' you."

Except a busted truck and a job that no longer existed. Tamping down his irritation, Clint turned toward the door. "I'm going to take a walk and do some thinking. You get that part ordered."

He jammed his hands in his pockets and wandered aimlessly down Main Street, past tired-looking trees and weather-beaten shops. Damn, he wished he hadn't lost that job. It paid well and he needed the work.

Now what? He did a quick mental calculation of the state of his finances. His meager supply of money would last a week or two if he was careful. But he'd need more to pay for the truck and to carry him until he landed another job. Preferably as far away from Flatville as possible.

Meantime he was stuck here.

Groaning, he massaged his forehead, where a pounding headache threatened. He didn't want to be in Flatville, and he sure didn't want to work here. But with the truck out of commission and his wallet nearly empty, there wasn't much else he could do.

He thought briefly about the insurance money sitting in his savings account, then tightened his jaw. No degree of desperation would make him touch that money. Like it or not, he would just have to tough this out.

Muttering a string of profanities, he kicked a rock off the sidewalk. It flew into the street, barely missing an old heap the same vintage as Alison's Chevy. His thoughts unwittingly turned to her. How much longer would her sickly car hold up, and what would she do when it broke down for good? She sure couldn't depend on Chuck to keep it running.

Clint frowned. That wasn't his concern. Still, as long as he was forced to stay in town, he had to pay for lodging somewhere. It might as well be at her place. She needed the money.

The thought of seeing Alison and her talkative kid again lifted his spirits more than it should have. Scowling, he pushed away the emotions he had no business feeling. Damned if he'd let himself care.

He heard an oldies rock song mixed with hammering and the buzz of a table saw as he neared Millie's restaurant. *Well, hell.* His legs had carried him here of their own volition. He recalled what Chuck had said about Rusty needing help, and headed forward.

At the door he hesitated. Inside, four men were hard at work, two hammering up sheet rock and two sawing more. Suddenly a tall, rangy man turned toward him. By the carrot-colored hair curling out from under his hard hat and his take-charge expression, Clint knew he must be Rusty.

"Can I help you?" the man asked, tipping back his hat and eyeing Clint.

Clint straightened his shoulders. "I hear you need a temporary hand."

"You heard right."

Extending his arm, Clint strode toward him. "I'm your man."

The songs of a jillion cicadas filled Alison's ears as she hurried through the park entrance two mornings later. Jenny had phoned and asked to meet her here. Since Alison had confided in her, their friendship had deepened. Jenny wanted to talk to Alison this morning, but only in person.

Her curiosity piqued, she'd dropped Hannah at Millie's and come straight here. Wandering down the path that cut through the grounds, she scanned every bench for her friend, nodding and stopping to greet half a dozen acquaintances. Partway through the park, she spied Jenny, sitting on an old green bench under a sprawling oak.

"Hi, Alison." The blonde waved and scooted over to make room. "Nice day, isn't it?"

"For now. In another hour, it'll be too hot to sit out here." Alison lifted an eyebrow. "Why all the mystery? What did you want to tell me?"

In no hurry to divulge her news, Jenny shrugged.

"I'll come to that in a minute. Let's talk about Clint first. It's all over town that he's still here."

Alison nodded and grinned, unable to hide her pleasure that he had returned. Not forever, but for now. She should be sorry his truck wasn't fixed and his job in Florida had fallen through, but she wasn't. The rent he paid helped with her cash-flow problems. And his taking the job at Millie's would help speed up the remodel. Maybe, just maybe, the restaurant would open on time.

But that wasn't all. Somehow, his coming back shored up her spirits. Even if he was gruff and more distant than ever. "Chuck couldn't find the parts he needed in Indianapolis. He had to special order them from some place back east. He says it'll take at least a week to get them and another few days after that to install them," she said.

"A whole week and then some, with Clint Strong sleeping under your roof? Have mercy." Jenny fanned herself.

"Jenny," Alison protested, albeit weakly.

Her friend smiled knowingly. Could she have guessed, somehow, that Alison liked Clint more than she should, that she couldn't stop thinking about those breath-stopping kisses, that she longed to kiss him again, and more? Her face heating, she shook her head. No, Jenny couldn't know any of those things.

Her friend eyed her as if she did. "You like him."

Alison had never been good at hiding her feelings. She bit her lip. "Too much," she admitted.

Jenny angled her head Alison's way. "He must be one happy guy."

"Come on, Jenny. The man needs a place to stay until his truck's fixed. He's not interested."

"I don't know about that. The day I picked up the living room furniture, I couldn't help noticing the way he looked at you. He's definitely interested."

Alison thought about how Clint had avoided her the past two days, and how when they were in the same room, he seemed tense and edgy, as if he couldn't wait to get away from her. "You're wrong." She shook her head. "Even if you weren't, he's a drifter. He'll leave as soon as he can. Who knows, he may not even stay long enough to finish the remodel. I've been through that before, with Hannah's father. I don't want to get hurt."

"Maybe you won't."

Jenny's suddenly narrowed eyes made Alison uncomfortable. To escape her friend's scrutiny, she leaned down and refastened the buckle on her sandal.

"Is there a chance the restaurant will open on time?" Jenny asked.

"A slim one, yes. The project is still behind schedule. But thanks to that new agreement Millie negotiated, they're working hard to catch up." Alison thought about the way Clint left at dawn and returned at dusk and crossed her fingers. "If they do, then there's a good chance I'll be able to get that loan and save my house."

"That *is* good news," Jenny said. "What about the bank?"

"I'm phoning Vincent Cahill this afternoon to make an appointment." Alison dreaded talking to the banker. But there was no point in delaying.

Jenny offered an encouraging smile. "Things will work out. With Clint part of Rusty's crew, it's a cinch you'll get that extension. I can feel it in my bones."

"I hope you're right." Alison tried hard to believe

her friend's words. She'd always considered herself an optimist. But lately, keeping a positive outlook on life wasn't easy.

"He will, especially when he hears about your good news." Grinning, Jenny leaned toward Alison. "I got an offer on your dining room set."

Alison's eyes widened. "So quickly?"

"It's a matter of being in the right place at the right time. You'll never guess how much they offered. After my fee, you'll net close to four thousand dollars."

Alison's jaw dropped. For a moment surprise rendered her speechless. That was more than she'd ever imagined.

"Well?" Jenny prodded. "Aren't you going to say anything?"

"Wow," she managed at last. "That's a lot of money."

"Worth every penny, too. The couple who want to purchase it live in one of those big old mansions in Indianapolis. The buffet and table will fit perfectly in their dining room, and I know they'll take good care of it." Jenny's eyes danced. "So, do you want to accept their offer?"

"You bet." Alison thought about the mahogany buffet that hadn't been cleaned in decades. "It'll take time to empty all those drawers. When do they want it?"

"Will two weeks work?"

"Perfect."

"Double perfect." Jenny beamed. "Be sure to tell Vincent about this. I guarantee you, nothing will sway him like cold, hard cash."

"I will." Alison smiled, feeling more upbeat than

she had in months. "Thanks, Jenny." She gave her friend a heartfelt hug.

"Hey, thank *you* for hiring me to sell your stuff. Be sure to let me know what the bank says."

"I will." The town hall bells began to chime, as they did every noon. "I've got to pick up Hannah." Alison stood up. "Millie took her to see how the re-model's going."

No doubt Clint wouldn't like seeing the little girl on-site. He was as stiff and uncomfortable around her as ever. But Alison had wanted time to talk to Jenny alone. When Millie had offered to take the little girl along with her, Alison had readily accepted. And Hannah had jumped up and down. "She couldn't wait to see the men working," Alison added.

"You mean Clint." Jenny grinned. "The kid's got good taste. Just like her mother."

"Enough already." Alison rolled her eyes. "That subject is closed, all right?"

Unfortunately her heart disagreed. It seemed to have a mind of its own; it seemed to agree with Jenny.

Caring for Clint was reckless. And dangerous. Alison's "good taste" had failed her once before with Hannah's father, and things didn't look any better this time. If she wasn't careful, her foolish heart would surely break.

With a heavy sigh she pushed those thoughts aside and headed for the car.

Chapter Seven

Clint strode through the woods, squinting in the gathering darkness. Ahead of him Barker dodged in and out of view. In the time since they'd left the house after dinner, the sun had slowly sunk until Clint could barely see. But tired as he was after long hours working at Millie's, he'd needed to stay out here, away from Alison and Hannah, where he could think in peace.

In the three days since he'd rerented the room, he'd watched Alison's morale sink lower and lower, until she seemed a shadow of the woman he'd met a week ago. It didn't take a genius to figure out why.

Worry about losing the house was eating her alive.

If Vincent Cahill would ease up on her and give her an extension until the restaurant reopened, she could qualify for a loan and pay off the note. He knew from Millie that Alison had called the banker and scheduled an appointment to ask for more time. Cahill must not have been very encouraging on the phone. Alison's drawn face was proof of that.

A mosquito bit Clint's neck. He slapped it as thoughts charged through his mind. Maybe Rusty should talk to Cahill, show him the tight work schedule he and his crew were adhering to.

If that didn't work, then what? For what seemed the millionth time in a week, Clint thought about the insurance money sitting in his savings account. He could never touch it, never use it. But what about Alison?

Stay out of it, the voice in his head warned, just as a tree limb smacked his shoulder. ''Dammit,'' he muttered.

Served him right. Rubbing his smarting skin, he ducked under the branch and whistled for the dog. ''Come on, mutt. It's time to go back.''

Barker woofed and raced past him, no doubt anxious to see Hannah. Clint scratched the bites on his neck and arms in a futile effort to make the itching stop. The little girl bothered him just like the bites. He hoped she'd be in bed by now, so he wouldn't have to answer her endless questions or listen to her constant chatter or that bubbly laughter. Or see her, clean and shining after a bath and full of spit.

Right now she was probably giving Alison a hard time about going to bed. Despite himself, he grinned. Hannah wasn't that bad. Hell, she was just a little kid. Still, he didn't care to forge a relationship with her.

Or with her mother.

He didn't deserve a relationship with them.

The past three days he'd avoided both of them as much as possible. He left for the restaurant at dawn, before either of them awoke. So far he only ran into them at dinner. Yet despite his distance, Alison left a sack lunch for him in the refrigerator each morning. Evenings, she cooked a meal too good to miss. And even though he didn't offer much by way of conversation, both females seemed to welcome him at the table.

For the life of him, he didn't know why.

Bone weary and tired of thinking, he entered the yard. Through the window he heard the soft cadence of the television. Alison must be watching something. Yet no light showed through the crack in the drawn curtains.

He frowned. It wasn't like her to sit alone in the dark. Scratching a bite on his arm, he trudged heavily up the front steps.

She sat huddled on the sofa, a shadowed form in the unlit room. Seeing her like that made Clint's chest hurt. "Hey," he said softly, moving toward her. "What are you watching?"

"Nothing yet. Hanna's finally asleep. I'm waiting for an old Steve Martin movie to start. He makes me laugh," she said, sounding as if she badly needed a night off from her troubles.

"Me, too," Clint replied. "Didn't your mother tell you that watching TV in the dark is hard on the eyes?" He flipped on a lamp. "Think I'll watch it with you."

"Okay." She wore that worried expression he'd seen more and more of, lately.

He wanted desperately to wipe it from her face. "You know," he said, "to really appreciate a Steve Martin movie, you need popcorn. Why don't we make some?"

"Yeah?" She shrugged. "We can do that."

"I like it dripping with butter."

"Me, too." Her lips almost turned up at the corners. "And cold beer to top it off."

It wasn't a smile, but it was a start. Clint smacked his lips. "Woman, you read my mind. All right, then, come on." Reaching for her hand, he tugged her up. Without letting go, he led her from the room. "My mouth is watering already."

In the brighter light of the kitchen, she looked up at him. Her eyes widened. "Look at your neck and arms. The mosquitoes must have eaten you alive tonight."

It was like her to put his discomfort ahead of her problems. Clint shrugged. "It's just a few bites," he said, rubbing the back of his neck.

"I'll get you something to stop the itching."

"Don't bother—" he started to say, but she'd already disappeared through the door. Moments later she returned, the tube of salve already open. Clint reached for it. "Thanks."

"Let me." She snatched it away from him. "Sit down, Clint."

He didn't want her to touch him, but at least the despair was gone from her face. For now. If taking care of his bites helped her disposition, so be it. He sank onto the nearest chair.

"Look at the floor," she directed. An instant later she brushed his neck.

Her fingers were gentle, and the cool salve instantly eased the itch. Clint closed his eyes. It seemed a lifetime since anyone had cared enough to do something like this for him.

She stood close enough that he felt the warmth radiating from her body. Her scent washed over him. Damn, she smelled good, like cinnamon and sunshine and woman. Her soft breaths fanned his forehead.

It was heaven, letting her minister to him. And hell. He wanted to touch her, too, wanted to pull her into his arms until they both forgot about mosquitoes and mortgages. But that would be dangerous. And stupid. Curling his hands into fists, he fought the urge.

"Now your arms."

Her hands continued their magic across his biceps. Heat shot through him. He shifted uncomfortably, hoping she wouldn't see his burgeoning erection.

"There." Thankfully she moved away, recapped the tube and set it on the table.

"Thank you." His voice was rough.

"You're welcome." She stood still a moment, her soft eyes searching his, her expression warm. God, she was beautiful.

And off-limits. Clint knew what would happen if he gave in to his desires. A piece of heaven. Then, pain and destruction, caused by him.

Alison deserved better. He cleared his throat. "We don't want to miss the movie. How about that popcorn?"

A few moments later they returned to the living room. Alison cradled a huge bowl brimming with hot-buttered popcorn, and he had two ice-cold beers and a handful of napkins.

It had been years since he'd sat beside a woman and watched television, years since he'd wanted to. Not that he wanted to now, he told himself, but Alison needed the company.

They dug into the popcorn with gusto. Clint was halfway through his beer when Alison let out a soft chuckle. The sound lifted his heart. "It's good to hear you laugh," he said.

The smile remained on her face. "It *feels* good, too."

They grinned at each other like fools. It seemed natural to slip his arm around her. When she rested her head lightly against his shoulder, he felt even better.

Warm, full, and strangely content, he yawned. He'd put in ten hours today, would do the same tomorrow. He should get up, go to bed and try to sleep. But he stayed right where he was.

His eyes drifted shut as he lost the battle to stay awake, and for a long time sweet oblivion swept over him. A singing commercial woke him. He glanced at the wall clock in amazement. Two-thirty. Tonight the nightmare had stayed away.

Alison lay across his chest, her face partially blocked by a thick curtain of hair. Drowsy, he brushed it back and gazed down at her. In sleep her lips were parted, and her face was smooth and free of worry. The way her long, dark lashes almost curled against her cheek gave her a sweet, peaceful air.

Tenderness filled him. In slumber she'd managed to escape the worries that plagued her during waking hours. He wanted her to sleep a long time. Shifting carefully to a more comfortable position, he managed to reach the remote and shut off the television.

The movement woke her. Her lids fluttered open, and then her eyes were on his. "Clint?" Her soft smile and sleepy voice stirred his body to life. "What happened?"

"We fell asleep," he murmured, watching her

mouth. Her face was so close. He could easily bend down and kiss her.

"Oh." She lifted her head from his chest. Her eyes were half-closed, but he saw the warmth in them. Leaning up, she kissed the underside of his chin.

His pulse hammered crazily. "Alison?"

Without answering, she closed her eyes again. Her tongue licked lazily over her full lower lip. *Damn.* Clint's blood heated.

"Kiss me, Clint," she whispered.

Unable to resist, his heart thundering in his chest, he complied. She tasted of popcorn and beer, and so sweet his heart ached. He wanted to kiss her again and again, so he did. Each time, his arousal grew, until finally, breathing hard, he drew back. "What are we doing?"

"Something we both want." She reached a hand behind his neck and pulled him toward her. Groaning, he captured her lips again. Her mouth moved under his, demanding more. Angling his head, he deepened the kiss. She opened to him, probing the inside of his mouth. Fire shot through him.

"Sweetheart," he whispered. He stroked her back, her hip. His hands traveled upward, to the sides of her breasts.

She gave a tiny gasp and stiffened. Instantly he stilled. "I'm sorry," he said, pulling away.

"Please, Clint, touch me." Locking her eyes on his, she placed his hands over her breasts. They were small and soft and filled his palms. Through her thin T-shirt, he felt the rigid tips and remembered glimpses of those rosy nipples the day she bathed Barker.

Suddenly he wanted to see her naked.

As if she read his thoughts and agreed, she grabbed the hem of her top.

"Let me," he said, and tugged it over her head. Then he slipped off his shirt and tossed it aside.

Alison's eyes were dark and luminous as she reached behind and unfastened her bra. Her unbound breasts tumbled out, white and round, the nipples pink and proud. Clint swallowed. For a moment he simply stared. "You're perfect," he finally stated, knowing the words were inadequate.

"I have stretch marks." She frowned down at the barely visible lines.

"They're beautiful." Leaning down, he kissed the soft skin.

"You really know how to sweet-talk a girl," she murmured in a deep, throaty voice. Her womanly scent surrounded him.

"I can do a lot more than talk." He drew a stiff, rosy peak into his mouth and suckled gently.

Moaning softly, Alison arched back, giving him full access. He thoroughly laved one breast, then the other. Her hands opened and closed on his shoulders, kneading like a hungry cat.

The passionate response inflamed him. He wanted to lie with her, but the couch was too short. Holding her close, he lowered her to the floor, then covered her body with his. Her beaded breasts, wet from his mouth, pressed against his chest in sweet torture.

His groin thick and heavy, he thrust a thigh between her legs and urged them apart. Alison's hands swept over his back in long, sensual motions. He stroked his hand up the smooth skin of her inner thigh. Sliding his fingers under the hem of her shorts, he easily breached the elastic on her panties. He found the tiny nub where he knew she ached. Making throaty little sounds that drove him wild, she lifted her hips. He slipped inside, where she was hot and moist. The moment he did, she came apart.

Watching her face, flushed with passion, feeling her muscles convulse around his fingers, aroused him so much that he almost joined in her release.

When it was over, she smiled. "Wow," she said in a wondrous voice.

The joy in her eyes filled his heart. Leaning down, he planted a kiss on the tip of her nose. "So you liked that."

"Mmm-hmm," she purred, and laid her hand across his rigid length. "Now I want to touch you, Clint."

She stroked his arousal through his jeans until he was ready to explode. He wanted to bury himself in her. Fool that he was, he wanted to make her his.

What am I doing?

Gritting his teeth, he lifted her wrist. "Don't, Alison."

"Why not?" She looked puzzled.

He sat up. "This isn't right."

"It feels right to me." She sat up beside him. Suddenly self-conscious, she folded her arms over her breasts.

Breasts he'd suckled moments ago. Already he wanted to taste them again. Fighting the urge, he grabbed her shirt and handed it to her. "Put this on."

She tugged it over her head. A lot of good it did. Without a bra, her nipples poked enticingly against the thin cotton.

Desire threatened to fog his brain. Clint forced his gaze upward. Rubbing a hand over his face, he searched for a way to explain. "You deserve better than me."

With her eyes wide, her coppery hair mussed and falling loose around her face, she looked like a wayward angel. "Let me be the judge of that."

He shook his head. "There are things you don't know about me."

"Why don't you tell me what they are," she coaxed.

He wanted to talk about Lynn and Erin and how he'd failed them. But he knew if he did, Alison would hate him. Or worse, feel sorry for him. He couldn't bear either.

He shook his head. "Look, it's late." He stood up. "I've got to be at the restaurant in a few hours. I need rest, and so do you." He offered her a hand.

With her lips pressed together, she looked as if she wanted to argue. Instead she let out a sigh. "I suppose you're right." Her eyes were filled with pain and confusion when she pulled herself up beside him.

He'd hurt her. Another reason to keep his distance. He released her hand. Or tried to.

She wouldn't let go. She stared at the ugly red burn scars that criss-crossed his palm and fingers of his left hand. The skin and the bones underneath throbbed, as if he'd burned them again.

"What are you looking at?" he growled. Jerking away, he shoved both fists into his pockets.

"Whatever you've done, I'm sure there's a valid reason for it," she replied. "You're a good man, Clint." Her eyes shone softly. "And you have good hands."

Her simple faith in him ripped him apart. To his

shame, moisture gathered behind his eyes. "Good night, Alison."

Swallowing hard, he turned away from her.

Late the following afternoon, after taking a much-needed break, Clint stretched his arms over his head. The muscles in his biceps and back twinged from the exhausting, nonstop labor he'd pushed them through over the past nine hours in an effort to empty his mind. But this time, the heavy physical work hadn't helped.

No matter how hard he drove his body, he couldn't get Alison out of his thoughts. Her body, her kisses, those little noises she made. More than that, her words.

You're a good man, Clint, she'd said.

He laughed bitterly. If she only knew.

You're starting to care for her. The thought scared him more than anything in a long time. Grabbing a hammer, he drove in a ten-penny nail in two pounding strokes. There was no way he could stay at her place any longer. It was too dangerous.

He glanced around the restaurant. It wasn't finished, but with the windows and insulation in, it provided enough shelter. He would move out of Alison's and sleep here until the truck was fixed. Then he'd drive away in it and leave Flatville forever.

But Alison needed the money. And she'd given him a room she could have leased to someone else. Clint picked up another nail. He'd pay her for two weeks, anyway. By then the restaurant would be nearly done.

Suddenly the room was quiet, and Clint realized the drone of the buzz saw had stopped. Billy Bob

Chapman, one of the three men he worked with, waved from across the room. "Hey, Clint, telephone." Covering the mouthpiece, he winked. "It's Alison."

Since Hannah's visit the day before, when Alison had stopped by to pick up the little girl, Rusty and the crew had teased him mercilessly. They thought he had something going with Alison. It was good-natured banter, and Clint appreciated that they'd accepted him so readily. But he aimed to put a stop to it. He rubbed his stiff lower back. There was nothing between him and Alison, and there never would be.

Her calling here didn't help matters. He frowned as he strode toward the phone. He hadn't seen her since last night. Maybe she'd had second thoughts about what happened. Maybe, like him, she'd decided he shouldn't bother coming back. Now was as good a time as any to settle things. Ignoring Billy Bob's thumbs-up sign, he took the receiver. "Hello?"

"Thank goodness you're still there." She sounded breathless and scared.

In the background he heard agonized cries. *Hannah's.* Heart in his throat, he gripped the phone. "What's happened?"

"There's been an accident. Hannah jumped off the woodpile and hurt her leg. I think it's broken. We're in the emergency room now, waiting for the doctor. I wanted you to know."

She didn't say it, but Clint knew she needed him. Hannah was hurt. He forgot about his decision to stay away from them. He hated hospitals, but he pushed that aside, too. "I'll be right there," he answered without hesitation.

When he hung up, the men were all staring at him.

He turned to Rusty. "There's been an accident with Hannah. Can someone drop me by the hospital? I'll make up the time later."

Thankfully, the foreman didn't argue. "Sure thing." He nodded to Billy Bob, the crew member who carpooled with Clint. "You drive him, then get right back here."

"Sure thing, boss."

Ten minutes later Billy Bob skidded to a halt in front of the hospital's emergency entrance. Clint's gut clenched with worry as he jumped from the truck.

Bile rose in his throat as he entered the waiting room. God, he hated hospitals. The smells, the orange plastic chairs filled with nervous people—all of it was painfully familiar. His hands balled into fists. The last time he was in a place like this, the two people he loved most had died. He swallowed hard and shoved away his anguish. This was no time for a walk down misery lane. He had to locate Alison and Hannah.

He found them in a small examining room, waiting for the doctor. Hannah wasn't crying, but her skin was pale and her face pinched in pain. Clint felt awful, seeing her hurt and so quiet. Sick to his stomach, in fact. Erin had been quiet, too, and she had died. *Oh, God.* He wanted to turn around and run. But Hannah wasn't facing a life-and-death situation. And she needed him. He forced himself to move slowly toward her. "Hey there."

"C-Clint." She sniffled, reaching a hand up to him.

A white-faced Alison stood on the far side of the bed, holding the girl's other hand. Relief filled her face when she saw Clint. "Thank heavens you're here."

Though he shook inside, he reached across the bed

and touched Alison's shoulder in a gesture meant to reassure. On unsteady legs, he hunkered down and brushed the little girl's wrinkled forehead with the back of his hand. "What happened to you, smart stuff?"

Two fat drops rolled down her tear-streaked cheeks. "I hurted my leg."

"Let's see." Her shin was red and already badly swollen. She definitely needed X rays. He tried a smile. "Don't worry, we'll get you fixed up in no time."

Suddenly her face screwed up in agony. "It hurts, Clint," she cried.

His heart ripped. She was so little to have such pain. Alison brushed her daughter's forehead and murmured comforting words. Clint glanced at the door. He'd give the medical staff ten seconds. If they didn't show up by then, there would be hell to pay.

Luckily, a white-coated doctor and a nurse showed up in time. As they approached the bed, Hannah's eyes were huge. "I don't like hospital people," she cried, shrinking against Alison. "Last time I was here, they hurted me."

"They're going to help you, honey," Alison soothed. She met Clint's gaze over her daughter's head. Worry etched her face.

Clint nodded. God knew, he hated this as much as Hannah did. But it couldn't be helped. "She's right, smart stuff. These folks will fix you up."

"Your mom can stay with you, okay?" the young, brown-haired doctor said as he prepared to examine Hannah's leg.

"And your dad," the nurse added.

Hannah frowned. "I don't gots a daddy. But I want Clint to stay."

He grimaced. He damned sure wasn't her father, nor did he want to be. He didn't want to stay, either, didn't want to see the little girl suffer. But he had no choice. He couldn't let Alison and Hannah down. "I'll be right here with you, smart stuff."

Swallowing back his fear, he stayed at her side.

Hours later, when Clint carried an exhausted Hannah up the stairs to her bedroom, Alison close behind, a thick, white cast covered the little girl's left leg from ankle to thigh. The poor kid had fractured her tibia and was stuck this way for at least a month.

Shifting her gently, he turned toward her room. It had been a long afternoon and evening, with Hannah frightened and in pain, and he never wanted to go through anything like it again. Now, as he approached her bedroom, she snuggled against him comfortably as if he'd carried her this way a dozen times, as if he were a trusted protector.

He almost laughed. The kid was sadly mistaken if she expected him to protect her. Yet, she'd clung to him since he'd arrived at the hospital. He didn't understand why, and he was too tired to think about it now.

"I'll turn on Hannah's light," Alison murmured, and slipped ahead of them.

Dread filled him. Four years ago his little girl's room had burned to ashes. He hadn't been in a child's room since, and he had no desire to stir up painful memories now.

But there was no way to avoid it. He hesitated in the threshold, steeling himself against the agony surg-

ing through him. Drawing in a breath, he squared his
shoulders and carried Hannah through the door.

As she had everywhere else in the house, Alison
had made Hannah's room a cheerful, welcoming
space. Disney characters in bright, primary colors
decorated one wall, with curtains and a comforter to
match. An open toy box revealed a tangle of dolls
and blocks, and the bookshelf overflowed with books.
The room teemed with life.

To Clint's surprise his pain receded. Here, in this
child's room, there was no place for old sorrow.

With practiced expertise, Alison turned down the
covers and swept aside a handful of stuffed animals
in one motion.

Clint set the girl carefully on the bed. "There you
are, smart stuff."

"Will you hold her up while I put on her nightie?"
Alison asked.

"Sure." Grasping Hannah's pint-size waist, he
supported her while Alison slipped a flowered nightshirt over her head.

"There. Lie down, sweetie." Alison plumped the
pillow, then eased her daughter back.

"Wait." Hannah struggled up. "Where's Barker?"

Hearing his name, the dog whined softly and lifted
his head. Hannah patted the dog's nose, then the animal settled down beside the bed. Satisfied, the little
girl relaxed.

Once her daughter was settled, Alison carefully sat
down on the edge of the bed. Her face full of a
mother's love, she smoothed Hannah's brow, then
planted a kiss on the little forehead.

Watching the intimate scene, Clint felt like an in-
truder. Alison and Hannah were a family. They be-

longed together. Barker, too. But Clint didn't. A hole opened in his chest. Because of who he was and what he'd done, he would never again be part of a family.

Suddenly he wanted out of this room. Compressing his mouth into a thin line, he backed away.

"Clint?" Drowsy from fatigue and pain medication, Hannah reached for him. Beneath the sun-browned skin, she was pale.

She'd been through so much tonight. How could he walk away now? Exerting monumental effort, he put his pain on hold and moved toward her, grasping the small outstretched hand and squeezing gently. "What is it, smart stuff?"

"Will you tuck me in and kiss me good-night?"

"All right." His voice was rough. Leaning down, he kissed her soft little cheek. Careful of her leg, he eased the cover over her. "Sleep well."

"I love you, sweetie," Alison murmured, performing the same ritual. Straightening, she switched off the overhead light. A Goofy night-light cast the room in dim shadow.

"I love you, too, Mama. And I love you, Clint."

I love you. God, how those words ripped him in two.

He didn't deserve love, especially from sweet little Hannah. His eyes moist, he retreated into the shadows. Within seconds the child drifted off to sleep.

"Thank goodness," Alison breathed. Together she and Clint crept from the room.

Her hands shook as she shut the door, leaving it ajar in case Hannah called for her. Relieved that ordeal was finished, Clint glanced toward his room. Now was his chance to leave. He would pack up tonight and move to the construction site first thing to-morrow. Then he wouldn't have to—

Alison's heavy sigh interrupted his thoughts. "This has been one of the longest days of my life." Looking up at him, she shuddered. "Thanks, Clint. I don't know what I'd have done without your help."

He stifled a grimace. If she only knew what that had cost him. "No big deal," he managed.

"Are you kidding? When I think what could have happened…" Swallowing, she looked away.

She was still badly shaken. Fueled by the need to comfort her, Clint slipped his arm across her shoulders. "Hey, it's okay now."

She sought his eyes, then let out a breath and collapsed against him. "I know. But, Lord, I was scared."

For some reason her weight against him eased some of his pain. Of its own accord his arm tightened around her. "What we both need is a good, stiff drink," he said, surprising himself.

"And how," Alison replied. "But all I've got is an old bottle of brandy left over from when Aunt Phoebe was alive."

"That'll do."

A few minutes later they sat across from each other at the old oak kitchen table. Clinking glasses, they sipped the rich liquor. For several moments neither spoke.

"I feel like I've aged ten years," Alison finally said. Exhaustion, worry and guilt flitted across her face. She was as easy to read as a book.

Reaching across the table, Clint touched her cheek. "It wasn't your fault."

"No?" She toyed with her glass before meeting his eye. "I let her play on that woodpile."

"Hell, I stacked that wood. Maybe it's my fault."

Alison rolled her eyes. "That's ridiculous and you know it."

"You're right, but so is your guilt. How could either of us know she would hurt herself?"

Alison shrugged. "As a mother, I should have watched her more carefully."

"You did nothing wrong," Clint repeated. "Hannah's a resilient kid. And, anyway, you heard what the doctor said. In a month or two she'll be good as new."

"I know, but I hate to see her suffer. Hasn't she gone through enough?" Her eyes flashed, and Clint knew she was remembering her daughter's heart surgery. "If I could, I'd take her pain into my body."

Clint had no doubt of that. He nodded, knowing exactly what she meant. He would have given his life gladly for Erin and Lynn. But things hadn't turned out that way. They were dead, and all he had to show for their suffering were a few pitiful little scars on one hand. And a huge, gaping hole where his heart used to be.

Grimacing, he reached for the brandy, refilled his drink and quickly drained his glass. He relished the burning sensation in his belly.

Alison frowned. "Are you all right?"

No. "I'll survive." He spread his hand on the table and stared down at the ugly red skin.

"That looks sore. You said you burned it. Does it still hurt?"

Not as bad as his heart, he wanted to say. "Sometimes. It happened a long time ago."

Her eyes rounded. "Did it happen at a construction site?"

"No." He dropped his arm to his lap.

"Oh?" Her eyes were full of questions he didn't feel like answering.

"Look, it's late." He pushed back his chair and stood up. "I've got to get some rest and pack."

"Pack?" Her brow furrowed.

Clint busied himself corking the brandy. "From now on I'm bunking at the site."

"What?" Shock and confusion played across her face. "But why?"

Because it was dangerous here. Because tonight had stirred up painful emotions he didn't want to feel. "If we're going to meet Millie's deadline, I'll need to put in longer hours. By sleeping there, I can start earlier and work later."

Alison wrapped her arms around her waist. "I see," she said.

"Don't worry, though, I'll pay you for a full two weeks."

"Keep your money." Her lips pressed together.

"No, you rented the room to me, and I intend to pay for it."

She raised her chin proudly. "I won't take money I haven't earned."

He should have figured she'd assert that stubborn streak. He also knew how badly she needed the cash. He threw up his hands. "Dammit, Alison, all right, if it makes you happy, I'll sleep here. But I'm warning you now, I won't be around much. So don't look for me at dinner, and don't expect me to keep you company at night."

''Fine,'' she snapped, and glared at him.

Good, she was angry. Maybe now she'd leave him alone. Turning away from her, Clint headed for the stairs.

Chapter Eight

Alison's bedroom was stuffy and too hot for sleep. Restless, she kicked off the covers. A moment later, cold, she pulled them up again and rolled onto her side. But that didn't work, so she tried her stomach. No luck. Darn it, after what had happened tonight, she was exhausted. Why couldn't she fall asleep?

Any fool knew the answer to that question. Clint Strong. Alison gripped her pillow as anger, confusion and frustration tore at her. And hurt, too, if she were honest.

He'd said he wanted to sleep at the site so that he could put in longer hours and try to finish the remodel on time. While that was a great excuse, she knew better.

The real reason was to avoid her and Hannah.

Alison bit her lip. That stung, but she was an adult, and she could handle rejection. However, Hannah was a little girl, and she was deeply taken with Clint. Especially after tonight. Alison had watched her daughter cling to him in the hospital, and when they had put her to bed, Alison heard Hannah tell Clint she loved him.

Clint had flinched at the words, as if he wanted to deflect them. Yes, he'd been gentle with Hannah, especially in the emergency room. Alison was truly grateful for that because, heaven knew, she couldn't have handled tonight alone. But once they were home, he'd seemed no friendlier or warmer to Hannah than before.

Tonight pain medication had kept Hannah from noticing. Surely tomorrow she'd sense his withdrawal. Her feelings were bound to be hurt.

Alison's protective hackles rose. In Hannah's short life she'd braved what most people never faced. Rejection from a father she didn't know and probably never would. Heart surgery. Now a fractured leg. Hadn't she suffered enough?

Angry, Alison sat up in bed. Clint had no right to trample on Hannah's feelings. True, he bore no responsibility to her or Hannah. Alison didn't want that. What she wanted was simple—an occasional smile for her daughter and a little show of warmth. Just until he left town.

Was that asking so much?

She pursed her lips. She intended to tell him, right now, while the words were fresh in her mind. Tossing on her robe, she strode toward his room.

But when she arrived at his door her courage faltered and she hesitated. Did she really want to do this, barge in and discuss Hannah now? Maybe he was sleeping, and he did have a long day tomorrow. She should probably wait until morning—

"Erin? Lynn?" Clint shouted from inside the room. "No-o-o-o!"

The agony in his voice frightened Alison. Who were Erin and Lynn? Forgetting why she was outside Clint's room, she rushed through the door. "Clint?"

He shot up. Breathing hard, he snapped on the lamp. The haunted look in his eyes had nothing to do with the sudden light in the room. His expression cut straight into Alison's heart. Something had shaken him terribly.

"Bad dream?" she asked in a low voice.

"Real bad." Shuddering, he scrubbed a hand over his stubbled chin. His hair stuck up, and the covers lay in a tangled mess. He glanced at Alison, then away.

"Are you all right?"

"Lady, that's a loaded question." His mouth twisted bitterly. "I will be."

More than anything, she wanted to brush the hair from his forehead and the shadows from his face, wanted to somehow erase his torment. And she wanted to know what had put it there.

But a sixth sense warned her against touching him right now. Uncertain what to do, she hovered by the door and locked her hands at her waist. "When I first moved here, I used to have nightmares. Actually, the same one over and over."

"What was that?" he asked, lifting his eyes to her.

She hadn't spoken of the dream for years. But he wanted her to talk, she saw it in his face. "I was lost and couldn't find my way home. No matter who I asked for directions, no one could help me. It was

BUSINESS REPLY MAIL

FIRST-CLASS MAIL   PERMIT NO. 717   BUFFALO, NY

POSTAGE WILL BE PAID BY ADDRESSEE

SILHOUETTE READER SERVICE
3010 WALDEN AVE
PO BOX 1867
BUFFALO NY 14240-9952

NO POSTAGE
NECESSARY
IF MAILED
IN THE
UNITED STATES

scary and lonely, and I always woke up crying. Aunt Phoebe helped me stop having that dream."

"How'd she do that?" Jerking back the covers, he swung his legs over the bed.

In a pair of navy boxers and nothing else, he was practically naked. Lord, his chest was broad. He had a hard, muscled torso and a flat stomach, the kind that came from heavy physical labor. And those legs, long and strong...

Alison swallowed and gave herself a mental shake. Now was hardly the time to notice the man's body. "She asked me to tell her the dream, and then we talked about what it meant. I was afraid I wouldn't be accepted in Flatville, that folks here wouldn't like me. Once I understood, I felt a whole lot better. And I realized that people liked me fine. I never had the dream again."

"Yeah?"

"So you see, if you talk about it..." She let the words trail off.

His expression remained shuttered. "You were a kid, Alison. I'm a man, and I'll deal with this my own way." He clamped his mouth shut, apparently finished with the subject.

Curiosity filled her. She wanted to question him, to find out what made him suffer. Who were Lynn and Erin? Had something bad happened to them? But Alison was a patient woman. She would wait until he was ready to explain. Wordlessly she nodded.

After a moment of silence he pushed to his feet and eyed her warily. "Anyway, it's over now. Sorry I woke you."

"You didn't." Standing up, he looked even better. Alison couldn't help noticing the way the hair on his chest tapered to a narrow line down his stomach and disappeared beneath the boxers, or the bulge below— Her face heated as she jerked her gaze to his face. "I...I came here to talk to you about Hannah."

"Hannah?" His face darkened as he crossed his arms. "So talk." His shoulders stiffened as if he expected a blow.

Alison swallowed. "She's only a little girl, Clint. What did she do to make you hate her?"

He bowed his head. "Look, I don't hate her. I— she's okay." He swallowed. "It's just, I'm not used to being around kids."

Alison believed him. And thought she understood. Children made some people uncomfortable. Unfortunately, Clint was one of them. Time and patience would take care of that, but he didn't possess enough of either.

"By now you know she doesn't bite," she teased, striving to lighten his mood. "And I'm not asking you to play with her or anything. Just be nice, and smile now and then, okay?" She moved closer to him and laid a hand on his forearm.

He smelled of pine-scented soap and man, and under his warm skin his muscle tensed. "I'll give it a shot."

"Thank you."

Now that they'd come to an understanding, Alison could go back to her room and try to sleep. But for some reason she stayed right where she was. Of its own volition, her thumb began to circle his skin in a light caress.

Clint stared down at her fingers, then raised his gaze. "You need to go, Alison."

His smoldering eyes were at odds with his words.

No look had ever heated her blood like this, and no man had ever made her feel so…so hungry. With a shock she realized she wanted to make love with Clint. Moistening her dry lips, she shook her head. "What if I want to stay?"

His gaze, full of hunger, sought her mouth, then rose to her eyes. "Don't tempt me," he warned, his voice husky.

The words, the timbre of his voice, pulsed through her. Leaning into him, she flattened her palms against the soft black hair on his chest. Beneath her hand Clint's heart thudded in a rapidly escalating rhythm matching her own.

"I want to tempt you, Clint. I want you to kiss me."

Groaning, he tipped up her chin. "You've got your wish." He captured her lips. His mouth felt so right on hers, so *good.*

"You are so sweet," he murmured, as if he'd read her thoughts. Slanting his mouth, he parted her lips with his, then plunged his tongue inside.

Alison's heart expanded until her whole body pulsed. Flinging open her robe, she pressed close, until her breasts flattened against his chest. Clint's hands anchored on her hips, hauling her tight against his arousal.

"Oh, yes," she whispered. "I like that."

"So do I."

He nuzzled her neck, then planted kisses at the sensitive hollow beneath her ear. Giving in to sensation, Alison tilted her head back and melted.

She barely noticed when Clint slipped the robe from her shoulders. Lifting the hem of her nightshirt, he slid his hands up her bare sides and cupped her breasts. She shivered.

"I want to taste you again, see if you're as good as I remember." Lowering his head, he took her nipple into his mouth and suckled.

Alison's bones turned to water. "Oh, Clint," she moaned, urging him closer.

"You're even better than before," he murmured against her sensitive skin. For a few blissful moments her thoughts disappeared. There was only Clint and the pleasure coursing through her body.

Suddenly he straightened. With a resigned sigh he backed away from her.

Alison opened her eyes. "Clint?"

"This is dangerous, Alison." His face was full of regret. "I'm at the point of no return. We have to stop now, while we can."

"I don't want to stop."

"Don't tease me. This isn't a game."

"I know." She let her need show in her face. "Make love with me, Clint."

His smoldering gaze caught and held her. "I want you more than you know. But I don't want to hurt you. You know I can't stay. And I can't make you any promises."

He was a drifter, like Hannah's father. And like Hannah's father, he would love her and leave her. Alison knew she'd suffer a broken heart later, but right now, she didn't care. "I'm not asking for a commitment. I know you'll leave as soon as your truck is ready. But, please, let's not think about that now."

His inner struggle played across his face. Hands on her shoulders, he searched her eyes. "Are you sure?"

"Completely," she stated, leaning into him.

Don't do this. She deserves better, the voice in Clint's head warned as he tugged Alison close. He pushed the warning away. Maybe so, but for some lucky reason she wanted him.

And, God help him, he wanted her.

Wordlessly, he tugged her nightie over her head.

God, she was beautiful. Her fiery hair streamed down her back and shoulders in shimmering waves that warmed him like the sun. Her lips were puffy from his kisses. His gaze dropped to her rosy nipples, still rigid from his attention. With her skin flushed and her eyes dark and full of need, she was the sexiest, most beautiful woman in the world. Just looking at her made him want to explode.

"Come here," he growled, hauling her close. Hungrily he devoured her mouth with kisses she eagerly returned. One foot hooked around his calf. The taut peaks of her breasts pressed against his chest, driving him to the brink of insanity. "You feel so good," he whispered, urging her hips closer.

"I know." Suddenly playful, she smiled. "You make my knees weak. I really need to sit down, before I fall over."

His heart brimming, he chuckled. "I can take care of that, darlin'." Scooping her into his arms, he moved to the bed. He sat her down gently and eased her onto her back. Her beauty awed him. With desire flushing her neck and breasts and her coppery hair fanned out over the pale-yellow covers, she looked like a goddess.

His. For now.

He cleared his throat. "Where were we?"

Her gaze moved to his swollen groin. "Here, I think." With a tug, she eased down his shorts. Eyes wide, she stared at his arousal. "You're so big," she whispered.

"That's because I want you so much," he said.

A pleased smile hovered on her lips. "I figured that out."

Her fingers closed over him. Intense pleasure flowed through him, sapping his strength. Groaning, he sank onto his knees beside her. He wanted to drive into her, bury himself in her softness right now, but she wasn't ready yet.

"Easy, Alison." Circling her wrist, he lifted her hand. "I don't want to go any further until we're both naked."

Without taking her eyes from his, she raised her hips. He slipped off her plain white panties.

The thatch between her legs was the same brilliant copper as her hair, a triangle of fire. "I'll be damned," he murmured as he leaned over her. He kissed her flat stomach, then moved lower.

She sighed as he parted her thighs. When he tasted her sweetness, she stiffened and gasped. "What are you—"

"Pleasuring you."

"O-h-h-h-h." She let out a low moan. Her hands tangled in his hair, urging him to continue. After a long moment she pushed him away. "Please, Clint, stop. I want us to…to be together."

"Hang on." He groped for his wallet and extracted a condom. Turning away, he sheathed himself.

When he faced her again, her eyes were dark and luminous. Without taking her gaze from his, she opened her arms to him.

His heart expanded until it filled his chest. He swallowed. He'd never wanted a woman so much. It scared him to death.

But his fierce desire overrode his fear. Aching for release, he slid between her legs. His erection nudged her moist warmth, and he knew he was going to lose it. "Alison, darlin', I wanted to take this slowly, but I don't think I can," he rasped.

"I don't want you to hold back," she pleaded, urging him closer. He plunged inside.

She was tight and hot and, oh, she felt good. Clint closed his eyes and tried to hold on to his sanity. But she wrapped her legs around his waist, squeezed her muscles around him and started making those little throaty noises. His mind emptied. In a dance as old as creation, he drove into her, harder and faster and deeper. Breathing raggedly, she matched him thrust for thrust.

Suddenly she gasped and clutched him. "Oh Clint, oh Clint," she cried as she convulsed around him.

Her frenzied movement pushed him over the edge. "Alison," he called out, and then his world exploded.

When his head stopped spinning and his heart slowed, he was holding her carefully against his chest. Snuggling close, she cupped a hand against his cheek. In that moment he felt a peace so profound it surprised him.

"That was incredible," he murmured, and kissed the flower-scented crown of her head. "Thank you."

She propped herself up beside him. "No, thank *you*. The pleasure was all mine." She looked at him through her lashes. "It's been a long time for me, since Hannah's father. And it was never like this." Her fingers traveled lazily across his belly.

"Me, too." His groin stirred. Damned if he didn't want her again.

He fought his feelings. What right did he have to want more? She deserved better than him. *Leave,* the voice commanded, but then Alison licked her lower lip in a slow, provocative motion that heated his blood.

"Clint?" Her voice low and throaty, she nipped his neck. "Let's do that again." Her hand closed around his new arousal.

Desire raged through him. Right or wrong, he wanted her, and she wanted him. For tonight, that was all that mattered.

Pushing away his thoughts, he reached for her.

Alison had always been a light sleeper, and tonight was no different. The moment Clint rose from the bed, her eyes opened.

In the gray, predawn light she watched his tall, dark form pad silently toward the lump on the room's lone chair that must be his jeans. The denim rustled as he stepped into them.

Oh, no, he was leaving. Please, not now, when she'd given him her heart. Yes, it was true. Sometime last night, she'd fallen in love with him, deeply, sweetly in love. She hadn't meant to, but she had.

Too bad he didn't feel the same. Instead he was sneaking out, as if he regretted last night. Her heart clutched painfully, until she thought about what had happened between them.

Images of fevered lovemaking followed by tender kisses and gentle caresses changed her mind. He wouldn't just walk away, not after making love with her. Two incredible, fantastic times. He was probably going to the bathroom. Smiling, she stretched.

Instantly he stilled. "You're awake."

Wanting to see his face, she leaned up on one elbow and flicked on the lamp. Blinking, she looked at him. "Where are you going?"

His expression shuttered, he stiffened. "It's almost dawn. I have to get to the site."

His voice bore none of the tenderness she remembered.

She'd been right the first time, then. He didn't want her anymore.

Alison stifled a cry. Anger and hurt bubbled up in her. She fought to hold them inside. Clint was a drifter. He'd always been honest about that, so what had she expected?

Maybe not promises of love or words of endearment, but more than the shabby treatment she was getting now. She remembered his nightmare last night and the names he'd called out. Erin and Lynn. Dear God, what if he had a girlfriend, or worse, a wife?

No. He wasn't the type to make love to her if he belonged to someone else.

Was he? She couldn't bear the thought.

Abruptly, she sat up, pulling the covers with her. "And you were going to slink away without a word, is that it?"

His hesitation and the guilty look on his face answered the question. "Look, Alison, last night was wonderful." His eyes flickered over her bare shoulders to the tops of her breasts. "But it was a mistake."

She ignored the surge of heat his gaze caused. "You didn't seem to think so a little while ago."

"Yeah, well, maybe if I'd been thinking with my head instead of my—" he glanced down at his groin "—this wouldn't have happened."

She had to know. "Are you...married?"

"Hell, no."

Relief poured through her. "Well, then, are you sorry we made love?"

He looked at her as if he was.

Lord, that hurt. Alison lifted her chin. "Well, excuse me for throwing myself at you."

"Dammit, Alison, I knew this would happen." He threw up his hands. "I told you I couldn't make any promises. What did you expect, a marriage proposal?"

"Of course not!" Crossing her arms over her chest, she glared at him.

He frowned. "Good, because that's not going to happen," he replied with equal force.

"Darn it, Clint, I'm not stupid. I know we made love because we wanted each other, and not for any other reason," she lied.

His scowl deepened.

"And I enjoyed it, too. A whole lot." She couldn't help noticing that the top button of his jeans was unfastened. Swallowing, she raised her gaze. "But I'm not some one-night stand you can have your way with and then leave without even a goodbye."

After a brief hesitation he nodded. "You're right. I was out of line when I tried to...to take off without saying anything." He plowed a hand through his hair. "I do have to leave, though. And in a few hours, when Hannah wakes up, you've got a tough day ahead. So, uh, get some sleep, okay? And don't wait up for me tonight. I'll be working late.'' He glanced at the door.

He couldn't wait to get away from her.

Alison swallowed back a cry. She wouldn't let him see how he'd hurt her. ''Sure,'' she said, shrugging. ''I'll just go back to my own bed and get some sleep.'' Holding the sheet in front of her, she walked across the room, toward her nightshirt.

Clint looked relieved. He opened the door. ''Tell Hannah I hope she feels better.''

Turning on his heel, he strode away. Alison waited until his footsteps faded and the bathroom door clicked shut. Then she hurried back to her own bed.

When the shower started, when she was sure he couldn't hear, the tears came.

Chapter Nine

"All right, Hannah, everything's ready to go." Alison fit the silver lid onto the old-fashioned ice-cream maker that had belonged to Aunt Phoebe. "Just a few turns of the handle, and in no time at all we'll have the best homemade peach ice cream you've ever tasted. Enough for dessert tonight and your birthday party." Alison glanced anxiously at her child, who sat silently beside her under the shade of the big elm. "How does that sound, sweetie?"

A few days earlier the little girl would have giggled and started singing one of her made-up songs. Today, on an old patio recliner, she shifted her leg gingerly atop the pillow supporting it and shrugged.

She'd never been one to sit still long. Too little for crutches, in the two days since the accident, she'd learned to navigate using the tiny walker the hospital had loaned her. But getting around was awkward and time consuming, and right after lunch Hanna had given up. Now, she looked miserable and bored.

Alison bit her lip, wishing for the hundredth time that she'd forbidden Hannah to jump off the woodpile. "Tell you what. When the mix starts to set up, you can add the sugared peaches."

"Okay," came the listless reply.

From his resting place beside Hannah, Barker wagged his tail hopefully and nudged her hand. She patted his head, but not with her usual fervor.

"I've got an even better idea. Why don't you help me mix it now?" Alison suggested, hoping to engage her daughter in the activity. "We can take turns."

"No." The little girl crossed her arms and puffed out her lower lip.

"But, sweetie…" Alison sighed and commenced turning the big handle. "You like to help, remember?"

Her daughter shook her head. "It's too hot. I don't want to help, I wanna go swimming."

Alison glanced at her daughter's cast. "You know you can't."

"But, Mama, I'm hot. Hot, hot, hot."

"So am I, Hannah." Her patience waning, Alison stopped cranking to wipe her brow. Even in the shade of the tree, the midafternoon air felt like a sauna turned up high. "Tell you what, why don't you color or play with your Pretty Pony?" She gestured toward the basket of toys she'd brought out earlier. "As soon as this mix turns into ice cream, you can have a taste. That'll help cool you off. And you can have a double-scoop cone after dinner. How does that sound?"

"I want it now, Mama. Now, now, now, because I'm hot, hot, hot."

"Stop it," Alison snapped.

Hannah popped two fingers into her mouth, something she hadn't done in over a year. Guilt stabbed Alison. For goodness sake, her daughter's leg was in a cast during one of the hottest summers in history. Hannah couldn't help it if she was whiny and hard to please.

Alison sighed. The truth was, with the heat and her problems weighing her down, she was almost as crabby as Hannah. "Sorry I scolded you, honey," she said. "Tell you what, we'll go to the pizzeria tonight. It's air-conditioned there."

She couldn't really afford the luxury of dining out, but Hannah deserved it. And they could eat the leftovers for lunch tomorrow. The child stared at her with big eyes, then nodded, but the fingers stayed in her mouth.

Alison turned back to the silver vat at her feet and resumed churning. Money wasn't her sole problem. If only she hadn't lost her heart to Clint. But she had.

A heavy sigh escaped her lips yet again. It was foolish and definitely one-sided, but it was the truth. Three nights ago, lying in his arms was the only thing that mattered. Now, in the light of day, she wished she'd kept her head.

Since that incredible night, true to his word, he'd come home late. So late Alison was already in bed. Not asleep, though. She'd listened to his footsteps as he entered the kitchen and found the plate set aside for him in the refrigerator, heard the water rush through the pipes as he cleaned up after eating. When the middle step on the stairway creaked, she knew he was headed upstairs. Holding her breath, she'd waited and wondered. Would he come to her? So far he hadn't. Which was probably for the best. Wasn't it?

Loving him definitely had its drawbacks.

Ka-thunk. Ka-thunk. Alison listened to the rhythmic sound of the churn without really hearing it. She'd even set her alarm an hour early, but Clint was always gone before it went off. The man was putting in over sixteen hours a day in order to finish the restaurant on time. How long could he keep that grueling pace?

She appreciated his efforts, really she did. All her hopes and dreams were pinned on that finish date. Unless the restaurant opened on time, she couldn't secure a loan to pay off the note.

But Clint was a man, not a machine. He needed a break now and then. Would it hurt to leave a little later in the morning or come home earlier at night?

It would if he were avoiding them.

He didn't want her.

Stung, she turned the crank faster. If only she hadn't thrown herself at him, like the world's neediest woman. He'd seemed a willing partner, but what else could he do?

What had possessed her, anyway, to go after him like that? A man she'd known only a week. She'd never behaved that way before. It had taken her months to decide to make love with Hannah's father.

Alison hadn't thought about Brent Jackson in a long time, but now she let her thoughts drift back to that crisp fall day nearly six years ago, when the tall, good-looking Brent had sauntered into Millie's in search of a fry-cook job. He'd said he was looking for a place to settle, and Flatville seemed like a good town for that.

Those words had wooed Alison better than the poetry or flowers he brought her over the next few months. By then Aunt Phoebe's second round of chemo was in progress, and things didn't look good. Alison remembered the fear and sorrow that had shrouded her like a black cloud. She'd needed comfort, and Brent had offered it. First, with warm embraces and later, in his bed.

Like a fool she'd assumed he would be there always, but she'd assumed wrong. Within twenty-four hours of learning she was pregnant, Brent had propped a note on the kitchen table, quit his job and left town. Leaving her to face her pregnancy and Aunt Phoebe's death alone. Alison released a heavy sigh. At the time, his abandonment had hurt terribly. But in the end she was stronger for it and better off without him. She'd confused love with need, she'd later realized. And she'd learned a much-needed lesson about independence and holding on to her heart.

A lesson she'd sadly forgotten as soon as Clint Strong showed up. Loving him hurt, worse than before. Alison snickered at her foolishness. She ought to know better.

Angry at herself and Clint, she pressed her lips together. Her only salvation lay in keeping her feelings hidden from him. Since they hadn't seen each other in days, that was proving easy. But it didn't solve her problems. Or ease the ache in her heart.

Darn it, she had to stop this. Taking a short rest, she stopped cranking and peeked inside the large silver vat. "Are you ready, Hannah? It's time to pour in the fruit."

"'Kay." With Barker watching, the somber little girl dumped in two quarts of fresh sugared peaches, then methodically licked the syrup off her fingers without the slightest spark of enjoyment.

Alison frowned. Why had she thought making ice cream would be fun?

"Mama, I want to take a nap. Where's my Pretty Pony?"

"In your basket, honey. See? Right under the cute little skunk Millie brought you."

Since the accident, many people had sent cards or stopped by with gifts and treats for Hannah. Not since her daughter's surgery three years earlier had Alison witnessed such kindness. The outpouring of concern and friendship touched her deeply.

Only one person was conspicuously absent. Clint. He hadn't seen or spoken to Hannah since the night she'd broken her leg.

Alison's mouth tightened. He made love with her, stole her heart, but he didn't give a rip about her or Hannah. That hurt more than anything, especially where her child was concerned. And it made Alison fighting mad.

She used her anger to move the crank, which was harder to turn now. Her arms were beginning to tire. She needed a break, but unless she wanted to ruin the ice cream, she couldn't stop. She glanced at Hannah and was glad to see her sleeping.

At least one person in the house was able to rest. Alison lifted her chin. Why should she lose sleep over Clint Strong? From now on she didn't care when he came and went. She wouldn't think about him anymore. She wouldn't.

Thirsty, she licked her dry lips. Lips Clint had branded. Oh, could he kiss. Everywhere. She couldn't stop the images that flooded her mind.

She leaned dreamily against the ice-cream maker's handle. His mouth had sent hot shivers through her body. And the clever things he did with his hands had made her feel wicked and sultry and aching. And those earth-shattering climaxes… She frowned. Why was she thinking of *that?*

Frustrated, she threw her weight against the crank. There was only one way to avoid all the useless fantasizing about Clint Strong. Keep busy. Later today she'd work on Hannah's party favors. Tomorrow there were two dozen cupcakes to make and frost. After that she'd clean out the buffet to ready it for Jen. And the garden needed weeding.

The list was endless and so was Alison's desire to rid her thoughts of Clint. If her body ached for him, well, in time even that would disappear.

Just as the ice cream set, Barker's ears pricked up, and Billy Bob's red truck spun into the drive. A moment later Clint emerged from the cab, his face as dark as it had been the night of Hannah's accident. Billy Bob waved at Alison and the sleeping Hannah, turned the truck around and drove off.

Clint looked as if he'd washed in dirt. Dust and grease streaked his face, his faded T-shirt and his pale, worn jeans. Bits of sawdust flecked his black hair.

Even so, he was handsome as sin. One smile and she would melt hopelessly at his feet.

Stop it, Alison. Returning her attention to the ice-cream maker, she watched him through lowered lashes.

Setting his jaw and narrowing his eyes, he stared at her and Hannah as if he were angry. Alison stiffened. Well, so was she. He'd better be civil to her daughter. But instead of approaching them, he wheeled toward the spigot, peeling off his shirt as he moved. Bending down, he turned on the faucet.

His arms bunched and flexed as he sluiced water over his head, neck and face. He looked fit and lean and gorgeous, and Alison couldn't tear her gaze away. Until he shut the water off. Then, her face heating, she gripped the ice-cream crank and pushed it down.

"Hey," he said, finally coming toward them. His hair and torso glistened in the fierce afternoon sun.

"Hello." She trained her attention firmly on the big silver container at her feet.

The voices woke Hannah. "Clint!" Her face lit up as she reached out for him. "I'm so glad to see you."

Alison swore he winced, but when he hunkered beside the child, he managed a smile. She let out a breath she hadn't realized she was holding.

He tweaked Hannah's pigtail awkwardly. "How are you feeling, smart stuff?"

"Good." She pointed to her leg. "Look at my cast, Clint. Mama and Millie and Jenny Ross and Mr. Farley auto—autodrafted it. Wanna sign your name, too? You can't use a regular pencil or pen, you need a marker. Mama gots one. She keeps it in the kitchen drawer." With barely a pause Hannah hurried on. "We're going to the pizzeria for dinner, and now we're making ice cream. Peach, my favorite. Want some? It's for my birthday party, but Mama says I can have some for dessert tonight. We're going to have cones, and Mama told Barker he gets some, too. He likes ice cream. Isn't that funny?" Giggling, she wrinkled her nose.

Alison's jaw dropped. Hannah sounded like her

normal self. Could it be possible that the fractured leg was only partly the cause of all that moping and whining? Could it be that she'd missed Clint?

Alison stifled an unhappy sigh. Clearly, Hannah was as crazy as her mother. They both pined for a man who didn't care and who would soon leave without a backward glance. Well, he'd never know, not if Alison could help it. She frowned at him. "We didn't expect to see you. What are you doing home so early?"

"It's been a day from he—ck," he told her, grim-faced. "I need to talk to you." He glanced at Hannah. "In private."

Alison's anger evaporated at his worried expression. She nodded and quickly stood. "The ice cream is almost ready, Hannah. Clint and I are going inside for a minute to get that marker and a tasting spoon. Will you take a turn churning while I'm gone?"

"'Kay. But when you come back, I want Clint to sit next to me. And I want him to sit by me at the pizzeria, too."

By the pained look on his face, Alison knew that wasn't what he wanted. Her anger flooded back. It was one thing to spurn her, but quite another to hurt her innocent child. "I don't think he can do those things, sweetie," she began. "He's busy."

"Oh." Hannah looked crestfallen.

Her disappointment seemed to reach the stiff-faced Clint. Shifting his weight, he shrugged. "Tell you what, Hannah, let me talk to your Mama and then clean up. Since I'm hungry and I like pizza, I'll go with you tonight. My treat." He glanced at Alison. "If that's okay with you."

Too surprised to speak, she nodded. Maybe he felt guilty about ignoring Hannah since the accident.

"Goodie. What about ice cream? Will you have some with us?" Hannah asked, her green eyes on his.

Don't push it, Hannah, Alison thought.

Clint shoved his hands in his pockets. "I guess I'll have time for that, too, especially if it's homemade."

"Yippee!" the little girl squealed.

Thank heavens. Alison released a breath.

While she and Clint headed toward the house, Hannah belted out a tuneless song. "Oh, we're making ice cream, ice cream, for my birthday party," she sang. It was good to hear that little voice raised joyfully again.

Clint paused outside at the front steps to brush the loose dirt from his jeans and remove his work boots and socks. Leaving them neatly beside the door, he followed Alison through the house. The moment they entered the kitchen, she turned to him. "Okay, Clint, what is it that you want to say?"

He quickly raised his eyes, which had been focused on her rear end. Alison caught the gleam of sexual interest smoldering there. So he wasn't immune to her, after all.

He glanced at a chair, then at his filthy jeans, and opted for leaning a shoulder against the wall. His eyes were dark as they sought hers. "I think you'd better sit down."

She didn't feel like sitting, but something in his voice scared her. She took the nearest chair and dropped onto it. "Was there an accident?"

"You might say that." He cleared his throat the way he did when he had something important to say. By the bleak expression on his face, it wasn't going to be good. "Sometime after the crew left Millie's last night, a water pipe broke. It ruined one wall, a good part of the underflooring, our table saw and our drill. Luckily, Tom Farley has some equipment we can rent."

Alison's eyes widened. "That's terrible. Poor Millie."

"She's plenty upset, but at least she's got insurance. But that's not the worst of it." He scrubbed a hand over his face. "We have to let the wood dry out and then replace what's ruined. That'll take several days. We were behind before, but this sets us back maybe one to two weeks. Even if we work round-the-clock, we won't be finished on schedule." He pushed away from the wall and came toward her. "I'm sorry, Alison."

"Oh." Numb, she sank against the chair. She *needed* the restaurant to open on time. But now that it wasn't… Her stomach pitched wildly as her last hopes of getting that loan died. She slumped in her chair as defeat, nausea and fear warred inside her.

She also felt like a spoiled child. Here she'd been, selfishly thinking Clint was avoiding her. Maybe he was, but he'd also wanted to finish the restaurant on schedule for Millie. For her.

He moved forward, stopping in front of her. If she kept her gaze level, she could look straight at his washboard stomach, see the tiny mole to the left of his navel. For some reason she wanted to touch it. She didn't.

"Alison?"

She looked up at him, vaguely registering his concerned expression. He grasped her shoulder gently.

A tremor passed through her. One little touch and

she wanted to sink into him, forget the horrible news he'd just delivered. But she couldn't do that. "I don't mind if you sit down," she babbled. "I made the cushion covers out of polyester. They're washable."

"Thanks." But he remained standing. "Look, don't give up hope."

"Don't give up hope?" she repeated dumbly.

"There *are* other banks, you know. If things don't work out at one, take your business elsewhere."

"I thought about that, but with the layoff my credit isn't so good. There's not much chance—"

"Mama, Clint? Where are you?" Hannah called from the yard.

Oh, God...Hannah. Sick at heart, Alison sucked in a breath. "Please, don't tell her."

Clint shook his head. "I won't. Look, I'm going to shower. Then I'll be back. Are you going to be all right?"

Alison's future flashed through her mind. Selling the dining room set helped somewhat, but short of winning the lotto, if she wanted to save her property, she'd have to convince Vincent Cahill to give her an extension at the meeting she'd scheduled for a few days from now. If he turned her down... But he wouldn't. She'd make him understand, get down on her knees if need be. What else could she do?

"Am I going to be all right?" Knotting her hands in her lap, she looked at Clint. "I'm going to have to be, for Hannah."

His mind full of Alison, Clint turned on the shower. Lifting his face to the spray, he thought about the way she had looked a few minutes earlier, her skin pale as an eggshell and her mouth drawn and tight with worry and fear. Her gaze had locked on his as if he were a lifeline. In her eyes he'd seen everything in her heart.

Defeat and despair, the belief that she'd failed Hannah. Those emotions looked out of place on Alison's beautiful face. He'd wanted to blot them out, to pull her close and take her troubles onto his own shoulders. He wanted to—

No. He soaped his body. He would not get mixed up in this.

Her problems weren't his business. He couldn't let himself care enough to get involved. Still, even knowing that, it had taken all his strength to keep from hauling her into his arms.

Clint uncapped the shampoo. He didn't dare touch her. Because once he did, he wouldn't stop with holding her. He would want to erase all those worries from her mind. And he knew just how to do that. First, he'd taste her lips. Then, when her breathing escalated, he'd fill his hands with those sweet little breasts, teasing the nipples to stiff points. Alison would moan her pleasure, and then he'd—

His body tightened like a randy teen's. *Damn.* Groaning in frustration, he turned off the hot tap and let the cold water needle his skin.

A fat lot of good that did. He still wanted Alison. More than that, he wanted to help her.

As if you can help anyone, the voice in his head chided.

Clint winced and scrubbed his hair vigorously in an attempt to shut the voice off. Alison had plenty of friends. Let one of them step in.

But none of them could give her the forty thousand dollars she needed. Only one person could do that—

that jerk of a banker, Vincent Cahill. Dammit, the man had to give Alison that loan.

If he didn't... Clint's hands fisted at his sides. He wouldn't let Alison lose her home.

As if you can do anything about that. Get real.

"Why don't you shut up," he scolded the voice. "I've got more than enough money from the insurance proceeds."

It was the first time he'd admitted it out loud.

Death money.

He tensed and waited for the familiar pain that accompanied the thought. When it sliced through him, he raised his head and let the shampoo run down his face. It stung his eyes and left a bitter taste in his mouth.

God, he hated having that money. And he hated thinking about it, which he'd done far too many times since meeting Alison. His hands curled into fists. Dammit, her troubles were none of his business. He turned off the water. He would stay away from her and her problems, he vowed as he toweled off.

But not tonight. He'd promised to join her and Hannah for pizza and ice cream. With that cast, Alison needed help getting her daughter in and out of the car.

Hell, it was only for a few hours. Somehow he'd get through it. Besides, Alison probably wanted some adult company tonight, to see her through the evening. To talk, if she wanted. To put a smile on her face, if possible.

He wasn't good at making people laugh, but tonight he'd damn well give it a try. Alison needed an evening away from her problems.

With luck, he'd lighten her burden. Just for tonight.

* * *

Clint gunned the engine. "All right, ladies, let's go get that pizza."

"Ladies?" Hannah crowed from the back seat. "Am I a lady?"

"Uh…" For a moment he looked stricken, as if bantering with her made him uncomfortable. But then he rolled his shoulders, visibly working to relax. "Sure you are," he said. He winked at Alison. "And so's your mama."

Alison lifted an eyebrow. When Clint had suggested they put their problems off-limits tonight, she'd had no idea what he meant. The cheerful, teasing manner he struggled to adopt didn't come easy to him. But his attempts to show both her and Hannah a good time touched and charmed her. So much so she'd even agreed to let him pay for dinner.

Shoving her problems from her mind wasn't going to be easy, but she'd decided he was right. Not counting today, there were three days until her appointment with Vincent Cahill. Other than worry, she could do nothing before that meeting. One night away from her troubles wouldn't make any difference.

"Which way now?" Clint asked.

"Turn left at the next light," Alison directed. "You'll see the sign on the right."

"I love pizza," Hannah said. "We hardly never go to the pizzeria 'cause it's too 'spensive. I'm so hungry, I'm going to eat a whole cheese and pepperoni pizza, and then I'm gonna go home and eat a great, big ice-cream cone. I want three scoops instead of two, as tall as my head. I wonder if Barker likes pizza? He has to eat his dinner if he wants dessert. Do you think they'll have a special chair for my cast?

Hey, maybe I'll get some new autodrafts. Autodrafts, autodrafts on my cast,'' she sang.

Alison couldn't help smiling. Thanks to Clint, Hannah's upbeat personality had returned, full force.

Once again he'd saved the day.

Too bad he couldn't help her save her home. Without that waitressing job at Millie's, securing a loan looked doubtful at best. The thought depressed her horribly. Her stomach knotted, and for a moment her shoulders bowed in despair.

Clint braked at the light. "Hey," he said gruffly and shook his head, "I thought we agreed."

Reaching out, he touched the corner of her mouth. Sun-browned, callused and scarred, his hands bore the stamp of hard labor and pain. Yet his touch was as gentle as a summer breeze. "No long faces tonight, okay?"

Alison's heart filled. She loved him more than ever. She nodded.

"That's better." He dropped his hand, but his gaze roved slowly over her face like a lover's caress.

Her breath caught. Suddenly the world faded, and there was just her and Clint. A deep longing filled her, to fall into his arms, to make love with him until she forgot everything but the joy of uniting with him. A fantasy she had no business entertaining, but she couldn't stop it.

"The light's green, Clint," Hannah said, breaking the spell. "Hurry up, hurry up, 'cause I'm hungry, hungry, hungry."

Frowning, he glanced in the rearview mirror. "Yeah, Hannah? I didn't know that." He sounded rough, almost angry. But then his mouth quirked. "We'd better feed this girl and fast, or she's going to talk us to death,'' he groused, and maneuvered the bulky station wagon into a space a block away from the eatery. ''Did someone say they were hungry?''

Hannah giggled. ''Me, silly.''

''Well then, let's go.''

''I'll get the walker from the back,'' Alison said.

Hannah's mouth tightened, and Alison braced for trouble. Her daughter hated the walker, but the doctors insisted she use it to prevent atrophy of the muscles in her healthy leg.

Alison had explained as much to Clint. She placed the walker on the sidewalk, then straightened. Over the top of the car, she met his gaze, silently warning him about Hannah, and begging his patience. Raising a eyebrow, he gave an imperceptible nod.

Before lifting the child from the seat, he rubbed his chin. ''I'm not sure you can use that walker, smart stuff. It looks too hard for you, and you're too little. Should I carry you instead?''

''I'm not either little, I'm big,'' Hannah retorted. ''Put me down and I'll show you.''

Clint set her inside the silver, U-shaped contraption, waiting until she grasped the padded handles to let go of her.

''See?'' She moved forward in jerky steps.

Pleased, Alison shot him a grateful smile.

He shrugged noncommittally, but the corner of his mouth lifted. ''Wow, kid. You're a pro.''

''Uh-huh.'' The little girl beamed.

As they headed slowly toward the door of the pizzeria, Alison's heart soared. Watching Clint with Hannah, teasing, encouraging, felt natural, *right,* as if the three of them were a family. She gave a mental sigh. If only they could be.

But Clint didn't want a family. He didn't want love, either. He was only acting like this because of what had happened at Millie's. Because he felt sorry for them.

Alison lifted her chin. She didn't want his sympathy, but she wasn't going to worry about that now. Tonight she would pretend he cared. Tonight she'd take whatever he offered.

There was time enough for reality tomorrow.

Chapter Ten

By the time Clint paid and they ambled out of the pizzeria an hour and a half later, night had fallen. True to her word, Alison had squared her shoulders and worn a smile that reached clear to her eyes throughout the meal. Clint admired her courage, her ability to put aside her troubles for her daughter's sake.

She'd even chuckled at his poor attempts at humor. He didn't feel half-bad, knowing he could do something for her, could make her laugh. Now, full and oddly content, he held the restaurant door open until Alison and Hannah moved through it.

In front of the pizzeria, the little girl leaned forward in her walker. "I'm gonna see how fast I can go."

"Careful, honey." Alison glanced around. "Stay on the sidewalk. And watch out for cracks."

Soft lights illuminated Hannah's path. Clint

glanced around. Though it was early, the street was deserted. "Where'd everybody go?"

"They're probably at home, watering the garden or sitting on the porch."

"How do you know?"

Alison laughed. "This is a small town, remember? That's what people do here on lazy summer nights. That and watch the stars." She nudged him. "Look up there, Clint."

He gazed into the darkness above. A silver moon hung over them, full and bright. Tonight he felt as if he'd swallowed it. Without thinking, he anchored his arm around her shoulders.

What do you think you're doing? the voice asked. Clint started to drop his hand, but then Alison leaned into him. "Hannah's happier than she's been in days. The dinner, the company, it was wonderful. I really needed this night." The eyes that sought and held his were warm. "Thank you."

"My pleasure," he said, meaning it. His arm stayed put.

Her soft sigh pleased him. It seemed natural to kiss the top of her head. She snuggled against him as if she belonged there.

Damn, that felt nice. He couldn't stop the smile. "Do you really think Hannah will eat a triple cone?"

Alison laughed. "After all that pizza, I don't see how she can. She tends to exaggerate."

A few feet ahead Hannah stopped. "There's Mr. Cahill across the street."

Alison stiffened. "Oh, no," she muttered. "He's the last person I wanted to see."

Clint swore under his breath. Couldn't she have

this one night away from her worries? He hustled her forward. Maybe the banker wouldn't see them.

"Hi, Mr. Cahill," Hannah called out, ruining that ploy. "I broke my leg and now I have a cast. Look at me, using the walker."

"Hello, Hannah. I heard about your accident. Looks like you're doing well." Glancing both ways, Cahill quickly crossed the street and strode toward them.

Damn. Offering his support, Clint tightened his hold on Alison. "You okay?" he muttered under his breath.

"Not really, but I'd better say hello." She wriggled out of his grasp. "Hello, Vincent."

The banker dipped his head. "Alison."

Clint crossed his arms and eyed the man curiously. So, this was the jerk who ran the bank. The stylish cut of his slacks and the initials embroidered on his shirt fitted right in with the image Clint held of him. Sporting a movie-star hairstyle and a thick, gold chain around his neck, he reminded Clint of a used-car salesman pushing middle age. Only this man reeked of money and expensive cologne. Instinctively Clint disliked him.

Alison tried to smile. "Clint Strong, meet Vincent Cahill."

Several inches shorter than Clint, even with the two-inch heels on his snakeskin boots, the banker somehow managed to look down his nose at him. Swallowing his distaste, Clint offered his hand.

"Pleased to meet you." Cahill shook it without enthusiasm. A Rolex flashed on his wrist. "You're new in town."

"Clint is working with Rusty and his crew," Alison explained.

"Ah, yes, Millie's restaurant remodel. I was sorry to hear about what happened over there last night," he said.

"What's wrong with Millie?" Hannah asked.

"The restaurant—" Cahill began.

Alison paled. "Please, not now."

Clint shot the banker a black look. Surely he realized that Alison didn't want her daughter to worry. "Millie's fine, Hannah," Clint said.

"Oh." Oblivious to the tension between the adults, the little girl inched the walker forward. "Guess where we went tonight, Mr. Cahill? To the pizzeria."

"How nice," Cahill replied absently. "Well, I've got a town council meeting to attend." He nodded his head. "Mr. Strong, it's been a pleasure." His cold eyes glittered as he honed in on Alison. "I'll see you in a few days."

"Right." Her posture was straight and her head high, as if the upcoming appointment was nothing more than routine. But the slight tremble of her chin gave her away.

"Good night." Cahill crossed back to the other side of the street.

"Thank goodness he's gone." Alison released a heavy breath. But she didn't move or take her eyes from the retreating banker.

Clint tensed. Damn, he hated seeing her like this. "Let's go, Alison."

"Okay." Her hands twisted at her waist.

Looking worried, Hannah pushed the walker closer. "Come on, Mama, Clint says it's time to go."

Alison pulled her gaze to Hannah. "Great idea,"

she said in an overbright voice. "It's time for ice cream."

She touched Hannah's shoulder, and they moved toward the car. Clint lifted the girl into the car and fastened her seat belt. When she was settled, he turned to Alison. Standing beside the car with her arms around her waist and her head bowed, she appeared lost in thought.

"Hey." He tipped up her chin. "You okay?"

The gnawing worry was back in her eyes. She swallowed and shook her head. "No," she whispered. "I'm scared, Clint."

Damn, he hated hearing that. "Hey." Cupping her shoulders, he stared into her eyes. "You promised to put those worries away tonight. The evening's not over yet." He touched his forehead to hers. "So, come on, show me that pretty smile."

Her lips curled weakly. "I'll try."

"That's good enough for me." He kissed the tip of her nose.

For this one night he was more determined than ever to wipe Alison's troubles from her mind. And he would.

No matter what it took.

The middle step on the stairs squeaked, signaling that Alison was on her way down after putting Hannah to bed. Clint leaned back in the chair and crossed his arms. From his vantage point at the kitchen table, he could observe Alison as she walked through the dining room, toward the kitchen. Despite her troubles her posture was proud and straight, her movements fluid and graceful.

Admiration filled him, and he silently renewed his

vow to make her forget her troubles for the night. He filled two glasses with the red wine he'd purchased on the way home.

Alison sank onto a chair and lifted her glass. "Thank heavens, Hannah finally fell asleep." She sipped the wine. "Making ice cream, dinner—the excitement wore her out. She'll sleep at least ten hours."

"Lucky kid," Clint said, and drank deeply. He couldn't remember the last time he'd slept through the night. A lifetime ago, before the bad dreams came and snatched away a full night's rest.

Alison let out a sigh. "I used to fall asleep the minute my head hit the pillow. But now…" Her brow furrowed.

"Hey." Clint lifted his glass. "I thought we agreed. None of that."

She offered an apologetic smile. "I'm trying, Clint. But it's impossible to just forget my problems and hope they'll go away. You can't imagine what it's like to lose your home." She shuddered. "When I was little, my mother dragged me from slum to slum while she struggled to make the rent. Sometimes we had to choose between food and a place to sleep. You've never been scorned and laughed at by people who don't understand." The eyes that sought his showed the depth of her pain and anguish.

He hadn't realized what she'd endured as a child. It shocked him. "That sounds grim," he said, wishing he could go back and change things for her.

"It was. It's a horrible experience, and I will not put Hannah through it." She lifted her chin. "I can't."

Seeing her like this, proud and struggling against

defeat, hurt. Knowing only too well what she felt, he swallowed. "I understand."

Arms crossed over her chest, Alison looked skeptical. "You mean, you feel bad about what's going to happen to Hannah and me. Anyone would, and I appreciate that. But you couldn't know the feeling of loss, the devastation, unless you were in my shoes. You're single, you move from place to place. You'd have to have a home and a family of your own, and lose that home, to truly understand."

The familiar pain shuddered through him. He understood, all right, more than she could ever guess. And dammit, he wanted her to see that. Angry, he leaned his forearms on the table and glared at her. "You think I don't know what it feels like to lose a vital part of yourself you can never get back? Lady, I've been there and then some."

Her mouth opened, but he didn't give her a chance to speak.

"You've loved your family and home, and you take your happiness for granted. Then one day, poof. It's gone. Everything's gone." The agony of speaking the terrible words wrenched his gut, and a ragged breath escaped his lips. "And there's nothing you can do to change that. Nothing." He raked his hands through his hair. "So don't tell me I don't understand."

Alison's eyes rounded. "You've lost someone, haven't you? I didn't know."

He saw by the curious look on her face that she wanted information. Locking his hands around his glass, he braced himself for her questions, not knowing if he could answer. But instead of speaking, she bit her lip.

Gratitude that she wasn't going to pry filled him, swiftly followed by blinding anguish. And the overwhelming need to finish the story he'd started, no matter what the cost. Hell, if his sick, ugly past didn't get her mind off her troubles, nothing would.

"I owe you an explanation," he said, staring at a scratch in the table.

He felt her eyes on him, waiting, as he reached for the bottle. "How about more wine?" he asked, wishing he'd bought scotch instead.

She shook her head. "No, thanks."

"Suit yourself." He refilled his glass, downed it, then repeated the process, hoping to dull the pain. Hoping if he delayed long enough, maybe she'd forget her questions.

From the intent look on her face, he knew she hadn't.

Finally he cleared his throat. "Once I had a little girl," he said, and gripped his glass so hard, his fingers ached. A vise squeezing his chest wouldn't have hurt more.

Silence shrouded the room. He reached for the bottle again.

"Had?" Alison asked, lifting one eyebrow fractionally. "Where is she now, Clint? With your ex-wife?"

He didn't try to hide his torment. "I'm not divorced."

"Then what—"

Wincing, he raised his gaze and looked her square in the eyes, bracing himself for the disgust and hate he knew would follow. "My wife and daughter are dead. And I'm the one who killed them."

* * *

Alison gasped, and Clint set his jaw as if he expected a fist in the belly. Had he really taken the lives of his wife and child?

He couldn't possibly have done that. He was brusque and short-tempered at times, but he would never harm the people he loved. Inside, he was kind and bighearted.

Alison's heart wrenched. To lose a wife and child must be unbearable, and, indeed, the deep anguish emanating from Clint was like a living thing. His eyes were dark and so haunted it hurt to look at him. Yet she couldn't lower her gaze from his face.

"That's right, I killed them." Tipping back in his chair on two legs, he stared into the depths of his empty glass.

She wanted to ask him what really happened, but the tension radiating from him kept her from doing so.

Suddenly the legs of his chair crashed onto the floor. Alison jumped, but Clint didn't seem to notice. "There was a fire," he said, and set down his glass. He spread his scarred hand on the table and stared at it.

"You burned yourself trying to save your family," she guessed.

His bleak expression confirmed her thought. A great sadness overwhelmed her, and her eyes filled. "I'm so very sorry," she said softly.

Clint's jaw tightened. "Save your pity for someone who deserves it."

Stung, she bit her lip.

Abruptly, he pushed his chair from the table, stood and moved to the sink. His back to her, he stared out the window at the blackness outside. Alison studied that long, straight, strong back, bowed under the weight of grief. His shoulders rose and fell as he sucked in and released a heavy breath.

"Hell, I may as well tell you the whole stinking story," he muttered, and suddenly the words gushed forth as if he couldn't stop them. "Before the... before, I was an insurance fraud investigator, specializing in arson. There was this local CEO, James Harridan. Old James was a real pillar of the community." Clint snorted. "But then his business started to fail. Harridan owed money to several prominent citizens. In order to pay them, he set his office on fire to collect the insurance. He swore he was innocent, but I was so damned good at my job," Clint sneered, "I proved him wrong. He went to prison."

Pausing, Clint drew in another breath and released it. "A few years later he got early release for good behavior. He found out where I lived."

Clint grabbed on to the counter in a white-knuckled grip. Alison could only imagine the painful images that must be going through his mind.

"You don't have to say anymore," she offered, giving him a way out.

"Yes, I do." Turning from the window, he faced her. "I want you to know what I am." He braced his hips against the counter and continued. "Erin was a month old at the time. She went through a dozen diapers a day." His mouth quirking, he glanced at Alison. "You know how that is."

She pictured the big man before her changing his tiny daughter. Sorrow filled her chest. Folding her hands around her glass, she nodded.

"I made a run to the drugstore to buy another case." He shut his eyes and rubbed the bridge of his nose as if his head hurt. "That's when the bastard decided to torch my house. By the time I got there, the place was a furnace."

His eyes open now and full of torment, he stared at something only he could see. Alison knew he was reliving that night. "I rushed inside, but I couldn't save them. Lynn and Erin—" His voice broke. He swallowed audibly. "They died." Drawing in a shaky breath, he covered his face in his hands, obviously working to control his emotions.

A sob caught in Alison's throat. So that was why Clint had called out those names with such anguish the other night. She longed to go to him, but something told her to stay where she was. A minute ticked by before he dropped his arms to his sides.

"That fire was meant for me. I should have died, not them." Shoulders slumping, he stared at his feet. "So you see, I was the one who killed them."

A beat of silence ticked by, and then a bitter laugh tumbled from his lips. "I'll bet you're not thinking about losing your house now."

"No," Alison whispered, aching for him, clear to her soul. Next to what he'd suffered, her problems were minor. Heartfelt tears streamed freely down her cheeks.

A moment later, still looking down, Clint shrugged. "I don't know why I thought I could help you with your problems when I can't even handle my own life. I don't blame you for hating me. Hell, I hate myself." Without looking at her, he turned toward the door. "I'll get my things together and leave."

"Wait." Her throat clogged with sorrow, Alison jumped up and moved toward him. "I don't hate you. Look at me." Framing his face in her hands, she forced him to meet her gaze. "Please. See what's in my heart."

She let her love for him and the pain she felt show in her eyes. "I...I care for you deeply."

"Then you're crazy," he said, shaking his head in disbelief. "I'm not worth the trouble."

"I think you are." She stroked his cheek. He needed a shave, and his skin was rough against her fingers. "From the moment you walked into our lives, you've done everything to help Hannah and me. In my soul I know you're a good man, Clint Strong."

He snorted. "So good that I let my family die. It should have been me." His eyes squeezed shut. "Oh, God, Alison, it should have been me."

"It wasn't your fault. You tried to save them," she whispered, hugging him hard. "Is the man who set the fire in prison?"

"Oh, yes. And I'm in hell." He stiffened and tried to draw back, but Alison held on. Finally, in jerky motions, his arms circled her.

They held on to each other for a long time. Clint's heart beat steadily against her ear, that big, warm heart he tried so hard to hide under a gruff demeanor. Now she knew why, and she wanted desperately to ease his pain. Turning her head, she kissed his solid chest, right over his heart.

It seemed to stop beating, so she carefully opened his shirt and kissed him there again. He smelled of pine-scented soap and man, and the sprinkling of hair on his chest felt springy against her cheek.

A beat later the mood shifted between them. Clint's heart began to thud rapidly, in a rhythm matching her own. His arms tightened around her.

"Hey," he said, his voice husky.

"Hey, yourself," Alison murmured.

"We shouldn't do this."

"Why not? You're the only man I want."

"Alison." Tipping up her chin, he crushed his lips against hers, hard, desperate, as if he wanted to obliterate his painful memories with passion.

She willingly became his partner. She could help him, do this for him. She didn't have to pretend to want him. The familiar desire flooded her, swift and awesome. Unable to stand on her now boneless legs, she sank against him. He was fully aroused, and his erection pressed against her stomach. Breathless, she slipped his shirt from his shoulders.

In tacit agreement, neither of them spoke.

Wanting to empty his mind of thought, she drew her palms over the warm, sun-browned skin of his hard, muscled chest. He quivered under her fingertips. Following her impulses, she licked his nipples. Clint stiffened and drew in a sharp breath.

His face a mask of desire, he stopped her. Grabbing the hem of her shirt, he tugged it over her head. Through heavy-lidded eyes he watched as she unhooked her bra.

"Heaven help me, I want you more than ever," he said, at last breaking their silence. Grasping her hips, he hoisted her onto the kitchen counter. Quickly, as though he couldn't wait, he parted her thighs with his leg, bent down and closed his mouth over one breast.

Alison's head spun as pleasure washed through her. Moaning, she threaded her fingers through his hair and urged him closer. Clint's groans joined hers as he held on to her like a lifeline.

Finally, panting, he pulled back. "Take your hair down."

Trembling, she lifted her arms to remove the tie at the back of her head. His eyes on her breasts, he growled. "Never mind, I'll do it."

His fingers shook as he pulled the band from her hair. Closing his eyes, he ran his fingers through her long locks.

Alison, too, shut her eyes. The feel of his hands, gently smoothing her hair down her back, over her sensitized breasts, sent heat pooling low in her belly.

"You're so beautiful," Clint murmured. "You look like an angel."

An angel wouldn't smolder with desire. "I don't feel like one."

"You are, though. My angel. Oh, no." He scrubbed a hand over his face.

"Clint?" Desperate to ease his agony, she ran her palms down his chest. "Are you okay?"

"No, dammit." He grabbed her wrists in his hands. "After the other night I promised myself we wouldn't do this again. But you tempt me to distraction." His burning eyes scorched her face. "If you want me to stop, say it now."

For the moment his eyes were free of pain. Thank heavens. Fevered with desire, she leaned forward, fervently kissing the underside of his arm. "Please don't stop."

"Why, Alison? You know what I am."

Staring straight into his eyes, she told him. "Because we want each other so much. Because we need each other. Because tonight neither of us should be alone."

"I'm always alone. That's the way it has to be."

The stark words matched his expression and cut her like a dull knife. Because she loved him, she pushed away the pain. Tonight the only thing that mattered was easing his suffering. "Let me hold you, Clint. Let me give you pleasure and release."

Let me love you.

He shook his head. "You deserve a lot better man than me—"

"Shh." She pressed her fingers against his lips.

A light flared in his eyes, and he kissed her fingers. "All right, but not here. You belong in a big, soft bed." Grasping her waist, he lifted her down.

Her swollen nipples brushed his chest, spiking her hunger for him. "Oh, Clint," she whispered, "I don't think I can wait. The kitchen is fine."

"What about Hannah?"

"She's upstairs, sound asleep. And her room is on the other side of the house. She won't hear us."

Groaning, he tightened his hold on her. "Are you sure you want this?"

In a haze of desire, she barely registered the question. "Positive," she managed.

Clint switched off the overhead light, bathing the room in dim light from the hallway. Then, grabbing her hand, he pulled her toward the kitchen table. Somehow, he cleared away the bottle and glasses. Then he stripped away what was left of her clothing and tugged off his jeans and boxers.

"Come here, Alison."

She obeyed and he lifted her, then laid her down and turned away to find protection and sheathe himself. The table felt hard and cold against her back, but only for a moment. Clint rejoined her and, locking his eyes on hers, he entered her.

The ache between her legs heightened. "Please,"

she whimpered. Wrapping her legs around his waist, she urged him deeper.

He growled and thrust deep. So deep he became a part of her. He slowly withdrew, then thrust again. Hard and fast, over and over.

"Yes, Clint. Oh, yesss," she moaned. A tidal wave of pleasure crashed through her, so intense, the world disappeared.

"Alison," he cried, plunging deep one last time. He collapsed against her.

Afterward, for long, mindless moments, they held each other. Heaven above, she loved this man. Tears filled her eyes and with them a sweetness so strong, she couldn't speak.

The way she felt, how could she possibly survive when he left? For the life of her she didn't know. But this was no time to think about that. She pushed the thought away. Tonight nothing mattered but loving Clint.

"Alison?" Frowning, he sat up and pulled her with him. "You're crying." He wiped her tears away with the pad of his thumb. "Did I hurt you, sweetheart?"

Sweetheart. The word had never sounded so beautiful. Though Clint hadn't voiced his feelings, he was acting as if he really cared, maybe even loved her.

She knew without doubt that she'd eased his pain. That she could do that, even for a little while, felt so darned good. Smiling through her tears, she shook her head. "No. You made me happy."

"Yeah?" He lifted an eyebrow. For once, no self-doubt plagued his eyes. "In that case, why don't we go upstairs? I can make you even happier in a nice, comfortable bed."

She didn't even have to think twice. "You're on."

* * *

Clint woke up tired. Another sleepless night. This time he couldn't blame bad dreams. He blamed himself. And Alison. He glanced over at her. Curled in the crook of his arm, her head was pillowed on his chest.

Dammit, he'd done it again, made love with her. Several times. And now here he was, in her bed, seriously considering another go-round.

There was no use denying it. She was like a potent drug. The more he tasted her, the more he wanted.

Her face was hidden under a riot of coppery-red hair. He couldn't stop himself from lifting a silken lock and sifting it through his fingers. The clean, flowery scent of it mingled with the musky smell of sex. Red-hot sex.

Heat surged through him.

She was a tigress and a temptress, eager and hungry. What a woman. *His*.

Get real. She's way above you.

He grimaced. Dammit, what was the matter with him? He didn't want a relationship, and he sure as hell didn't plan on sticking around much longer. He'd call Chuck today and push him about getting the truck repaired.

Alison stirred in her sleep and snuggled closer, bringing her soft, round breasts flush with his chest. Her stomach pressed against his hip, warm and inviting. Just like that he was on fire. He stifled a groan. He didn't think he'd ever get enough of her.

This wasn't supposed to happen. It wouldn't have if he'd kept his big mouth shut. What in hell had possessed him to tell her about his past? He didn't talk about that, not to anyone. Yet it had all spilled out last night.

He recalled her reaction, the way she'd touched his face and looked at him with such warmth. *I care for you deeply,* she'd said, but he knew better.

She felt sorry for him, that was all. Plus, she was scared about losing her home. What had happened between them grew out of mutual pain and the desire to forget for a while. Lust, pure and simple.

You'd best remember that.

Grim-faced, he eased his arm from under her and sat up. He nearly fell off the mattress. He was a big man, and her double bed was too small. Funny, he hadn't noticed that last night.

Alison's lids fluttered open. In the early-morning light, her eyes were as green as the dew-laden grass. "Mmm, good morning," she murmured in a voice husky with sleep.

Her slow, sexy smile stirred him like a hot caress. Fool that he was, he wanted to forget his thoughts and bury himself in her sweet, welcoming body. And by the sultry look on her face, she wanted the same release.

This was no time to act like a randy kid. Steeling himself against his raging desire, he crossed his arms and frowned. "We need to talk."

"Oh?" A pucker of worry appeared between her eyebrows. She sat up beside him, pulling the sheet with her. "If this is about last night, there's nothing to fret about. You didn't make any promises. I know that."

"Good." Her words should have eased his mind. Strangely, they made him feel worse.

The sheet didn't cover nearly enough of her. He

glanced at the creamy expanse of skin above her breasts, then the soft mounds beneath. Though covered, the sharp points of her nipples nudged the cloth.

His body responded immediately. Damn. He had to get out of bed, get away from her. He glanced at his clothes, tangled with hers just inside the door. Last night, in a haze of passion, Alison had scooped them from the kitchen and dropped them here. Swinging his legs over the side of the bed, he rose and snatched up his shorts. "I have to get to the site," he growled, stepping into them.

Alison's eyes widened. "It's too early. Besides, I thought you wanted to talk."

"I changed my mind." He jerked on his jeans.

Misreading his expression, she reached out her hand. "I care about you, Clint, and I hate to see you hurting."

To his dismay her eyes filled with compassion. She pitied him. He recoiled. He could take anything but that. With an effort he struggled to stop a howl of rage and spun toward the door, pausing only to grab his shirt off the floor. "I'm outta here."

"Don't you dare run away from me, Clint Strong!"

Damn. He shoved his arms into his shirt and pulled it over his head. "Run away?" With a snort, he pivoted to face her. "Lady, you don't know what you're talking about."

"Don't I?" Red circles flamed on her cheeks. "I trust you, Clint, and last night you trusted me back. Now you don't. I want to know why."

She trusted him. Shoving the knowledge away for now, he glowered at her. "Dammit, Alison, this isn't about trust, it's about pity. I don't want it, and I don't need it."

"Fine." She crossed her arms over her chest. "But that doesn't excuse you from taking off like a convict on the run when you're uncomfortable."

He glared at her. "What the hell is that supposed to mean?"

"Isn't it obvious?" She jerked out of bed, holding the sheet in place with her arms. "Whenever something comes up that you don't want to deal with, you leave. That won't solve your problems, Clint." Her blazing eyes seared him. "You can't outrun yourself."

The truth of her words hit him smack in the gut. "Is that right?" He scoffed. "Since when did you become a shrink?"

"A criminal set that fire, Clint, not you. Stop blaming yourself for something that wasn't your fault." Her quiet statement enraged him.

"Bull," he bellowed. Hands on his hips, he marched toward her. "I put that bastard in jail. And when he got out on parole, I didn't do anything to secure my family. Dammit, I was at a drugstore when he found my house." He laughed harshly. "The damn drugstore. Want to know why? Because I'd forgotten to pick up diapers earlier. If I hadn't been so damned caught up in my job—"

"Stop it!" Her nostrils flared as she faced him. "You aren't God, Clint, you're a man. How could you know?" She blew out a frustrated breath. "Listen to me carefully. What happened is not your fault," she said, clearly enunciating each word. "It was never your fault. And that's the plain truth."

"Now you're a priest." His lip curled in scorn. "Thank you for absolving me of my sins, Father

O'Hara.'' He gave a mock bow. "If you'll excuse me, I'm going to shower and get to the site."

Alison pressed her lips together. "Not before you eat. Part of your rent includes a home-cooked breakfast. It's time you started getting what you pay for."

Clint's jaw dropped. This new, stubborn side of her surprised him. He would have preferred to eat a quick bowl of cereal alone, but with her chin raised and her eyes shooting fire, he figured he'd never get out of there unless he gave in. He shrugged. "Have it your way," he grumbled.

He left before she could reply.

Chapter Eleven

Two nights later, after a sixteen-hour workday that had started at dawn, Clint trudged wearily toward Alison's house. His muscles ached from tearing out and replacing the water-damaged floor and walls, but at least the repairs were done. Knowing that the crew could move forward again on the remodel felt good.

Though his stomach was painfully empty, he was too dirty to go inside yet. He brushed off his jeans and T-shirt, then sat down on the front step and removed his work boots and socks. Even out here, he smelled the rich aroma of fresh-baked chocolate. Salivating, he licked his lips. Man, was he hungry.

Inside, lights blazed. As he neared the kitchen, the sounds of water running and the soft strains of an old sixties song on the radio beckoned him forward.

He stopped in the doorway. Alison was bent over a sinkful of dishes. Wearing a yellow T-shirt, short cutoffs that showed a nice expanse of leg, and a pink chef's apron, she looked sexy as hell. Clint's barely subdued hormones jumped to life. He swallowed a groan.

Dinner could wait. He needed a cold shower. Ice-cold. He started to back away.

Suddenly Alison spun around. "Clint. I didn't hear you come in."

"What are you doing up so late?" he grumbled.

Her eyes widened in surprise. "Have you forgotten? Hannah's birthday is tomorrow." She glanced at the chocolate cupcakes cooling on the counter. "I waited to bake until it cooled off outside."

"Looks like it'll be some party." He eyed the sacks of favors and decorations piled on the floor, then focused on those cupcakes. His stomach growled loudly.

"You must be famished. I'll get your supper. I hope you like fried chicken." Wiping her hands on the apron, she tugged the refrigerator open and reached for the plate inside, giving him a perfect view of her shapely backside. *Damn.*

"First, I need to clean up." His jeans uncomfortably tight, he headed upstairs for that ice-cold shower. Fifteen minutes later, his body firmly under control again, he sat down at the table and dug into his meal with relish. "This is delicious," he said around a mouthful.

"Thanks." Alison looked pleased. "Hannah's so excited about the party I could hardly get her to sleep. Millie's coming over right after lunch tomorrow to help put up decorations."

"Good idea," Clint replied, then focused on his dinner.

Alison turned back to the sink. For long moments only the clatter of dishes and the song on the radio broke the silence. Yet Clint felt comfortable enough. By some unspoken mutual agreement, since their argument two mornings ago, neither had mentioned what had happened between them. Not the incredible lovemaking or that he'd shared his ugly past.

Fine with him. He grabbed a napkin from the wooden holder in the middle of the table. He'd just as soon forget the whole thing, pretend he'd never told her anything.

But he couldn't forget the look on her face or her words that morning. *What happened was not your fault.*

He chewed absently. Her words had both shocked and amazed him, as had the lack of scorn in her eyes. She didn't hate him for what he'd done. She didn't even blame him.

For one brief moment he'd seen life through her eyes, and his world had brightened. God, he wished what she thought was true, wished he could throw off the burden weighing him down. He wished she was right.

And there's a pot of gold at the end of every rainbow.

Clint swallowed. Nothing could change the past, not even Alison. Because of him, Lynn and Erin were dead.

His appetite ruined, he frowned and stood up. He tossed the chicken bones in the trash and scraped the rest of his dinner into the bowl reserved for Barker. Then he carried his plate to the sink.

"Anything wrong?" Alison asked, glancing up at him. A faint pucker appeared between her eyebrows.

She wrung out the dishcloth and hung it neatly on the faucet.

"No," he growled, snatching it up again. He felt her curious gaze on him as he squirted soap onto the plate and washed it.

The silence and her skeptical expression mocked him.

"It's been a long day, all right?" Dammit, he was tired. He wanted nothing more than to go upstairs, fall into bed and get some much-needed sleep.

"Don't I know it, and it's not over yet." Alison sighed as she pulled the plastic cover from a mixer that looked older than she was.

Her mouth was drawn with fatigue, and there were shadows under her eyes. She looked as exhausted as he felt. Clearly, caring for a kid with a broken leg and worrying about holding on to the house had taken their toll.

Aw, hell. Clint wiped his hands on his jeans, then folded his arms across his chest. "Need help?"

Alison's eyes widened in surprise. "Thanks, I could use a hand. I'm about to make frosting, and then I've got those party favors to divide up. Want to ice the cupcakes?"

"Why not?"

Deftly she measured and dumped sugar, cocoa, butter and milk into the glass mixing bowl. While the machine whirred noisily, Clint moved the cupcakes to the table.

After a moment Alison shut off the motor. "Now for the taste test." Swiping a glob of chocolate on her finger, she sucked it off, closing her eyes in pleasure. "Mmm, this is perfect."

Clint couldn't help imagining her mouth on him

the same way. Swallowing, he pushed away the thought. There would be none of that. Since their angry exchange two days ago, she hadn't invited him back to her bed.

He didn't want to be with her, anyway. They'd made love enough that she was out of his system. Completely.

Liar. Frowning, he glanced down at his stirring groin. Stupid hormones. When they'd kicked back in, it had been with a vengeance.

"Want a taste?" she asked, oblivious to his tormented state.

He cleared his throat and sat down. "Uh, no, thanks."

"Okay, then. You'd better get started before this stuff sets." She handed him a knife. "Here."

He felt clumsy under her watchful eye, but she seemed satisfied enough.

Grabbing a bag from the floor, she dropped onto the chair opposite him and emptied the contents. Brightly colored balloons, stickers, washable tattoos, spinning tops and yo-yos clattered onto the table. "Isn't this stuff great? It was all on sale," she said as she began to fill ten fancy plastic bags for Hannah and each of her nine guests.

For a few moments they worked in silence. "I talked to Millie today," Alison said. "She says the restaurant is really shaping up."

Clint nodded. "Now that we've replaced the wood damaged by water. Rusty's been pushing, and we're all putting in long hours."

"Millie says your can-do attitude is wonderful and that it's affecting them all. She's awful glad you came along."

"Yeah?" Pleased in spite of himself, he shrugged and dipped his knife into the frosting.

"She bought Hannah the cutest Pretty Pony stable," Alison continued. "The birthday girl will be thrilled, and so surprised. She's been asking for that since last Christmas."

Clint could almost hear the little girl's delighted giggles. Without realizing it, he grinned. "That'll be a sight to see."

"You can, if you come to the party. It starts at three," Alison said, "so don't be late."

He paused in the middle of icing a cupcake. Well, hell. "Uh, I don't think Rusty will let me off early. There's too much to do at the site."

Alison's jaw dropped. "But Hannah's been looking forward to this day for months. She'll be crushed if you don't show."

Lately it seemed as if everyone expected something from him. Rusty and the crew needed him to put in extralong hours. Hannah expected him at the party. And Alison... He shook his head. He didn't have a clue what she wanted.

"Everyone you know is going to stop by," Alison cajoled. "Millie, Tom Farley and his wife, Marie, and Jenny Ross. They'll want to see you."

Clint swore silently. He didn't want to see them, didn't want any ties to Flatville. He wanted to leave the way he'd come, unknown and forgotten. But each day he was stuck here, that seemed less likely.

Alison dropped a handful of toys into another party bag. "You don't have to stay long, and you don't have to bring a gift. Just come for a little while, for Hannah's sake. It'll be fun."

"Fun?" Just the thought of ten little rug rats, all

in the same place, made him edgy. "It's a kids' party," he growled in disgust. "They'll be everywhere."

"Please."

Clint frowned. If he didn't show, Alison would accuse him of running away. That accusation still rankled.

Her big eyes implored him. Dammit, when she looked at him that way, how could he refuse? Besides, Hannah was a good kid. With that broken leg and Alison's money worries, the girl had been upset enough lately. He didn't want to make it worse. He gave in with a grudging shrug. "Look, I'll talk to Rusty. But I can't promise anything. I don't want him or the rest of the crew resenting me for taking off early."

That was only part of the reason. Other than Hannah, he'd never spent time around kids. They made him uncomfortable. And watching them, imagining what might have been if Erin had lived, hurt too much.

"If I know Rusty and the rest of the crew, you can bribe them with cupcakes." Relief lit Alison's face. "Thanks, Clint. You won't be sorry."

He doubted that. Plunging his knife into the frosting, he loaded it up.

The party was going to be tough going. Then there was the gift. He'd have to buy something for the kid, but he wanted no part of that Pretty Pony stuff. What the hell did a man like him buy a child like Hannah?

Alison shot him a pleased smile that was strangely reassuring. Clint spread frosting over another cupcake. For Hannah and Alison, he'd make it through that birthday party. Somehow.

* * *

By the time Clint headed for the backyard the following afternoon, Hannah's party was in full swing. Children's laughter and excited shouts rang through the air. For some reason the sounds scared him spitless.

Why had he decided to come? Ill at ease, he stayed back, out of sight, and observed. Alison and Millie had decorated everything in the yard. Pink and white streamers wrapped around the porch railing and tree trunks. Large pink balloons hung from the rafters.

The adults were busy. Jenny, Millie, and Marie Farley arranged plates and hats on a picnic table covered in a paper Pretty Pony tablecloth. Off to one side, Tom snapped pictures.

Clint's gaze settled on Alison. Not far from Hannah, she focused on her daughter with unfeigned joy. Clearly, she'd put away her troubles for the day.

His heart thundered in his chest. With her face clear of worry and her eyes softly glowing, there was no prettier woman in the world.

Hannah's face was flushed with excitement. Looking like a tiny queen in her cardboard gold birthday crown, she held court on the old lawn chair. Barker and nine chatty, giggling children sat gathered around, watching as Hannah gleefully shook, smelled and opened her gifts. Nine shakily scrawled autographs, written in red-and-blue glitter, decorated her now-dingy cast.

"I'm ready for another present," Hannah sang. "Oh, ready, ready, ready." She laughed.

Her happiness was infectious. Clint couldn't help grinning. It was about time the kid had some real fun.

"Here you go, honey. This one's from Andrea."

Alison smiled at the fair-haired, mop-top girl who must be Andrea, then handed her daughter the gaily wrapped present.

The love between mother and child shone on both faces. Clint swallowed past the sudden lump in his throat. He felt like a voyeur, viewing a very private moment. A moment that had nothing to do with him.

Hannah and Alison belonged together. They were a family. He glanced at the smiling guests, the friends and community who genuinely cared about them.

Clint would never have a family, let alone a community where he belonged. For a moment he forgot that he spurned those things. Loneliness engulfed him and the urge to turn around and leave now. Hell, he didn't belong here, didn't deserve to take part in the little girl's happiness.

Suddenly Alison looked up, directly at him. Her eyes rounded and her smile widened in a welcome that took the edge off the emptiness inside him...that made him want to stay.

She touched Hannah's shoulder. "Look who's here, sweetie."

"Clint!" The child's face lit up. "I'm so glad you came to my birthday party." She giggled. "Everybody, this is Clint. He's our boarder man," she said proudly. "He brought me Barker and he taked me home from the hospital when I broke my leg."

"Hi, Clint," nine childish voices called out. Tom, Marie, Millie and Jen echoed the greeting.

"Hey," he said to the faces raised his direction. Feeling awkward, he clutched the gift he'd wrapped himself and moved toward Hannah.

He picked his way around wrapping paper and brand-new stuffed animals, Pretty Pony accessories, books and games, wishing he'd bought Hannah a glitzy toy like one of those surrounding her. But it was too late for that.

"Happy birthday, smart stuff." He handed her the clumsily wrapped gift. The lopsided clown paper and sagging bow looked pathetic. Barker could have done a better job. Clint should have let the clerk wrap it.

Hannah didn't seem to notice. In a scant minute, she tore off the paper and discarded the bow. Clint shoved his hands in his pockets, steeling himself for her disappointment. To his surprise she crowed with delight.

"Look, a harmonica and a music book." She held up the small silver instrument and slim booklet.

The other kids oohed and aahed as if she clutched a nugget of gold.

Hannah's grin grew until the dimple appeared in her cheek. "It's just what I wanted." She beamed at him. "Thank you, Clint."

To his embarrassment he flushed. He shifted uncomfortably. It was only a silly harmonica. "The way you're always singing, I figured you could use something to help you make music," he managed.

"What a neat idea." Millie looked as pleased as if she'd thought of the gift herself.

Tom Farley threw him a thumbs-up sign. "Wish Marie and I'd thought of that."

"Ditto," Jenny said, and grinned.

Alison looked at Clint as if he were something special. His chest swelled.

"I'm gonna try it right now." Eyes crossed, Hannah lifted the instrument to her lips and blew.

The inharmonious noise startled Barker. Jumping up, he angled his head and watched her quizzically.

The giggles of nine children mixed with adult laughter and filled the air.

A beat later, Clint joined in. He felt damn good.

"It's time to start the games," Alison said. "Let's choose teams for Red Rover."

"Grown-ups, too?" a small, towheaded boy asked.

"Everybody," Alison said, glancing at Clint.

He frowned. This was where he drew the line. Wasn't being here enough?

The boy shyly approached Clint and looked up at him. "Can I be on your team?"

Clint didn't have a chance to refuse before Hannah, barely hampered by the walker, hurried over. "I want to be on Clint's team, too."

"Me, too," chimed two more children, who latched on to his legs.

For the next hour kids pulled him, tussled and giggled through Red Rover, hide-and-seek and Pin the Tail on the Cat, games he hadn't played since he was a kid. Hannah's friends were a lively bunch, full of spice and fun. Between them and Barker, Clint didn't have a moment to stop and think.

Later, after the hot dogs, cupcakes and ice cream, the party wound down. Alison moved everyone to the front yard so children could watch for their parents. Clint stayed in back to pick up the paper and confetti that littered the yard. Amid the mess he found a soggy birthday hat and chuckled. A wild water balloon toss had left him more wet than dry. Still grinning, he dropped it into a trash bag.

Alison was right, he'd enjoyed the party. So had she. Her eyes had sparkled and her melodic laugh had frequently filled the air. She'd needed this party, needed to relax before tomorrow's meeting with Cahill.

And she had. In fact, he'd never seen her so relaxed. The six adults had kept conversation lighthearted, discussing their favorite movies and teasing each other over how funny they'd looked playing the various games. When they weren't teasing one another, Hannah and her friends provided a constant source of chatter and amusement. Once Clint got used to the little guys, it wasn't so hard being around them.

In fact, romping around the yard with them was fun. He hadn't enjoyed himself this much in years.

What right do you have to feel this good about anything? Guilt needled him, and his smile faded as the familiar pain tightened his gut and darkened his heart.

"Hell," he muttered. Grabbing a balloon, he squeezed until it popped in his fist. He winced at the loud noise.

From the front yard, a car honked. "Bye, Andrea," Hannah called cheerily. "Thanks for coming to my party."

A tuneless harmonica song followed, floating through the air. A beat later, Hannah's laughter rang out. The little voice, so sweet and innocent, so full of happiness and life, squeezed past Clint's pain and touched his heart.

His chest swelled with feelings he didn't understand. He swallowed. Maybe he didn't deserve happiness, but Alison and Hannah did.

For them that meant living right here, on the property that belonged to them, the property they loved. They couldn't lose their home. They wouldn't, if Cahill gave Alison that loan. But she needed her old job back to secure it. Until the restaurant reopened, that wasn't possible. Unless...

Maybe she was looking at this from the wrong perspective. If she presented her case a different way, there was a chance she might get that loan. Clint's eyes narrowed. Yes, that just might work. After the party he would share his ideas with her.

Watch it, you're getting involved, the voice in his head warned. He ignored it. Giving Alison a little advice wasn't the same as getting involved; it was merely lending a hand when she needed help.

Wasn't it?

In the dim glow from the light on the back porch and half a dozen citronella candles, Alison and Clint cleared the dishes from the picnic table in companionable silence. All around, crickets serenaded them. Alison barely noticed. She felt as if she hadn't slept in weeks. The party had been a huge success, but it had taken all her energy to relax and have fun. Not only for the afternoon, but the entire evening, as well. This was Hannah's special day, and Alison refused to ruin it by worrying.

She dropped paper napkins into a trash bag. She'd managed to keep her spirits up after the guests had left and through the light supper Millie had stayed for.

Shortly after dinner Hannah had collapsed. Exhausted and happy, with her new toys gathered around her and Barker in his customary place beside the bed, the child had drifted off to sleep. Then Millie had quickly departed, her eyes twinkling.

Alison scraped dinner scraps onto a paper plate for Barker, then glanced at Clint. He'd definitely come through this afternoon, helping make Hannah's day special. For a few hours his dark, haunted look had disappeared. Without it, he looked years younger, and so handsome her breath caught.

He even seemed to enjoy Hannah's friends. Alison had never seen him smile so much or have such a good time. Had he been as easygoing before the fire? She imagined he had, and ached for his positive mood to last.

She would never forget Hannah's pleasure over his interesting and thoughtful gift. Still warm from the thought, she smiled. "Hannah really likes that harmonica."

Beside her, Clint stopped stacking paper cups and shrugged. "Let's hope she learns how to play the thing before we all lose our minds, Barker included. If I hear one more tuneless wonder..." His mouth quirked in that way that made Alison's heart thud wildly and her pulse race.

She laughed. "The poor dog doesn't know whether to howl, bark or hide."

"Don't worry about him. He's got a good deal here, and he knows it."

Clint was right. The animal had a home and a little girl who doted on him. In the midst of collecting plates, Alison pulled in a sigh, catching a whiff of citronella. The pungent candles helped keep the mosquitoes away.

Even though it was too dark to see much beyond the glow of the candles, her gaze swept over the backyard. She knew every inch of it, from the mole holes near the garden, to the knot in the old elm, to the untamed meadow and woods beyond.

Home. She loved it all, even the pesky bugs. And,

heaven above, she didn't want to lose it. Her eyes filled. *Please.*

Clint frowned. "Please?"

She hadn't realized she'd spoken. Without answering, she pressed the plates to her chest.

He pried them from her hands and set them down. Then he pushed her gently onto the picnic bench. "I'll finish this. You sit."

His voice was rough. Puzzled, Alison glanced at him, but in the dim light, his expression was unreadable. Too tired and miserable to argue, she complied.

He finished clearing the table in silence. Then he dropped down beside her, straddling the bench so that he faced her. The familiar scowl was back on his face. Alison toyed with the candle in front of her, staring into the flickering flame. Was he angry?

"Nervous about tomorrow?" he asked.

She thought about the appointment with Vincent Cahill, the fateful meeting to determine whether she got that loan extension and kept her home. Fear knotted her stomach. Unable to speak, she nodded.

Clint crossed his arms. "Want to talk about it?"

In the candlelight his eyes looked like black coals. She couldn't read his expression, but she sensed his concern. She wanted to be brave, wanted to face her problems alone, but she couldn't resist the chance to once again share her burden with Clint. "Counting today, I've got exactly eleven days left to pay off the note on my house."

"What happens if you don't?"

"The bank will start foreclosure proceedings." The thought turned her stomach. Shuddering, she lifted her chin. "I can't let that happen. I won't. Jenny Ross sold the dining room set. She's picking it up in a few days. That'll give me four thousand dollars toward what I owe. If I can just get a loan to cash out the rest of the note…''

She let the words trail off. The hopes of that were slim to none.

Clint eyed her, then leaned forward, resting a forearm on the table. When he spoke, his voice was low. ''What would it take for Cahill to give you that loan?''

''If the restaurant opens on time and I can prove I'm working there as much as I did before the remodel, he'll approve the loan.'' She swallowed. ''But that's not going to happen.''

Clint met her gaze, then grimaced. ''No, it's not.'' He scrubbed a hand over his face. ''I'm sorry, Alison.''

''It's not your fault Rusty fell behind and the water pipe broke. Heaven knows you've worked as hard as possible to catch up. I'm grateful for that.''

But all the hard work in the world couldn't help her now. She buried her face in her hands as the full weight of her problems crushed down on her again. *What am I going to do?*

''Hey,'' Clint said softly.

Alison knew he wanted her to look at him, but she didn't want him to see the utter despair in her eyes…and shame that she couldn't save her home. Hannah's birthright.

With his fist he gently nudged up her chin until she was forced to meet his eyes. ''What's your plan?''

''P-plan?'' she repeated dumbly.

He dropped his hand. ''What are you going to do to convince Vincent Cahill to give you that loan?''

''Millie promised to call tomorrow and talk to him.

She'll guarantee that the minute the restaurant re-opens, I'll have my old job back, with the same hours.''

"Good idea." Clint nodded approvingly. "Get her to put that in writing, on official restaurant letter-head." He rubbed his chin thoughtfully. "I've been working with Rusty and the crew for long enough to know they're focused on finishing the job as soon as possible. What if Millie also gets you a copy of Rusty's time line? She can add in the days she needs to prepare for opening. When Cahill sees her letter and Rusty's schedule, he'll know that giving you a loan poses no risk at all. He'll loan you that money.''

Clint sounded so sure of himself. His words gave her hope. And surprised her. She didn't expect anything from him, but she welcomed whatever he offered. She managed a weak smile. "It's worth a try.''

Clint's mouth quirked. "That's more like it.''

She stared into the darkness. Vincent Cahill wasn't the kind of man who accepted documents at face value. No doubt he'd ask plenty of questions. She imagined sitting across from him at his huge mahogany desk, trying to answer his questions. Dread filled her. What if he didn't like her replies? What if he turned her down?

"Talk to me, Alison," Clint prodded.

"I...he makes me nervous." She moistened her dry lips, then met his gaze. "Don't worry, though, I'll handle this.''

Clint shifted against the bench. "What time is the appointment?''

"Right after lunch, though heaven knows, I won't be able to eat. Millie's promised to watch Hannah. I don't want to take her—''

"I'll meet you there." Looking as shocked by his offer as she was, he clapped his mouth shut.

"You don't have to do that, Clint. This is my problem. I can take care of it alone. Besides, Rusty may not let you come."

He set his jaw stubbornly. "He won't mind, as long as I make up the time. Look, I know you can do this alone, but I want to come." He lifted an eyebrow. "You go into Cahill's office by yourself. But I'll be waiting outside, in case you need a shoulder to lean on. And if he wants information about the remodel, I can answer questions you might not be able to."

For the first time in weeks Alison felt hopeful. "You'd do that? Why?"

Clint's eyes locked on to hers. "Because you and Hannah deserve to keep your home," he said softly.

He cared about them, really cared. Her heart full, she touched his arm. "Thank you," she whispered.

Squirming uncomfortably, he cleared his throat. "Hey, no big deal."

"Yes, it is, Clint. It's a great big deal." Wanting very much to feel his arms around her, but unwilling to ask, she hugged herself.

Clint frowned and rubbed the back of his neck. "The citronella isn't working anymore. A mosquito just bit me. Let's go in."

He scooted off the bench, then reached for her hand and pulled her up beside him. Together they blew out the candles and headed up the back steps.

Just inside the door she reached up and touched his cheek. "I need…would you hold me?"

His arms circled her, warm and comforting. Alison snuggled gratefully against his solid chest.

"It's going to be all right," he said, the steady beat

of his heart echoing the reassurance. His breath fanned her face, and his lips pressed softly against her forehead.

Today something had shifted and softened in him, but Alison didn't try to understand why or how. For now, for however much time they had together, she would savor every moment, remember every detail.

Later, when he was gone, the memories would warm her lonely nights. Because one day soon, he *would* leave. On that day her heart would break.

Unwilling to dwell on that bleak thought, Alison pushed it away. She lifted her face and planted a soft kiss on the warm underside of Clint's chin, where his pulse raced. Threading her hands through his hair, she urged his head down.

"Alison," he murmured, then claimed her lips.

He was already hard, and his arousal pressed against her stomach. The familiar desire raged through her, wiping her worries and fears from her mind. She longed to lie down with him, take his body into hers. But she couldn't, not again. Not after the argument they'd had. Not when she loved him so, and he didn't return that love.

Not when he was leaving.

Hands on his chest, she pushed away. "No. We shouldn't."

Clint released her immediately. "You're right," he agreed, breathing hard. Shoving his hands into his pockets, he backed up a step, then closed his eyes, as if to collect himself. When they opened, he'd managed to bank the desire that had smoldered there. "You're right. We shouldn't make love again."

Alison swallowed. "I think that's a wise idea."

After a beat he cleared his throat. "Tomorrow could be rough. You'd better get some sleep."

She only hoped she could. "You, too. Good night, Clint."

"Back at you." He turned toward the stairs, then hesitated. "I think I'll stay down here awhile."

Alison nodded, though he couldn't see the gesture. That sounded like a good way to put some much-needed physical distance between them. Yet, as she felt his gaze follow her up the stairs, she knew that it would take more than space to keep her from wanting him.

Chapter Twelve

Without speaking, Clint and Alison headed toward the bank. Pale and tense, she'd been unusually quiet since they'd met up a short while earlier. She was nervous, and he didn't blame her. Grasping her arm, he gave a reassuring squeeze. She leaned into him as if glad of the support.

Outside the double glass doors of the bank entrance, she hesitated. Clint looked down, into her troubled eyes. "Ready?"

"In a minute." Using the glass as a mirror, she tightened her ponytail and smoothed back a few short tendrils that refused to be tamed. Her brow puckered with uncertainty, she glanced up at him. "Do I look okay?"

Before this afternoon he'd never seen her in a dress, and he took his time examining her. The sleeveless cotton shift was belted at the waist, with a straight skirt that stopped a mouthwatering two inches above the knee, showing off her shapely legs. Not too tight or short, nevertheless, it emphasized her small waist and clung to her curves enticingly. The soft-teal color brought out the green in her eyes and the copper in her hair.

"You look great," he said, meaning it.

"Thank you," she said, and as he'd hoped, her eyes lit and a quick smile flashed across her face. Too soon her lips straightened, and doubt replaced the warmth in her eyes.

Hating her uncertainty, he touched her cheek. "You can do this, Alison."

He handed her the folder that held the loan application, Rusty's time schedule and the letter from Millie. "Once Cahill sees these, he'll know you're a good credit risk. He'll give you that loan," Clint predicted, hoping he was right.

Alison searched his face a moment. Then, clasping the folder against her middle, she nodded. "I'm ready." Head high, she preceded him into the bank.

In contrast to the muggy heat outside, the air inside seemed frigid. Gooseflesh rose on Alison's arms as they crossed the near-empty lobby.

"Afternoon, Alison, Clint." The young teller who cashed Clint's weekly paychecks grinned, looking both pleased and surprised to see him with Alison.

"Hey, Jessica," he replied.

Word had gotten around that he'd taken Alison and Hannah for pizza the other night, and now people seemed to think there was something between them.

Perhaps there was truth to that, though Clint refused to consider the possibility.

Alison offered the teller a tremulous smile, then bit her lip. "Is Mr. Cahill in? I've got an appointment."

"He's in his office." The teller glanced toward Cahill's closed door. "I'll buzz him on the intercom and let him know you're here." She gestured toward a small waiting area in the center of the lobby. "Why don't you two make yourselves comfortable."

"I'm too nervous to sit," Alison confided to Clint in a whisper.

"You don't want Cahill to know that." Clint kept his voice equally low. "Take a seat."

She complied, but perched stiffly on the edge of the armchair. With her back ramrod straight and her hands gripping the folder, she looked anything but relaxed.

Clint frowned as he took the opposite chair. Until she settled things with the bank, nothing was going to make her rest easy.

Suddenly Cahill's door opened. Alison jumped, but managed to keep her seat until the banker strode toward her. In a hand-tailored summer suit and tassel loafers, he looked rich and far too elegant for the small-town bank.

His eyes widened as he glanced from her to Clint. "Good afternoon, Alison," he said, offering her a perfunctory handshake. His chilly smile didn't quite reach his eyes.

"Hello." To her credit she sounded calm and assured.

Cahill turned to Clint and shook his hand. "Nice to see you again." His eyes gleamed with speculation. "Are you here on bank business?"

Clint exchanged a look with Alison. "Just keeping Alison company."

"Ah. Well, this shouldn't take long." The banker sounded as if he'd already made up his mind.

Foreboding filled Clint, and he wished he were going into the meeting with them. But Alison hadn't invited him. She wanted to do this alone. Uneasy, he watched her walk forward, graceful despite her nervousness.

His gaze strayed to Cahill's door and beyond, and he caught a glimpse of the banker's office. Like the man himself, the plush Oriental carpet, dark mahogany trim and expensive paintings looked out of place in the small bank. Intimidating, Clint decided.

In less than half an hour the door opened. An apologetic smile on his face, Cahill again shook Alison's hand. The minute she moved through the door, he shut it firmly behind her. At the loud click she flinched. She held her head high, but her face was ashen.

It didn't take a rocket scientist to figure out what had happened. Despite Alison's supporting documents, Cahill had turned down the loan.

Alison and Hannah were going to lose their home, and the bank owner didn't give a damn.

Clint swore, not caring who heard. Outrage tightened his hands into fists. He wanted to storm into the plush office and show the jerk just what he thought of him and his decision. But one look at the despair in Alison's eyes, and he shoved his anger aside. Decking Cahill might help him feel better, but it wouldn't help Alison. She needed something else. Support and a shoulder to lean on.

He slipped his arm around her waist. "Let's get out of here."

Chin quivering, she nodded. The fine tremors that

shook her alarmed him. Quickly he guided her through the door.

The hot afternoon air hit them like a blast furnace, a thick, oppressive heat that immediately sapped Clint's fury. It was too hot to hold on to Alison, but he didn't dare release his hold on her. She was too shaky.

Moments later, a block down the sidewalk, in front of Flatville Lumber and Hardware and the half dozen townsfolk on the street, she slumped and fainted.

"I've never seen Alison faint before." Tom Farley knotted his big hands anxiously and peered down at her. Stirring, but still unconscious, she lay on the old green sofa in the hardware store's cluttered back room, where Clint had gently deposited her after catching her. "Will she be all right?"

"I hope so."

The few seconds since she'd passed out seemed like hours. Had she eaten today? Hunkered down beside her, Clint cast a worried gaze at her limp body. Her skin was pale, the deep shadows under her eyes a testament to too many sleepless nights. Guilt pricked him. He should have done more to ease her worry.

Her forehead was beaded with sweat. He frowned. "Have you got something cool to put on her head?"

"I know just the thing." Looking relieved at having something to do, Tom hurried into the bathroom. Moments later, he handed Clint a wet paper towel.

"Thanks." Clint draped it gently over her fevered skin and frowned down at her. "Wake up, honey."

She stirred, but her eyes remained shut. That scared

him. What if this was more than just a fainting spell? Maybe they should call a doctor.

"I saw you come out of the bank," Tom said, interrupting Clint's thoughts. "That gol-durned Vincent Cahill turned down her loan, didn't he? He's a cold one, not one bit like his daddy."

Clint shrugged. Though Alison hadn't told many people about her problems, he wasn't surprised at the hardware owner's knowledge. In a town the size of Flatville, people knew each other's business.

Suddenly, to his immense relief, Alison moaned softly and rolled her head. Leaning closer, he stroked her cheek. "Thank God, she's coming out of it."

"Hallelujah." Tom released a breath. "I'd best get out front again and tell all those worried folks that it was just the heat. You need anything, holler." He disappeared through the door, closing it softly behind him.

Alison's eyes fluttered open. Blinking, she frowned, pulled the wet toweling off her forehead and tried to sit up. "What happened? Where am I?"

Clint gently pushed her back again. "Lie down. You fainted in front of Tom's store. We're in the back room."

"Oh." Though still pale, faint pink tinged her cheeks. She touched her stomach as if it hurt.

Clint frowned. "When did you last eat?"

She thought about that. "Last night. I haven't had much appetite today."

"That's not good. As soon as you feel up to it, we'll find you some lunch."

She didn't reply. Her brow wrinkled. "I suppose Tom knows what happened?"

"I didn't say anything, but I won't lie to you. He saw us leave the bank."

At the mention of the bank, anxiety clouded her eyes. "What am I going to tell Hannah?"

"Give her some credit." Clint smoothed back tendrils of hair that clung to her forehead. "You're her world. If you're okay, she will be."

"I don't feel okay, I feel rotten." Alison squeezed her eyes shut. "Dear God, I'm going to lose the house."

She turned her head away, but Clint saw the tears spill from her eyes and run down her cheeks. She made no attempt to wipe them away.

He panicked. He was no good with crying women. Awkwardly he patted her back. It tore him up, seeing her suffer. The thought of her and Hannah, turned out on the street, made his chest ache. They couldn't lose their home, their heritage.

And they wouldn't.

In that instant, he made up his mind. He would give Alison the insurance money. Hell, he'd been mulling over that idea for weeks, hadn't he? It was more than enough to cover that note, and he sure didn't want or need it.

The more he thought about it, the more he liked the idea. And in his heart he knew Lynn and Erin would approve. What better way to use their money than to do something good with it, for two people who deserved a break? Two people he cared about.

"To hell with the bank," he said, his voice rough. He handed Alison a tissue. "I can get you the money you need."

There, the offer was on the table with no way to call it back. He was stuck now.

Stuck? Who was he kidding? He *wanted* to help Alison and Hannah. And dammit, he would. He waited for the voice to taunt him, to call him a fool, but it didn't.

Alison sat up. Her gaze, bright with moisture, sought his. "But you don't have that kind of money."

"Yes, I do." He dropped onto the sofa beside her. "It's sitting in a bank in Seattle, earning interest and gathering dust."

Her mouth dropped open, and he knew she wondered how a man as poor as he was had come across so much cash.

"But where—"

"Insurance proceeds." He swallowed and cleared his throat. "From the fire."

"Oh, Clint." Awareness filled her eyes. "I know how you feel about that. I couldn't—"

"I'll never use it. I can't." Clint stared down at his scarred hand as the familiar pain sliced through him. But along with the pain came the feeling that this was a good decision, and the right thing to do. He met her sober gaze straight on. "I want you and Hannah to have it. I wouldn't offer it if I didn't."

Alison shook her head. "You've already given us so much, Clint. We can't take your money, too. It wouldn't be right."

It *was* right, for him and for her, but the stubborn tilt of her chin warned him she wouldn't buy that explanation. "Then borrow it from me, if that makes you feel better."

He had no intention of asking for any of it back, but from the look on Alison's face, he knew he'd piqued her interest. "We'll draw up an agreement, if you want, but there's no need to do that. Unlike Cahill, I know you'll make good on the loan." She still looked doubtful, so he added, "If not for yourself, take the money for Hannah. The kid needs a house with a yard and woods. And so does that mutt of hers."

To his dismay, Alison's eyes shimmered with fresh tears. "Oh, Clint." She bit her lip, then slowly shook her head. "I don't know what to say."

Not again. He wiped the big droplets away with the pads of his thumbs. "Come on now, this is good news. It's supposed to make you smile. Please don't cry anymore."

"Okay." She sniffled and managed a watery smile that made his own mouth quirk.

"That's my girl."

With soft, gentle fingers, she touched his cheek. "You are the kindest, most wonderful man I've ever known."

His face warmed. No man was less worthy of her praise. Uncomfortable that she thought so much of him, he frowned. "Hell, it's only money." He searched her eyes, almost afraid to ask. "Well, what do you say? Will you take it?"

"I—can I think about it?"

Hope lit her eyes, hope he'd put there. His dark thoughts lifted. Then the realization hit him. For some reason he needed her to take that money.

"Sure." He nodded. "You've got ten days before the note is due, so take your time. Now, how about something to eat?"

"I'd like that," Alison replied. "Suddenly I'm starved."

Alison was still in shock when, half an hour later, she and Clint headed to the playground behind the town's lone school. They'd stopped at the Flatville grocery and bought ready-made sandwiches, pop and cookies, then walked the two blocks here.

She still couldn't believe what had happened. Clint had given her a way to save her home. His gesture stunned her. Knowing the source of the money and his guilt and pain over what had happened to his family, Alison could only imagine how difficult it must be for him to offer it. Yet he *had*. He wanted to help her.

Maybe he didn't love her, but he cared deeply about her and Hannah. Giddy at the thought, Alison wanted to throw her arms around him and shower his face with kisses. But that would only embarrass him. He didn't do well with compliments. Every time she told him what a nice guy he was, his face reddened and his back stiffened.

He didn't know how special he was, how wonderful. Her heart filled at the thought. Oh, how she loved this man. What she'd felt for Hannah's father was nothing compared to this.

That didn't mean Clint returned the feeling, or that he planned to stay in Flatville. Chuck expected the truck parts soon. Then, just as with Hannah's father, it was only a matter of time before Clint left town, left her. When he did, he would take her heart with him.

Alison released a heavy sigh and willed away the depressing thoughts of a lonely future. Today there were other things to focus on.

Shading her eyes, she searched for a good place to picnic. They settled on a spot under a huge maple. Its lofty, leafy branches spread out in a wide, natural umbrella, providing much-needed shelter from the sun. Yet, though automatic sprinklers watered the area regularly, the relentless heat had leeched the moisture from the ground, and the grass was dry and dusty.

Clint glanced down, then back at Alison with a lifted eyebrow. "Maybe we should picnic somewhere else. You don't want to ruin that pretty dress."

Alison shrugged. "It's washable, so I don't mind. Besides, I'm too hungry to wait any longer." Toeing off her flats, she sat down, careful to keep her knees straight and tug her short skirt over her thighs, and wishing she'd worn a dress with a longer, fuller skirt. "Let's eat."

"Yes, ma'am," Clint drawled. His appreciative glance at her legs changed her mind about the dress.

He hauled out the sandwiches, cookies, pop and napkins, then used the grocery bag as a tablecloth between them. For the next few moments they concentrated on eating. Other than an occasional birdcall and the usual cicadas, no sounds interrupted their meal.

"It's so quiet here." Alison glanced at the deserted grounds and the unused slide, swings and jungle gym. "Without children, this place seems lifeless."

Clint chewed in silence, and for a moment his expression darkened. Alison tensed, wishing she could call the words back. Was he thinking of his daughter? Had she made a mistake, bringing him here?

"Is it a good school?" he asked at last, turning to her.

To her relief his eyes were clear and free of shadow. "It's our *only* school. But we've got great teachers, and the kids seem to like it. Hannah will start kindergarten here in the fall."

He nodded, then reached for his pop. Head back, he downed it thirstily. Fascinated, Alison watched his throat work. Even in this pose, he was gorgeous. When he wiped his mouth with the back of his hand and crumpled the can in his fist, she continued to stare.

Dropping the can, he angled his head her way and gave her a wry smile. Both eyebrows lifted. "What are you looking at?"

Caught...mooning over him. Her face flushed. "I've been thinking about your offer." She moistened her suddenly dry lips. "Are you sure?"

"About the money?" He shot her a glance she couldn't fathom. "Yeah, I'm sure." Very still now, he studied her through slightly squinted eyes.

Alison knew what he wanted her to say. For whatever reason, he wanted her to take the money. She hated this, hated having to borrow from him, but he was her only hope. And she couldn't refuse this chance to save the property that belonged to her and Hannah. She nodded slowly. "Then I accept. I'd like to borrow what I need from you."

For a split second, deep emotion flashed in his eyes. It vanished so quickly she wasn't sure what it meant. And she didn't have time to ponder it.

"Smart woman." Clint gave her a thumbs-up sign, then leaned his forearms on his knees. "Tomorrow I'll have the money wired from Seattle. It should be here in a few days."

"In the meantime I want to draw up a legal document with the amount and terms."

"We don't need anything like that." His sober gaze hooked on hers. "I trust you."

Alison lifted her chin. "I can't take your money unless we sign an agreement."

His mouth tightened, and for a moment she thought he might refuse, but then he shrugged. "If that's the way you want it, no problem."

She released a breath. "I'm so grateful for what you're doing, Clint." The simple words didn't begin to express her appreciation. She touched her heart. "How can I ever thank you?"

His gaze hooked on hers. "Holding on to your house is thanks enough."

Overwhelmed with gratitude and love, she bit her lip. Her eyes filled. "Oh, Clint—"

"I changed my mind. You can thank me by keeping a smile on your face," he teased. "No more tears, okay?"

"I'll try." Alison smiled and swiped at her eyes. "I'll be able to pay back some of what I owe you in a few weeks. Jenny's picking up the dining room set the day after tomorrow. As soon as I get the check for it, I'll sign it over to you."

Clint frowned. "Better save that for emergencies, like the hospital bill for Hannah's broken leg."

Clapping a hand to her forehead, Alison groaned. "I'd forgotten about that. I'll give you whatever's left over."

"We'll see." He compressed his lips and started to stand.

"Wait a minute." Alison touched his arm, stopping him. "There's one more question. When I start paying you back, how will I know where to send the money?"

"We'll work that out later."

"But when? Your truck will be ready in a few days. You'll be leaving—"

Clint focused on stuffing trash into the grocery bag. "I've decided to stick around until we finish at the restaurant."

He was going to stay awhile longer! Alison's heart lifted at the news.

"That'll take a few weeks at most," he said, as if he'd read her thoughts and didn't want her getting any ideas about him settling down. "Rusty needs my help. It's only fair to him and Millie that I help finish the remodel."

Alison nodded. "You don't have to pay me room and board, Clint. We can deduct the rent from what I owe you."

"Uh-uh. I want to pay. You need the cash."

"But—"

"End of discussion." His jaw set stubbornly. "Now, I'd better head back to work, before Rusty and the crew come looking for me." He stood and carried the trash to the dumpster near the building.

Alison stood, too, slipping into her flats and brushing the dust and grass off her skirt. She glanced at her watch. "I've got a little while before I have to pick up Hannah. I think I'll stop at the lawyer's office."

"Why don't you wait until the money comes in?" Clint asked. "Meantime I could use a ride to the site." Hooking his arm through Alison's, he walked with her toward the car.

Chapter Thirteen

"Want to help me clean out the buffet?" Alison asked Hannah late the next afternoon. "Jenny's coming in the morning to pick it up, and I want to be ready."

The little girl blew what sounded like the shaky notes of an alphabet song on her harmonica, then nodded. "Okay, Mama."

Alison's eyes widened. "You're making real music, Hannah."

Her daughter beamed. "Clint taught me how."

"Oh?" Pleased that he'd spent time with her child, Alison laughed as she had many times over the course of the day. "Well, he's a darned good teacher."

She thought about all that he'd done for her and Hannah and added, "And a very special man."

If only she didn't have to borrow money from him. But she needed it, and his offer was too wonderful to

refuse. Thanks to Clint, she could hold on to the
house. The knowledge lifted a huge load from her
shoulders. Once again life was sweet.

Humming, she slid two dining room chairs together, plumped a large pillow on one and helped
Hannah get comfortable. Sometime today Clint would
stop at the bank to request a wire. Alison had already
set up an appointment with a lawyer to draw up a
repayment schedule. As soon as Clint's money came
in, she'd pay off the old note and sign a new one with
him. She intended to pay it back as quickly as possible and then never again go into debt.

Pivoting around, she surveyed the buffet. But her
thoughts lingered on the man she loved. She would
never forget the pleased look on his face when she
agreed to take his money. She smiled to herself. Who
would have guessed that borrowing money from him
would make him so happy?

Heaven above, how she loved him! A dreamy sigh
escaped her lips. If only things could stay this way
forever.

That wasn't going to happen. When Clint finished
the remodel, he'd move on to another town, and
maybe even another woman. Jealousy pricked Alison.
She pushed it away. Just because she loved Clint
didn't mean she held claim to his heart. For now she'd
make the best of things and enjoy his company for as
long as he stayed.

Bending down, she grasped the burled wood knobs
on the top drawer of the buffet and pulled. In this and
the other two drawers, Aunt Phoebe and those before
her had stored doilies and dozens of linen tablecloths
and napkins. Alison caught a whiff of old wood and
stale air, and suddenly her head filled with memories

of birthday and Christmas dinners, of her high school graduation party. Aunt Phoebe had liked to use the "good" linen whenever she had the chance. Those were happy times, and Alison smiled.

Just as her aunt had done, Alison used the linen for holidays and special occasions. She'd done so on Clint's first night here. But she'd never used the doilies, and she didn't remember her aunt ever using them, either. They were too old and fragile.

Sliding the heavy drawer along its cast-iron rollers, she carefully tugged it all the way open. "Look at these doilies, Hannah. They're handmade and very old."

The little girl's brow creased as she studied the pile of lace-edged circles and ovals. "What are they for, Mama?"

"Oh, I don't know." Alison set the linens carefully into a tissue-lined box. "Fancy parties, I guess."

"Like my birthday?"

Alison laughed. "Sort of. Only the parties I'm talking about were a long, long time ago, way before your birth. Even before mine. Right here in this house, around this table."

A bittersweet longing to hold on to the dining room set gripped Alison for a moment, but she pushed it aside. The money from the sale of the furniture was worth an empty dining room. And she'd still have the tableware. She stroked a hand lovingly over the delicate fabric of the top doily. It felt cool and soft. "These were made and used by your great-great-grandma Rose. I'll bet some were even made by her mother."

"Oh." Hannah's eyes widened. "I want to tell her what we found. Help me get up, Mama."

Alison angled her head. "You mean, talk to Grandma Rose's portrait?"

"Uh-huh."

Smoothing tissue over the linens, Alison frowned. "She won't hear you, sweetie. She's been in Heaven a long time."

"I know that." Hannah huffed. "I want to talk to her, anyway."

What harm could that do? "All right." Alison pushed to her feet and held the walker steady while Hannah grasped the handles.

"I'll be back in a minute." Hannah zoomed off as if she'd used a walker all her life.

Smiling, Alison shut the top drawer and tugged open the middle one. Large and heavy and slightly warped, the drawer jerked open slowly. The musty smell reminded her that it hadn't been opened in decades. Though both it and the bottom drawer also contained linens, they were so hard to open she rarely delved into either.

She knelt down and peered inside at the neatly stacked tablecloths and matching napkins. Just as she had with the top drawer, she carefully removed the contents, piling them gently into a box. She tucked fresh tissue paper around the precious linens. When she tried to push the drawer shut, it resisted, moving in fits and starts. Finally she managed to close it.

Hannah hobbled back into the room. "I told Grandma Rose about the doilies. She smiled at me."

"Did she?" Hands on her hips, Alison eyed the bottom drawer. Would it be as difficult to open and close?

"Grandma Rose said wait until we looked in the bottom drawer. Let's open it now, Mama."

Alison frowned. "Hannah Rose O'Hara, you know paintings can't talk. And we already know what's in there. More tablecloths and napkins."

"Can I see, anyway?"

"I suppose. You'd better sit down here, on the floor." Alison grabbed the pillow from the chair and plumped it on the rug in front of the buffet. Then she sat Hannah down, settling her leg on the pillow.

Kneeling beside her daughter, Alison grasped the knobs. This drawer was even harder to manipulate. The wood complained squeakily as she slowly urged it open. Suddenly, with only a few inches of space showing, it stuck fast. Alison blew out a breath. "It's no use, I can't budge this thing another inch."

Curious, Hannah leaned on the rim of the drawer and peered inside. "You're right, Mama, there's more tablecloths in there."

"I know, sweetie. And we've got a problem. Somehow, we have to get them out. Maybe if I try again, it'll open enough for me to empty it."

Ten minutes later she gave up. Her arms ached from pulling, but the drawer remained stuck. She wiped her brow. "Clint will be home soon. He'll fix it."

"Thanks for the ride, and see you tomorrow." With a wave, Clint exited Billy Bob's truck.

Whistling, he shoved his hands in his back pockets and sauntered up Alison's driveway. It was muggy and hotter than hell, but he barely noticed. His thoughts were on the house and the beautiful, sexy woman who waited for him inside, the woman he couldn't stop thinking about or wanting.

His body stirred, but by now he was used to his

constant state of semiarousal. Alison wanted him, too. He saw it in the warmth of her eyes, in the soft smile she favored him with. That only made it harder to stay in his own bed at night. But they'd agreed to keep their distance, and he was bound to abide by that decision. But even with his body thrumming uncomfortably, knowing he'd helped her and Hannah filled him with a strange contentment he hadn't felt in ages.

The thought struck him that over the past few days, some of his bitterness had faded. That surprised him. He couldn't change the past, could never forgive himself for his part in Lynn's and Erin's deaths. And he'd never, ever forget or stop loving them. But maybe it was time to move on, to focus on life instead of death.

Guilt needled him. Was it wrong to want that? "Tell me," he pleaded aloud, staring upward at the gathering dusk.

But the voice in his head remained silent. The first star appeared in the sky, winking at him. He took it as a sign. Slowly his guilt receded, and a sense of peace settled over him. This was a good decision.

Just then Barker yipped wildly and loped forward to greet him. Chuckling, Clint rubbed between the mutt's ears. "Hey, fella. I'm glad to see you, too. Come on, let's go."

He was beat, yet strangely energetic. It had been a great day, starting at the site, where things went so well that the crew accomplished more than they set out to. Then at lunch he'd stopped at the bank and sent the request for the insurance money. Knowing what that meant, he grinned. In three days, when the funds arrived, Alison's money worries would be over.

If she insisted on paying him back, he'd open a

savings account for Hannah and deposit the money there. Maybe the kid could go to college someday, or open her own business. Why not?

Still smiling, he stopped at the front steps, sat down and removed his work boots and socks. The sparkle was back in Alison's eyes, and he'd helped put it there. Damn, that felt good.

Yes, things were turning about better than he'd imagined. This was one town he'd leave feeling better than when he came.

Suddenly Barker cocked his ears and jerked his head toward the woods. Giving a joyful woof, he took off running. Clint chuckled. Even the dog seemed happy.

Clint climbed the front steps feeling lighter than he had in years. He looked forward to a great meal and another evening with Alison and Hannah.

The moment he stepped through the door, the little girl rushed at him as fast as she could, given the walker. "Clint, Clint, guess what?"

Even the overzealous kid couldn't dampen his high spirits. Pausing in the threshold, he tugged her lopsided pigtail. "Hello to you, too, smart stuff. What?"

"Mama and I tried to clean out the buffet but the drawer got stuck. We can't open it, but we have to before Jenny Ross comes to take it away. Mama says she'll be here tomorrow morning, and we gots a big problem."

He held up his hands, palms up. "Slow down there, kid. What's the trouble?"

"Come on, I'll show you."

Clint followed her through the hall and into the dining room. The walker clicked and thumped across the throw rugs and hardwood floor.

The table was set for dinner. Other than the open boxes beside the buffet, filled with what appeared to be linens, things seemed as they always did. "Looks like dinner's almost ready," Clint said.

Mouthwatering aromas floated toward him from the kitchen. He sniffed appreciatively. "Smells like it, too." Wanting to see Alison, he turned toward the kitchen. "Where's your mama?"

"Cooking dinner, but wait a minute, Clint. Look." Hannah pointed to the buffet. "There's tablecloths and napkins in the bottom drawer but the drawer's stuck and we can't get them out. I'll bet you can open it, 'cause you can do anything."

The adoration in the little girl's eyes bothered him. He sure as hell wasn't worthy of that. Frowning, he shook his head. "I can't do everything, but I can probably help you with this."

"Hannah Rose, what are you doing?" Wiping her hands on her apron, Alison strode into the dining room with a pucker between her eyebrows.

"Hi," Clint said, his voice slightly husky. He couldn't help ogling her long, shapely legs. "I like that outfit."

"This thing?" Alison waved a dismissive hand over the blue T-shirt, shorts and thigh-length pink apron, but her cheeks flushed prettily.

For a brief, sizzling moment, desire and promise smoldered in her eyes. Clint's blood heated, and he knew his eyes reflected the same need. They both quickly looked away.

Alison turned to her daughter. "Didn't I tell you to let Clint clean up for dinner before you jumped all over him?"

The child popped two fingers into her mouth. "Yes, Mama."

Over her bowed head, Clint winked at Alison. "No sweat, Hannah." He shrugged. "I'll take a quick shower and be down in a blink. You can tell me more during dinner and help me fix that drawer. How does that sound?"

"Goody!" Hannah shouted.

Later, when the meal was over and the dishes cleared and washed, Clint signaled to Hannah. "Okay, smart stuff, let's take a look at that drawer."

Alison gestured toward it with a flashlight. "It won't open any wider than that. You'll need this to see inside."

"I'll hold it for you," Hannah offered.

Hunkering down, Clint tried to pull open the drawer. Nothing happened. While Alison supported Hannah and the child shone the flashlight into the drawer, he peered inside, then shook his head. "It's too full to see if anything's in the way. It's probably just warped. Don't worry, though, I'll fix it."

He grasped the drawer in both hands and prepared to force it open. Alison's hand on his arm stopped him.

"Be gentle, Clint. This is an expensive antique. I need it to stay that way."

He nodded his understanding. An undamaged piece would bring more money. He rubbed his chin. "Then I'll just have to coax it open."

It took awhile, but by putting even pressure on both sides and pulling firmly but gently, the old drawer groaned and slowly inched open.

Finally, when it was wide enough, Alison touched

his arm. "I think I can get my things out now. Thanks, Clint."

She reached in and began to remove linens. Hannah quickly lost interest and wriggled off her lap. "I don't want to do this anymore, Mama, 'kay? I want to play my new song. I practiced all day, Clint. Want to hear it?"

"Sure, smart stuff, if your mama doesn't mind." Chuckling, he shook his head and glanced at Alison. "I suspect she's been listening to you all day."

"Go ahead." Alison's smile was a brilliant thing that made her eyes sparkle and did crazy things to his blood pressure.

Clint swallowed. She was killing him.

He helped Hannah to her feet and onto the dining room chairs they'd rigged up for her.

While Alison emptied the drawer, he sat nearby with her daughter, enjoying the concert. Enjoying the three of them, together.

A man could get used to this.

The unbidden thought both surprised and unnerved him. God help them all, but he was falling for Alison, and Hannah, too. Admitting it scared him to death. He scrubbed a hand over his face, earning a puzzled look from the little girl and an inquiring, sideways glance from her mother.

He pretended not to notice. All along he'd believed they deserved better. Yet for some crazy, lucky reason, they seemed to want him.

"Look at this strange thing that was under the tablecloths." Alison's voice cut into his thoughts. She pointed to the right inside corner of the now-empty drawer.

"What is it, Mama?" Hannah grabbed her walker and hobbled over. Clint followed along behind her.

Alison shook her head. "It's a tiny wood knob." She frowned and bent down, peering at it. "Attached to a tiny little drawer."

"Yeah?" Clint shrugged. "Maybe it's a secret compartment. You know, a place to hide valuables."

"Could be, but I certainly didn't know it was here." Alison grasped the knob and pulled. This door slid open much easier than the others. "There's something inside."

Hannah's eyes rounded as she leaned forward. "What is it, Mama?"

"I don't know." Alison held up a yellowed bundle, secured with string. Looking puzzled, she weighed it in both hands. "It's too heavy to hold papers."

A musty smell permeated the air. Clint eyed the yellowed cloth and age-darkened twine. "Whatever it is, it's been there awhile."

He helped Hannah onto a chair, then tugged Alison to her feet. She, too, sat down, placing the packet on the table in front of her. Clint stood behind her.

A beat of silence ticked by as they all stared at the mysterious package. For once even Hannah seemed speechless.

"What do you suppose is in it?" Alison finally asked.

Clint placed his hand on her shoulder and squeezed gently. "Why don't you open it and find out?"

Her fingers trembled as she grasped the string. Dry and brittle, it snapped at the first touch. Slowly she unfolded the cloth.

Clint caught a flash of gold, then deep, glittering

green. By the time Alison smoothed back the last bit of fabric, he'd guessed what it was.

The stunning diamond pendant, circled with emeralds, confirmed his thoughts. He whistled. "Look at that."

Alison gasped. "Grandma Rose's necklace."

Hannah, too, seemed dumbfounded. "The one in the picture," she said, her mouth hanging open.

"All those years, we thought it was gone." Alison stroked the finely woven gold chain reverently. "Oh, my." She swallowed. "It's even more beautiful than I imagined. A wish come true," she murmured.

From behind, Clint couldn't see her face. No doubt the fanciful tone of her voice matched the look in her eyes. Hell, looking at that piece of history and those dazzling jewels, he felt a little dreamy himself. He moved to a chair and sat down.

"It's so bee-ootiful." Hannah's face was full of awe as she reached out and touched each of the four emeralds and the large, oval diamond at the center. "What are we going to do with it, Mama?"

A wistful smile on her face, Alison stared at the necklace. Grasping it in her hand, she hugged it to her chest. "Keep it a few days, maybe take pictures of each other wearing it." She set it back down in front of her, then swallowed. "Then we've got to let it go," she stated quietly, her expression filled with regret.

Clint watched as she shook off her nostalgia and lifted her head with determination. "We'll have it appraised and sell it. We'll use the money to pay off our debts and set up a college account for you, Hannah."

Clint covered her hand with his. "You don't have

to sell it, Alison.'' He squeezed her knuckles gently. ''You shouldn't. This necklace belongs to you and Hannah. You can get the money you need from me, just as we agreed.''

Her eyes filled. Pulling her hand from his, she grasped the pendant. ''Don't you see? Selling this necklace will set me free. I know Grandma Rose would understand. I won't need to borrow money from you or anyone else ever again. That's what I want Clint, freedom from debt. You understand, don't you? It's wonderful, isn't it?''

Clint should have felt relief that she wouldn't need his money. His ties to Flatville had just loosened considerably. Instead he felt numb. ''Peachy,'' he muttered.

Excited now, Alison jumped up. Laughing, she dropped lightly onto his lap, threw her arms around him and kissed him. Then she sprang up again. ''I'm going to call Jenny right now, and tell her I'm not selling the dining room set or any other furniture.''

Clint watched her dance out of the room, and suddenly he felt as if he'd been run over by a cement truck.

The greatest gift he'd had to offer Alison, she no longer needed.

By the time Clint sat down on the steps to remove his boots the following evening, darkness had edged out the dusk. Tonight clouds obscured the moon, making the sky as black as his mood.

The weather people predicted much-needed rain soon. He wondered if he'd be here long enough to see it. The way things were going, that was doubtful.

The whole town was abuzz about Alison's necklace. Less than twenty-four hours after she'd unwrapped the thing, the *Flatville Daily News* had printed a story, complete with pictures. Soon jewelers from Indianapolis and Chicago started calling in bids. Two antique jewelry experts were due in town the first of next week, along with a newspaper reporter from the *Indianapolis Star*. Alison stood to realize a hefty sum from the sale of the valuable antique.

She didn't need his money anymore. She didn't need him.

Not that he cared. Scowling, he leaned down and jerked his bootlaces loose. Above him the screen door whispered open. Without looking up, he knew it was Alison who stood there.

"Clint?"

He grunted and tugged off a boot, dropping it heavily beside him before glancing up at her.

"It's late." Hands on her hips, she frowned down at him. "Where have you been?"

The day from hell wasn't over yet. He grimaced. "I don't have to report to you," he snapped.

She bit her lip. "I was worried. When I phoned the restaurant, Millie said you'd left hours ago."

"Well, don't be." He yanked off the other boot and tossed it aside. "I walked home."

"What?" Her eyes widened. "I could have picked you up, if I'd known. I thought Billy Bob—"

"I felt like walking." He stood and glared at her. "Is that a crime?"

"No." Her mouth tightening, she opened the screen door and gestured him inside. "Hungry? I kept your plate warm."

"Hell, yes." He glanced around. "Where's Hannah?"

"In bed. With all the excitement last night and to-day, she was worn-out."

"Humph. I'm going upstairs to shower."

A short while later, clean but in no better a mood, he wandered into the kitchen. Alison set a plate in front of him, poured iced tea for them both and sat down.

He stabbed a forkful of salad. "You don't have to keep me company."

"I want to." She shifted in her seat. "Unless you'd rather eat alone?"

"Doesn't make any difference to me." Thirsty, he drained his glass.

Alison arched an eyebrow, then refilled his glass. "Chuck phoned a little while ago with good news. Your truck will be ready Friday afternoon."

For some reason the news further darkened his already foul humor. "It's about time," he grumbled.

He speared a chunk of potato and popped it into his mouth.

Alison leaned her forearms on the table, watching him chew. "How did things go at the site today?"

"Just great." Clint scowled. "Rusty added another man to the crew. Some cousin, new in town and looking for work."

"Oh?" Alison's eyes widened. "Millie didn't mention that when we talked." She frowned at Clint's expression. "Isn't that a good thing?"

"What do you think?"

"Since things are behind schedule, it sounds smart to me. If the man is competent, I'll bet Millie's pleased."

"Oh, he's competent, all right." He shoved a

mouthful of red snapper into his mouth. "This is delicious," he grudgingly admitted.

"Thanks." Alison smiled. "I splurged and bought fresh instead of frozen."

He did not return the grin. "I guess you can do that now, since you've got the money."

Confusion lit her eyes, and Clint knew she wondered about his black mood. Thankfully, she didn't pry.

"I take it you don't like the new guy," she observed.

He took his time chewing and swallowing before answering. "He's okay. Now if you don't mind, I'd like to finish my dinner in peace."

"Fine."

Pain flashed in her eyes, and he knew he'd hurt her. At least he'd silenced her.

The picture of contriteness, she pressed her lips together, locked her hands together on the table and stared down at them. She allowed him a few moments of blessed silence, then ruined what was left of his meal with the question he both dreaded and expected. "What's wrong, Clint?"

Everything. "Not a damned thing." Releasing a frustrated breath, he pushed his chair back and stood. Not bothering to dump his half-eaten dinner into Barker's bowl, he set his plate in the sink.

"Don't shut me out, not after what we've shared," Alison entreated.

She thought he was running away. The irony struck him as funny. With a harsh laugh he spun around. "Here's the deal." Crossing his arms, he cocked a hip against the counter. "You've got all the money you'll ever need, and with this new man, Rusty's got plenty of help. I guess that frees me up to leave town.''

He saw by the shock on her face that she hadn't expected his words. Her eyes wide, she clasped her hands to her chest. ''But I thought…you said you'd stay until you finished the restaurant. Several weeks at least.''

He'd planned to, back when Alison needed him and Rusty was short of help. But he was no fool. Those days were over. Alison didn't need him. She never really had. He shrugged. ''Things change. I'm not the kind of man who likes to stay in one place too long. It's past time to leave.''

''I see.''

Her big eyes, full of pain and caring, held his. Looking at her reminded him what he was, so he stared down at his feet. Where did he come off thinking he could help a woman like Alison? He certainly didn't resent her good fortune. Yet, he was acting like a jerk. The sad truth was, Alison no longer needed him. That stung like hell. He didn't belong here. Why had he ever thought he did?

''Where will you go?''

''There's a big construction project in Texas. They need men like me.'' Day laborers who worked hard, finished the job and moved on. ''After that, who knows?''

''When?'' she asked so softly he barely heard.

''As soon as the truck's ready.''

Her jaw dropped. ''But that's only two days from now.''

''That's right.''

''What about the insurance money, Clint? It's coming Friday. What will you do with it now?''

"It's all yours. Keep it or give it to someone who needs it. You decide." He pushed away from the counter and nodded. "Friday afternoon I'm out of here."

Chapter Fourteen

Friday, on Clint's last morning at work and his last day in Flatville, Alison lifted her chin, squared her shoulders and pretended her heart wasn't about to shatter into a million pieces. Forcing a cheerful smile, she dropped Hannah at a friend's. Then she bought groceries. But when she reached the checkout stand, she realized she'd picked up way too much food. With a heavy heart she put half of it back. Mealtime wasn't going to be nearly as interesting without Clint. Nothing was.

Stifling a heavy sigh, she wheeled the grocery cart toward the car. In her mind's eye, her life stretched out before her, lonely and empty. But whose fault was that? From the beginning, Clint had told her he wasn't the kind to settle down. She'd always known that one day he'd leave. She just hadn't expected it quite so soon.

Alison unloaded the groceries into the back seat and returned the cart to the store. Knowing that he would someday leave hadn't stopped her from hoping, or from falling in love with him. And it didn't take away the awful ache in her heart.

Unbidden, tears gathered in her eyes, as they often had the past few days. Mustering control, she covered her face with her hands. She'd expected to hurt, but not this much.

Thunder rumbled overhead. Alison glanced at the sky, surprised at the sudden darkness. The air carried the scent of moisture and the promise of rain, the long-awaited and much-needed first downpour all summer. How fitting that it would come on Clint's last day here.

Biting her lip, she slid into the car. She was a survivor, she would make it through this. Once she'd read that if a person acted happy, eventually they would feel that way. Determined to try it, she pasted a smile on her face and drove to Flatville Lumber and Hardware.

Thankfully, she was the only customer in the store. This morning, with tears ready to fall at any moment, she wasn't up to chitchat with townsfolk.

She found what she needed and carried her purchases to the cash register. Tom's head was bent over a large box as he busily checked the contents off an inventory list. Alison was glad he looked busy. He probably wouldn't notice her dismal mood.

"Hello, Tom." Careful to keep her smile firmly in place, she set the square of plywood and small wood stake on the counter.

"Why, Alison." He looked pleased to see her. "I

didn't expect to see you this morning, it being Clint's last day in town.''

Not surprisingly her eyes filled as she accepted his grandfatherly hug. Hastily she blinked them back. Darn it, she *would not* cry again, not until she was alone.

Tom frowned at her like a worried parent. ''You okay, honey?''

Resolve firmly in place, Alison nodded. ''I'm fine, thank you.'' She gestured toward the counter. ''I'd like to buy this wood. Would you mind cutting it for me? Make it the same as last time.''

Tom's eyes widened behind his bifocals. ''Sure thing.'' He rubbed his chin. ''Making another sign?''

''I'm afraid so. I can't find the old one, so I'm starting fresh.''

''I see.'' He eyed her curiously. ''Does this mean you're planning to rent out that spare bedroom again?''

''That's right. I need some way to bring in money until the restaurant reopens.''

Though her heart wasn't in it.

''Now, why would you want to do that?'' Tom hooked his thumbs under his red suspenders. ''I thought that necklace you found was going to make you rich.''

''Not rich, but secure. After I pay the bills, I'm putting what's left *away,* Tom. I never want to get into a mess like the one I just had.''

''Smart girl.'' Pulling a stubby pencil from behind his ear, he measured the plywood. ''I'm real sorry about Clint leaving,'' he said with a sad shake of his head. ''I liked him.''

''So did I, Tom.'' *I still do. More than that, I love*

him. Afraid the older man might see the misery in her eyes, Alison dug through her purse for her wallet.

Tom pulled off his bifocals and replaced them with plastic safety glasses. "I was kinda hoping he'd stick around," he said, and positioned the cutting saw. "I'm not getting any younger, you know."

Alison watched him slice neatly through the plywood and wondered what his age had to do with Clint's leaving.

"I need someone to run the store, buy me out," Tom continued. "It's a shame my boys live in Albuquerque and Chicago and neither of 'em wants to take over the old man's business. Flatville's a fine place to raise a family, and the man who buys this store will make a nice living."

Surprise widened Alison's eyes. "I didn't know you wanted to retire."

Tom nodded. "Don't get me wrong, I like my work. But Marie's been at me to slow down, and I think she's right. We want to travel, see those grandsons of ours." He propped his safety glasses on top of his head. "I've been thinking and thinking on what to do about this store. Marie helped me figure it out. We found the right man to take over Flatville Lumber and Hardware. He knows a heck of a lot about construction and seems to have a good head for business. We want Clint to buy our store."

"Clint?" The wallet slipped from Alison's fingers as Tom's words spun through her head. Change spattered over the counter. "Did you—did you tell him?"

"Sure did. Yesterday, the minute I made up my mind. I even closed down the store at lunch so I could talk to him." Tom scooped up the quarters, dimes and pennies and handed them to Alison. "For a minute there he looked interested. Thought I had him." The balding man gave a heavy sigh and a slow shake of his head. "But he turned me down, said he couldn't stay here."

"Oh." Disappointment speared Alison, but she wasn't surprised. Clint's future didn't include settling in one place or owning a business. Dipping her head, she dropped the change into her wallet.

Tom patted her arm and looked at her kindly. "You like him a lot, don't you?"

Why try to hide what was obvious? Alison bit her lip. "I love him, Tom."

"I thought so. Have you told him?"

She shook her head. "I can't. He's not interested."

"Are you kidding? Every man wants love. I saw the way Clint looked at you at Hannah's party. And the other day, when you fainted, nothing could have made him leave your side. He's so crazy for you, he's busting with it."

Alison thought about the past two days, remembering Clint's dark, closed expression and the way he'd avoided her. For a while, when he'd seemed more open, she'd hoped that maybe he could learn to love her. But now? No. He couldn't wait to leave. She shook her head sorrowfully. "You're mistaken, Tom."

Clint didn't want love. He didn't want Hannah. And he didn't want Alison.

"I don't think so." The older man laced his fingers over his round belly. "I've got a hunch that, deep down, Clint wants to stay. He just doesn't know it yet."

Alison didn't believe Tom, but she grabbed on to the notion, anyway. "Do you really think so?"

He nodded knowingly. "What Clint needs is a good reason to stay, more than a job offer. You're the one who can give him that reason."

She must have looked as doubtful as she felt, because Tom's brow creased. Leaning across the counter, he beckoned her close with a crooked finger.

"I may be an old man, but I know a thing or two about love." He chuckled. "I've been married forty-six years, I ought to." He patted her shoulder. "You talk to him, honey. Tell him what's in your heart."

Alison shook her head. "It won't do any good. There's not much time left, and he's a stubborn man."

Tom dismissed her words with an impatient wave of his hand. "When is he leaving?"

"Sometime after lunch. As soon as his truck's ready."

"Then you don't have much time to convince him." Tom winked. "Go to it, girl. I'll be rootin' for you."

Clint drove away from Chuck's in his newly repaired truck, shaking his head.

He couldn't believe the people who'd stopped by the mechanic's shop to say goodbye. Millie, Jenny Ross, Tom and Marie Farley, and other townsfolk he'd met over the past few weeks. Surprisingly, they seemed genuinely sorry to see him go.

He couldn't imagine why. A man like him didn't usually make much of an impression with people, nor did he strive to. But with Flatville such a small town, any outsider was bound to make a few ripples. Especially one who stayed too long.

Clint signaled and turned onto Main Street for the

last time. For all Chuck's bumbling, in the end he'd done a great job. The engine purred like new. Clint knew he'd have no further trouble with it. Driving to Texas should be a snap and a pleasure.

He drove past the bank, catching a glimpse of Vincent Cahill through the glass doors. The banker had dropped by the site earlier to wish him well and to let him know his money had arrived. Clint had advised him to transfer the funds to Alison's account. She could bury it in the backyard for all he cared.

At the intersection near the hardware store, the light turned red. While his truck idled there, Clint's thoughts turned to Tom Farley. Clint liked the store and the man, but yesterday's unexpected offer had dumbfounded him. He shook his head in amazement. Who'd have thought the store owner would ask *Clint* to take over the business?

He'd been flattered and almost tempted. But owning a business and settling down weren't part of his plans. When he explained this to Tom, the man seemed sorely disappointed. Clint felt bad, but he knew Tom would have no trouble finding a buyer. Not with such a successful business.

While Clint waited for the interminable light to change, he watched two men saunter into the store. What did they plan to buy? Did they need advice on construction or repairs? He imagined helping them, imagined ordering supplies and managing the business. Then, when the shop closed for the night, going home, where Alison and a great dinner awaited him. And Barker, yipping a friendly hello. Hannah, full of youthful exuberance, would meet him on the porch steps, yakking his ear off before he even got through the door.

A car behind him honked, and he realized the light had turned green. Cursing himself six ways to Sunday, he sped off. Why was he wasting time on such thoughts?

Alison no longer needed him. She had what she needed—a family of her own and money to pay her bills, plus a town full of people who cared about her. He thought about the sorrow in her eyes the past few days. If she seemed sad that he was leaving, she'd get over it.

He slowed to let a dog cross the street. No, he didn't have to worry about Alison. He could leave here footloose and carefree, and he intended to do just that, as soon as he picked up his things and said goodbye to her and Hannah.

As he turned the corner and headed toward their house for the last time, melancholy filled him. He shook his head. What the hell was wrong with him?

That new job and the open road were calling to him like a siren's song, and what was he doing? Feeling sorry for himself. No more of that. He pushed the accelerator to the floor and felt the engine vibrate beneath him. Ah, that was more like it. He couldn't wait to leave.

The sooner, the better.

The rain started as he turned into the driveway. Thunder roared and lightning crackled in the distance. Thick, fat drops spattered the windshield and bounced off the hard, dry earth, and a fresh, clean smell permeated the air.

He rolled to a stop, staring at the big, old house through a curtain of rain. The roof didn't look so good. Alison probably needed a new one, or at least a patch or two. Maybe he'd take a look up there....

He saw the Room for Rent sign propped against the house. His lip curled into a sneer. She hadn't wasted much time. Though why she wanted a new boarder puzzled him. She sure as hell didn't need money.

Maybe she needed a man to keep her company on lonely nights. Jealousy stabbed him. His jaw set. He didn't own Alison. What she chose to do was none of his damn business.

He walked slowly up the steps. Rain pelted his head and shoulders, but he didn't hurry. For once he did not remove his shoes, instead wiping them carefully on the mat. Drawing in a breath, he stepped inside for the last time.

Just as he'd pictured, Barker woofed an excited welcome, and Hannah met him at the door, a pleased grin on her face and one hand behind her back. "Hi, Clint! It's raining, and you're all wet. Mama's in the kitchen, making lunch. I played with Melody and Christie this morning. Then I came home and maked you a present."

Her arm shot out from behind her. Beaming proudly, she handed him a large brown envelope. Across the front, his name was scrawled in shaky, barely legible letters.

A pang shot through him. He was going to miss the pesky kid. He accepted the gift, then tugged a pigtail. "Thanks, smart stuff. You didn't have to do that."

"Are you gonna open it?"

Her face, so anxious to please, touched him. He swallowed past the sudden lump in his throat. "I think I'll save it for later, when I'm on the road. Right now I need to get my things. Then I'll say goodbye to you and your mama.''

As always the middle step squeaked as he climbed the stairs and creaked again when he came down with his suitcase and duffel bag. For some reason the sound further lowered his spirits. He'd gotten used to that warped step. He set his bags by the front door.

''I don't want you to go yet, Clint.'' Looking worried, Hannah clumped her walker toward him. ''Mama's making us a fancy lunch. Fried chicken and potato salad and debilled eggs and carrots and brownies for dessert. Yum, yum.''

Clint sniffed appreciatively. Maybe he should stay, for one last meal. With a frown he stiffened his resolve. It was that kind of fool reasoning that had started the whole mess with Alison in the first place. He rubbed his chin. ''I don't have time to eat. I'll grab something on the road.''

The little girl's lower lip stuck out disapprovingly. Then she popped two fingers into her mouth. Guilt needled Clint and with it the urge to pick her up and coax a smile from her. He pushed it away. Once he left, she'd forget him soon enough.

He crouched down beside her. ''Now, Hannah, you've always known I wouldn't stay forever. There's a job for me in Texas. I have to take it.''

''But, Clint, you can't. I don't want you to go, and neither does Mama.'' Her big eyes filled.

Aw, hell. He felt like a jerk. Chucking her chin up, he wiped away the tears with the pads of his thumbs and cleared his throat. ''Don't cry, smart stuff. You don't want to upset your mama, do you?''

Hannah shook her head. After a moment the tears stopped.

Thank God. He released a relieved breath. "That's more like it. Now, I'd better go talk to your mama." When the little girl started to follow him to the kitchen, he hesitated. "I want to talk to her alone, Hannah. Can you find something to do by yourself?"

One little shoulder shrugged. "'Kay."

"Thanks."

He found Alison in the kitchen, focused on a skillet full of frying chicken. He'd seen her in the same familiar pose, leaning over a pot or a pan, her hair tied back loosely at the neck, dozens of times over the past few weeks. There was nothing glamorous or sexy about her loose T-shirt and shorts or the pink apron, yet desire rippled through him.

He wanted to grab her by the waist, pull her against him and kiss the sensitive crook of her shoulder. Instead, he shoved his hands in his pockets. "Hey."

"Clint." Her head jerked up. The gaze that met his quickly veered away. "I didn't hear you come in."

Clutching a long-handled fork, she deftly stabbed a chicken leg and deposited it onto a plate piled high with crisp, brown chicken pieces. "Lunch is almost ready." Her cheerful voice didn't match the sadness in her eyes. "I thought you'd like one last decent meal before you hit the road."

"That sounds great." Regret slashed through him that he couldn't share any with her. He quickly pushed it away. "But I can't stay. I want to make it to the Indiana border before nightfall, and that's at least a four-hour drive. I'd best head out right away."

Alison busied herself with removing the last of the chicken from the sizzling grease. "Then let me pack something for you."

He was hungry and couldn't turn her down. He shrugged. "If that's what you want."

"You want to know what I want?" Biting her lip, she glanced at him. "For you to stay."

Fool that he was, he wanted that, too, more than he had a right to. He combed a hand through his hair. "Like I said, I've got a long way to go. I can't afford the time."

"Not just through lunch." She straightened her shoulders and looked him straight in the eye. "Tom Farley told me about his offer."

"Yeah?" Clint frowned. Why had Tom told Alison? "What else did he tell you?"

"That you seemed interested, but you turned him down." She deftly wrapped six pieces of chicken in foil. "You could stay a few days longer and think about it." She tried a smile. "Just to make sure you're making the right decision."

For a beat Clint considered the suggestion. It was definitely tempting. Until he remembered that sign out front. Stick around here, like some fool? No thanks. He crossed his arms. "What's with that Room for Rent sign? You sure as hell don't need the money. Not mine, anyway."

Alison flushed. "Is that what's bothering you? That I don't need your money? Maybe not, but I need *you,* and so does Hannah." She swallowed. "And you need us, too, only you're too stubborn to see it."

Clint snorted. Her words only proved how different they were from each other. "I'm not stubborn, I'm right. I'm a loner, Alison, and I always will be. I don't need anyone," he said in an effort to convince them both. Awkward now, he kicked his toe against a worn spot in the linoleum. "Look, I didn't come here to argue. I came to say goodbye."

As she searched his eyes, the hope faded from her gaze. God, he hated seeing that. But he wasn't the kind of man she needed. She deserved better, and if she didn't realize that now, she would in time. Unable to bear the miserable look on her face, he glanced away.

Finally she nodded and turned toward the stove. "I'll finish making your lunch, and then you'd best go."

He watched in silence as she packed a meal fit for a king into a large paper bag. Finished, she wiped her hands on her apron and handed him the sack. "Here," she said solemnly.

Her fingers brushed his. Warmth stole through him. *Damn.* He drew back. "Thanks. I'll let myself out." Before he could stop himself, he touched the smooth skin of her cheek. "Take care of yourself, Alison. I'll never forget you."

Her eyes filled, and for one awful moment he thought she would break down. With the strength he'd grown to recognize and admire, she swallowed and took control of her emotions. "I'll never forget you, either," she whispered.

He had to taste her, one last time. Lowering his head, he kissed her. She was warm and soft in his arms, and the familiar hunger rolled over him. For a beat he wanted nothing more than to stay here with her forever. The thought scared him spitless. Releasing her, he spun away.

While he was still reeling from that kiss, Hannah ambushed him in the hallway. "Clint? Please, please

don't go," she cried. Her little arms circled his knees.
"I love you."

To his surprise, moisture gathered behind his eyes.
He blinked and patted her head awkwardly. "You be
good, kid, and do what your mama tells you to."

Pivoting away, he grabbed his bags and hurried
down the steps.

He drove off without looking back.

Halfway out of town, just about where his truck
had broken down a little over three weeks earlier, he
slowed, pulled over and stopped at the side of the
road. He was too shook up to figure out why, only
knew he couldn't drive right now. From the passenger
seat he picked up the fat brown envelope Hannah had
given him. For some reason the sight of his name
scrawled in her childish handwriting across the front
tugged at his heart. He carefully lifted the flap.

She'd crayoned a picture book for him, fastened
together with pink yarn. Clint could almost hear her
sing-song little voice, urging him to read it. Swallowing, he flipped to the first page.

A man with longish black hair, like his, stood in a
crudely drawn house. His outstretched arms held a
hammer and a drill, and he wore a large, blue frown
on his face. Clint rubbed his chin. Was that how Hannah saw him?

Grimacing, he flipped to the next page. This one
showed a woman clasping a large green bowl. With
the cherry-red ponytail and pink apron, there was no
mistaking who she was. Alison. Her mouth turned
down, too, and tears that looked like birds' feet
marked her cheeks. A sharp pang made Clint's chest

ache. Apparently, Alison hadn't been as good at hiding her worries from Hannah as she'd hoped.

Page three showed a little pigtailed girl, wearing a fat white cast on her leg. She, too, frowned, as did the funny-looking dog she hugged.

Disappointment shot through Clint. Well, hell, nobody in Hannah's story seemed happy. He realized that he'd wanted a laugh, that right now, he felt just like the guy on page one. Sad and lonely. With a heavy sigh he turned to the last page.

She told a different story here, a happy story. The man and woman held hands in front of the same house. At their feet, the pigtailed girl clutched a silver harmonica. The dog sat by her side. A vivid blue sky filled the background, and a bright yellow sun shone overhead. What put the lump in Clint's throat were the joyful smiles on every face, including the dog's, and the big red hearts filling every chest.

Then he saw the words at the bottom, penned in glitter in Hannah's awkward script. *My family.*

"Family," he murmured aloud. The word thrummed through him, settling in his aching heart like a healing balm.

Without explanation, Clint suddenly knew that wherever Lynn and Erin were, they understood. And they wanted him to be happy. Giving a solemn nod, he glanced upward and saluted the heavens. He would never forget them, and they would forever hold a place in his heart and his memory. But it was time to stop mourning, time to stop wishing for things that couldn't be changed. It was time to move on.

Just like that, the twin burdens of guilt and sorrow lifted. At the same time, realization hit him like a bolt of lightning. He thought he could drive away, forget

Alison and Hannah and go back to the way he used to be. A loner who didn't need anyone.

But he'd changed. He knew that now.

Hannah's crude drawing proved that she knew what should have been obvious to him, what Alison had tried to tell him, what had taken him until this moment to figure out.

He loved Alison and Hannah. He wanted to be part of their family. God, how he wanted that. Admitting it felt good and made his heart surprisingly full and light at the same time.

"I'll be damned," he said aloud. From somewhere deep inside, a chuckle broke loose and bubbled from his lips.

After a euphoric moment, panic claimed him. What if Alison didn't want him, after all?

In that case he'd do everything in his power to win her back. Clint checked for traffic, then made an illegal U-turn and pushed the accelerator to the floor. He had to get back to them right away. He had to get home.

Alison tiptoed down the stairs. For the first time in months Hannah had picked over her lunch, then asked to take a nap. She seemed as blue as Alison.

Who could blame her?

She glanced at her watch. Clint had left only half an hour ago, but it felt like forever. With a sigh she called to Barker. "Let's go outside and put up our new Room for Rent sign."

The downpour had softened the earth, hopefully making it easier to place the sign. Alison searched for a rock to pound it into the ground, while the dog romped playfully in the wet grass.

Her back to the road, she hunkered down and positioned the sign close to the road. In the distance, the rumble of an approaching car sounded. She paid no attention to it. Probably someone passing by on the way to someplace else.

Barker, however, yipped excitedly, obviously hoping for company. Alison frowned. Not now, when she felt so blue.

"Hush," she scolded, then turned her attention back to the sign. She began to pound it into the ground, but it was slow going. Despite the rain, the soil under the surface was still hard. Behind her, the car stopped. A door opened, then slammed shut. She jerked around.

She knew that truck. She knew the man, too. *Clint.*

"Hello." Her hand over her rapidly thudding heart, she dropped the rock and the sign.

"Hey," he replied, his voice strangely hoarse as he headed toward her. "Are you taking that down or putting it up?"

The hopeful expression on his face did funny things to her stomach, making it flip-flop. "That depends," she said. "Are you looking for a place?"

His eyes locked on hers, and the light shining there lifted her heart. "Not to rent, no." He shifted his weight and cleared his throat. "I, uh, changed my mind about leaving. I'm sticking around here."

"Oh?" Considering how fast her pulse raced, she sounded amazingly calm. Hands on her hips, she lifted a skeptical eyebrow. "I thought you liked to drift from place to place."

"Not anymore. I want a home of my own, and I want it here with you."

They were words she'd dreamed of for weeks now,

and she wanted very much to believe him. But he was a drifter and she was wary.

She must have looked doubtful, because Clint's chest lifted as he drew in a breath. "I was almost out of town before I got it through my thick skull. I belong here, with you and Hannah. If you'll have me, I'll call Tom Farley and accept his offer to buy Flatville Lumber and Hardware."

Certain she misunderstood, Alison shook her head. "What did you say?"

Clint swallowed. "You were right, I can't outrun myself or the past. But I *can* put it behind me. I don't want to be alone anymore. I want to be a family with you and Hannah." His gaze was full of warmth as he tipped up her chin. "I love you, Alison, and I want to spend the rest of my days showing you how much. I love Hannah, too. Will you give me the chance to prove it?"

She leaned into him. "I—are you saying what I think you are?"

Clint nodded and cupped her face gently between his hands. The love in his eyes melted her doubts. "I'm asking you to be my wife. Will you marry me?"

She didn't have to think about that. Her heart full to bursting, she smiled up at him. "Yes."

While Barker danced and yelped in circles around them, they sealed their love with a kiss.

Epilogue

One Month Later

From her place at Clint's side, Hannah sighed and clutched her flower-girl basket. "Doesn't Mama look bee-ootiful?"

He glanced across the backyard to the old oak tree, where his soon-to-be bride huddled with Millie and the minister and the string quartet Jenny had brought from Indianapolis. They were in earnest discussion, probably ironing out last-minute details before the guests arrived. In an antique lace gown, with her copper hair pulled back and a halo of flowers ringing her head, Alison looked stunning.

His heart swelled with love. "You've got that right, smart stuff. Your mama's the prettiest woman in the world."

"And you're the bestest, handsomest daddy in the world," Hannah replied.

Daddy. Clint grinned. He doubted he'd ever get tired of hearing her call him that. And he'd never take for granted this second chance. He fully intended to love, cherish and protect Hannah and Alison for as long as he lived.

He touched the head of the child he'd soon legally adopt as his own. "Thank you, Hannah."

Guests began to arrive. First among them were Tom and Marie Farley. Over the past month, as Clint took over the hardware store, he and the older man had grown close. Now, as his best man, Farley was dressed in a tux much like Clint's.

Grinning widely, Clint approached him. "I hardly recognized you, Tom. Welcome to our home," he said.

Tom grinned back. "Glad to be here. Where's the bride?"

"Over there." Again Clint turned his attention to the woman he loved.

Suddenly she looked straight at him, as if she felt his gaze on her. A brilliant smile lit her face. Her eyes softened with promise as she blew him a kiss. Clint knew his own expression matched the warmth in hers. When he made love to her tonight, he would show her how much she meant to him.

The musicians tuned up, and guests quickly took their seats in the folding chairs Billy Bob and the other crew members had set out. Clint and Tom took their places under the shade of the oak tree. Clint waited as Jenny and then Millie walked down the makeshift aisle to join them.

Then came Hannah. A lump formed in Clint's

throat as the little girl walked slowly toward them, proudly scattering flowers.

"All set?" Tom whispered.

Clint didn't think he'd ever been more ready for anything in his life. Too overwhelmed to speak, he merely nodded.

The moment he'd been waiting for finally came. Alison walked gracefully toward him, her eyes fastened on his.

Clint smiled around the lump in his throat. He was home, and it felt damn good to be here.

* * * * *

You're not going to believe this offer!

In October and November 2000, buy any two Harlequin or Silhouette books and save $10.00 off future purchases, or buy any three and save $20.00 off future purchases!

Just fill out this form and attach 2 proofs of purchase (cash register receipts) from October and November 2000 books and Harlequin will send you a coupon booklet worth a total savings of $10.00 off future purchases of Harlequin and Silhouette books in 2001. Send us 3 proofs of purchase and we will send you a coupon booklet worth a total savings of $20.00 off future purchases.

Saving money has never been this easy.

I accept your offer! Please send me a coupon booklet:

Name: _____

Address: _____ City: _____

State/Prov.: _____ Zip/Postal Code: _____

Optional Survey!

In a typical month, how many Harlequin or Silhouette books would you buy <u>new</u> at retail stores?

☐ Less than 1 ☐ 1 ☐ 2 ☐ 3 to 4 ☐ 5+

Which of the following statements best describes how you <u>buy</u> Harlequin or Silhouette books? Choose one answer only that <u>best</u> describes you.

☐ I am a regular buyer and reader
☐ I am a regular reader but buy only occasionally
☐ I only buy and read for specific times of the year, e.g. vacations
☐ I subscribe through Reader Service but also buy at retail stores
☐ I mainly borrow and buy only occasionally
☐ I am an occasional buyer and reader

Which of the following statements best describes how you <u>choose</u> the Harlequin and Silhouette series books you buy <u>new</u> at retail stores? By "series," we mean books within a particular line, such as *Harlequin PRESENTS* or *Silhouette SPECIAL EDITION*. Choose one answer only that <u>best</u> describes you.

☐ I only buy books from my favorite series
☐ I generally buy books from my favorite series but also buy books from other series on occasion
☐ I buy some books from my favorite series but also buy from many other series regularly
☐ I buy all types of books depending on my mood and what I find interesting and have no favorite series

Please send this form, along with your cash register receipts as proofs of purchase, to:
In the U.S.: Harlequin Books, P.O. Box 9057, Buffalo, NY 14269
In Canada: Harlequin Books, P.O. Box 622, Fort Erie, Ontario L2A 5X3
(Allow 4-6 weeks for delivery) Offer expires December 31, 2000.

PHQ4002

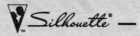

If you enjoyed what you just read,
then we've got an offer you can't resist!

Take 2 bestselling
love stories FREE!

Plus get a FREE surprise gift!

#1357 A MAN ALONE—Lindsay McKenna
Morgan's Mercenaries: Maverick Hearts

Captain Thane Hamilton was a loner who'd closed off his heart long ago. But when this strapping Marine returned home to recover from his most dangerous mission, he couldn't deny the fierce desire unassuming nurse Paige Black was arousing with her tender loving care....

#1358 THE RANCHER NEXT DOOR—Susan Mallery
Lone Star Canyon

A long-standing feud had forced rancher Jack Darby to end his clandestine affair with sweetly innocent Katie Fitzgerald. Now he wanted to win her back. But he'd have to do more than unleash his pent-up passion—he'd have to prove that this time he'd be hers forever!

#1359 SOPHIE'S SCANDAL—Penny Richards
Rumor Has It...

One unforgettable night long ago, Sophie Delaney had given rakish Reed Hardisty the precious gift of her virginity. But then their scheming families cruelly wrenched them apart. Now, years later, was it possible for these high school sweethearts to recapture the love they once shared?

#1360 THE BRIDAL QUEST—Jennifer Mikels
Here Come the Brides

Runaway heiress Jessica Walker went into hiding as a nanny for handsome Sam Dawson's darling daughters. But could the sheriff's little matchmakers convince Jessica their daddy was the husband she'd always longed for?

#1361 BABY OF CONVENIENCE—Diana Whitney
Stork Express

In a matter of days, Laura Michaels had gone from struggling single mom to married woman living in a mansion! But could Laura and her adorable son transform Royce Burton—her stubbornly sexy husband of convenience—into a devoted husband and father?

#1362 JUST EIGHT MONTHS OLD...—Tori Carrington

Rugged bounty hunter Chad Hogan had lost the fiery beauty he'd fallen for when he'd given her a sports car instead of an engagement ring. And when Hannah McGee reappeared with a beautiful baby—*his* baby girl—he was determined to claim his woman and child.